$18 DT

M000308660

Front cover image by Shafran
Book design by Stephanie Van Orman
Author photograph by Alison Quist

https://tigrix1.wixsite.com/stephanievanorman
stephanievanorman.blogspot.com
tigrix@gmail.com

HIS SIXTEENTH FACE

By Stephanie Van Orman

For my husband, who still has that curious look in his eye.

INTRODUCTION

"What's going on?" I whispered, startled in the darkness.

"I'm holding you," Christian explained evenly.

Though he was familiar, the feeling of his arms around me was not. He lifted me clean off the bed as if I weighed nothing. In the rocking chair, he settled my head into the space between his chin and his shoulder. His breath feathered down my nose to settle on the moist curves of my lips.

I had to remain calm. If I showed I was excited, even with my heartbeat, the monitors would show it, the nurses would come in and the moment would be lost. I had to stay steady, pretend his warmth, his shape and his closeness meant nothing.

"Why would you do that?" I asked. Though I had never been given this much of him, already I wanted more—his voice. "Did the doctor tell you something about my surgery that he didn't tell me?"

"No," Christian said, brushing my hair away from my face.

It was the blackest blue in the hospital room, but there were dashes of light everywhere: my monitors blinking my condition, the lights from the building across the courtyard, and the strip of yellow light under the door. We swayed in a waltzing rhythm in the rocking chair, almost like we were dancing. The chair was in the room because I was still young enough to be in the pediatric wing of the hospital. When I looked at it, I tried not to think about all the dead children who had been rocked, and felt their last moment of comfort, before they took those fateful steps into the world of spirits. I thought about the bodies they left behind and wondered how long children had continued to be rocked, even after they had left their fragile bodies behind.

Christian, my would-be guardian angel, held me like a princess in that chair, close to my monitors. He had never rocked me before, and certainly never visited me in the middle of the night. He should not have been there outside visiting hours, but he was there—the greatest gift I had ever been given. Nights alone in the hospital were the hardest. How many times had I dreamed someone was there with me, holding me? I shivered in my happiness. He pulled a blanket over my body and tucked me in like a little girl, except I was being tucked into

5

his arms—enjoying every moment. He smelled expensive and like the grown-up man he was.

He was not holding me because of my girlish dreams. He simply didn't have the heart to stay away. Teenage girls dying of heart disease were irresistible, in that they couldn't be left alone. His feelings for me could not be what I wished. He sat in the chair and held me, a girl so perfectly on the cusp of womanhood, and rocked me as if to lull me to sleep.

If I had been dying under ordinary circumstances, perhaps he would not have visited me after midnight. My tragedy was deeper than the death that loomed ahead of me. Three months before, my parents had both been killed in a car crash. It was a thoughtless accident. My mother had been driving my father on a slick rainy night and while applying her lipstick, she slammed into the support beams of a bridge. She killed them both instantly.

The wreck never seemed real to me.

The problem was that I had never had much to do with my incredibly rich parents. I was always away from them, with nannies or tutors who tried to teach me ballet and how to play the piano. I was only mediocre at any of these paid-for activities. My mother wasn't good at anything, except looking pretty, which she was skilled at beyond belief. Sadly, I contrived to look nothing like her.

The closest I had ever been to my parents was when they first found out I was sick and that my life was in danger. They pawed over me and petted me, making a fuss. It didn't last. It couldn't last. Not only were children incredibly boring company for socialites, but the gloom that came with the frequent hospital stays took an incredible toll on them. They couldn't handle it. I wasn't getting better and my decline was not fast enough to be a source of drama meaty enough to feed them.

That was when my father gave me a gift. He didn't understand much about me or my specific needs, but he understood that I shouldn't be alone. He asked an acquaintance who worked near the hospital, Christian Henderson, to look out for me. Dad needed my companion to assume guardianship since neither of my parents lived in Edmonton, where I was receiving my treatment. He needed someone he could understand, so he didn't get another nanny. He gave me Christian.

And Christian was glorious. He was patient, thoughtful, bright, so charming and heart winning, it was impossible to explain. I liked him better than all the doctors. He was a young man, not yet thirty. He wore button-down vests that suggested lean muscles underneath and had a habit of turning his entire body into nothing but angles. He would rest his elbow on his knee and place his forefinger on his temple to make triangles and diamonds of his limbs. Speaking through breaks in his fingers, his words always sounded better. Sometimes he'd place one finger on his nose bridge and the other between his eyebrows and look at me through the angle of his fingers like he was looking at me through glass that helped him see better. Truthfully, I realized that until he looked at me that way, I had never been seen. When my eyes shly met his, I thought that neither my parents nor I were off to a terrible place in the hereafter. After all, there had to be a heaven since there was a Christian.

He took the news of my parents' passing hard. I knew that was why he had snuck in that night. I had surgery coming up in a few days and there was a very real possibility that I might not wake up from it. He held me and I couldn't feel alone, because he was there.

I tucked a strand of hair behind my ear and said to him softly, "You don't have to worry about me this much. It doesn't matter."

His eyes flicked toward me.

"It doesn't," I said, continuing listlessly. "I'm going to die soon. You know the odds I'll live through my next operation aren't good. That was why my parents weren't here. My mother couldn't stand to watch me die, and now she won't. Like the little match girl, there will be plenty of people to greet me when I slip out of this world. It doesn't matter, because I was hardly even here." I hoped my words would ease some of the pressure he felt, but I was only fourteen and didn't know how to spin it to make him feel the relief I wanted for him.

Christian looked at me and his eyes were all compassion and personal unrest. "And what if I was your fairy godfather and could twirl you around and make one final wish come true?"

I scowled. "The last thing I want is for you to be my father." My chest hurt and I put a hand to it.

Christian lifted my free hand and took my heart rate. He never paid attention to the monitors and insisted on feeling my heart for himself. My body betrayed me by showing my enthusiasm. Christian could feel the difference. He didn't like the result and reached for the call button.

"Stop it," I said, putting a hand to his chest. "Can't I have a different heart rate when you offer me a wish? What's your heart rate?"

He laughed slightly and offered me his wrist.

"Can I listen to your heart instead?" I whispered.

"Is that your wish?"

I nodded solemnly.

He smoothed out his shirt over his heart and allowed me to hear it. Listening to the soft pounding made my insides melt, but then another sharp pain flared in my chest.

I gasped and curled myself into a ball.

"Are you all right?"

"It's passing," I gasped, rubbing my chest. "It's passing. It's okay."

He put a hand to his forehead and tried to smooth out his concern. I had pains in my chest so often, and the small ones didn't mean much. "I'm sorry, Beth. When your father asked me to watch over you, I hoped I'd bring you flowers once a week, along with some contraband, and we'd laugh a bit."

"This level of tragedy was not what you expected?"

"No," he breathed. "This is exactly what I expected. Exactly what I've already gone through many, many, times. Only this time, it feels worse. Like you're mine and I should be able to save you. Like I should be able to stand as a fortress between you and death, and I can't. I can't do anything."

I had to think of something for him to do that would comfort him, and make him feel like he had done something for me. My brain settled on a thought I had every time I closed my eyes for a procedure. "If I can have one more wish. There is something I want. Something you can do."

Christian's fingers ran in little patterns down my arm. "Tell me."

"You could kiss me."

"I can't," he said, his voice clipped in the darkness.

"It's the middle of the night. No one would know. I would carry it to my grave. I don't want to die without being kissed and there is nothing else I want."

It was silent as I waited for his answer. Finally, he said, "If I do this, you can never tell anyone."

I gave my promise.

He shook his head slightly like he didn't want to before he turned, bent his head, and touched his lips against mine. At first, he stayed perfectly still with his lips sealed shut and the slight fluttering of our breath intermingling. Then ever so slowly, he began moving his lips, and it was completely wonderful. He understood! I didn't want a little girl kiss like a peck on the forehead. I wanted a full-blown, romantic kiss that would leave me windblown long after it was finished. I responded by kissing him the way he kissed me. It was only seconds before he had taken it too far and my heart was hammering out of control. My monitors began beeping wildly and Christian suddenly let go of me.

He looked at my flushed cheeks and the smile on my face.

"This is wrong," he said defiantly.

"I won't tell anyone," I reassured him and tried to think of something to say that would make him kiss me again.

Before I could say another word, I was neatly deposited back in my bed, Christian had flicked my bed lamp on and a nurse had entered the room to check on me.

"I'm going to be moving Beth to a different hospital," he informed her curtly.

"You can't," she stuttered. She had been my nurse for a long time. "She can only be moved by her legal guardian."

"That's me. I'll be removing her tonight."

The nurse was appalled but took him to the front desk to make the necessary arrangements. There was a lot of work to do to get me transferred to a different hospital.

Something inside Christian had snapped. I had never seen him like that before. He had always been friendly. When my parents died, he had been both crestfallen and charming to make my pain less, but in those moments after he kissed me, he had changed completely to a man I didn't know. The boyish charm was gone in a single breath. Suddenly, he had become someone who knew all about action and even how to change the entire world.

My head was spinning as I was detached from my machines and bundled into the backseat of his car, where he had set up a bed for me. He buckled my seatbelt and closed the door. I pulled a gray wool blanket over my legs and gazed at him as he got behind the wheel. I had never felt so safe in my whole life. Then we were on the road with the stars being the only things moving as quickly as we were. Where we were going, I didn't know. Why he thought a different hospital would be better didn't make sense to me. I was already at a better hospital, which was why I wasn't near my family in Toronto, but in Edmonton.

It didn't matter.

What happened next has always been a blur in my mind. I don't even remember getting out of the car. I remember green walls and the operating room lights in my eyes. Then, nothing. In my haze, I knew they were going to cut me and I didn't know if I would wake up again. I looked around for Christian, but I didn't see anyone. There seemed to be no one there but the doctor. Then the anesthetic kicked in and there was blackness.

That was my last operation. I had another scar down the center of my chest to add to my collection, but I never closed my eyes on an anesthetic again. My recovery felt slow, but was fast according to the new doctors in Mexico when I awoke. To my astonishment, I was recovering at a private hospital in a tiny village on the coast and spent most of my days lounging on the beach and sipping something cold.

What treatment did these doctors have that the doctors in Edmonton didn't? Aside from my scars, I felt perfect.

The whole while, Christian was there, reading to me, then diving into the water for a quick stretch. He needed a lot of quick stretches.

I asked him questions in those days. What happened? How was I healed? He always pretended he didn't hear me and if I pressed the question, he would walk away, promising to be back soon. I was too weak to hound him and eventually I understood that he would never tell me what happened, or what he had done.

In his silence, I finally understood that he had done something unthinkable, possibly criminal, something he did not believe he could do to stand as a fortress between me and death. It was a secret. He would look at me across a room and I could feel secrets simmering between us, secrets we had together and secrets we kept from each other.

My secret was the love I felt for him because my feelings for him had to be caged. We couldn't be lovers. He was a man thirteen years older than me, and he had become my legal guardian. The reality of that fact meant that everyone believed that our relationship resembled parent and child, even if he was not my biological father. How unsavory it would be if the people around us got an inkling of my feverish longing. It had to be hidden from everyone: from him, from the world, and sometimes from myself.

Alone, I could acknowledge my true feelings. I loved him completely. I dreamed of the day when the secrets that stood between us would crumble to dust and only we would be left.

CHAPTER ONE

Runaway Girl

"I'm not sure if I should pity you or envy you," Trinity said thoughtfully as we spied on the alumni garden party. From the balcony above, she eyed Christian's impeccable shoulders and smacked her tongue stud on her front teeth. "Remind me. Is it a good thing Christian Henderson is your dad?"

I sighed. "He's my legal guardian. That doesn't make him my father."

"He may as well be for all the fun you can have with him. How long have you been living with him?"

I corrected her. I hadn't lived with him at all.

Leaning over the railing, I fixed my eyes on Christian. As I looked at his face, his mysterious face, I felt my resolve harden. My time with him was almost up. Once I turned eighteen and graduated from high school, he would cut me loose. I was almost finished grade eleven and the reality that I had to drastically change our relationship loomed over me.

It was time to stop doing what he asked. That, in itself, was going to be difficult. I took immense pleasure in doing exactly what he suggested. I took the classes he suggested, wore the clothes he thought looked best on me, reread his messages, and thought constantly of what would please him. The problem was, if I kept playing by his rules, he would keep me firmly within the boundaries he found the most comfortable.

Those boundaries did not please me.

I looked down on him working the crowd and thought of who he was and what I had learned during the past three years.

What did he look like? His hair was wavy, tawny shade of blond. He kept quite shaggy until he swept it off his brow with mousse to expose his perfect widow's peak. He could come off as boyish until his forehead was exposed, and then he looked like a man who could be suave or ruthless as the situation dictated. His eyes were hazel but never seemed exactly the same color as the time before. It was like his eyes didn't know if they were green or brown or gray. Color didn't matter. They were his eyes and they could be any color as far as I cared. To me, he was made of perfect shapes: like the triangle of his collarbone, the lump of his Adam's apple in his throat, the angle of his widow's peak, and the squareness of the back of his hand.

If his mood was right, I didn't even see the shapes. He had wonderful eyes for making me excited. Whenever he spoke, he made me feel like he was letting me into a world where only the two of us existed, promising a delicious closeness between the two of us.

Except it didn't last. He always went away.

The longest he had ever stayed with me for a vacation had been the time I was recovering from my final surgery. After that, the holidays were a week at the most. When we were vacationing, I was in paradise, but the time always passed quickly. Soon I was sent back to school, or summer camp, or something intended to enrich my life and keep me away from him.

Christian never hesitated to send me away.

I had to be protected. From what? You would think he was a playboy with mountains of women that had to be hidden from me. I knew he dated from time to time, but those fleeting relationships weren't what kept him from me. His work? He had long since moved along from his desk job in Edmonton. He was a director in charge of international marketing for a communication company in England. He liked his work and he was good at it, but that wasn't the clincher either. The problem was that wasn't his *only* job.

The fact was, Christian Henderson wasn't his real name.

At the garden party, I watched him shake hands with my English professor. The façade that covered Christian's face was perfect, like everything about him. It was a hair off the forehead night, where the crispness of his shirt paired with the white flash of his smile oozed wealth, education and worldly wisdom. His signature brand of luxury marked him as the best-dressed man in the room, even if he wasn't wearing the most expensive suit. It was the way he walked, the way he presented himself, and the way he gave away his attention. No one could buy or replicate his style because it wasn't real. As I watched him, I didn't see the flawless gentlemen everyone else saw. I only saw the

13

conman who knew how to leave a good impression and wondered what I would exchange for half an hour of the kind of attention he gave others. He never looked at me like he wanted to fool me, charm me, or seduce me.

He was a liar and a gentleman. Everything he was doing, saying, was for my benefit. He had nothing to gain by sweet-talking the faculty. Even if he was a liar, I believed my father would not have been disappointed in his choice, but he was not Christian Henderson.

If he was not Christian Henderson, who was he? What was his real job?

I wished I knew.

Once, when I was staying at a hotel with him in New York, he accepted a phone call for Damen Cross. He didn't realize until after he hung up that I overheard his conversation. I was fifteen then, and suspicious, so I read a few of his messages on his laptop. He had a unique operating system and unfamiliar programs. I found a request for him to go to Israel.

He was furious when he caught me. I was terrified when he slammed the laptop shut. For a split second, I thought he was going to hit me. He didn't, but he sent me back to the boarding school that evening. Before he sent me away, he gave me an incredibly father-like lecture on snooping. I wouldn't treat my father's things that way, would I? I had no idea. I had no father.

On the plane, *I* was furious. Christian wasn't my father and his imitation of him made me sick to my stomach. The thing was, he felt like he had to put me in a box where his 'other lives' didn't affect me. There was no need for the partition. It didn't matter to me what Christian had done or was currently doing in his double, or triple, life. Whatever power he had, he had used it to save my life. I knew the sacrifice had been too much. Though he did everything he could to stop his discomfort from showing, something was bothering him that had not bothered him before my operation. Maybe he owed money. Maybe he was running from someone. Whatever was happening, at fifteen years old, I didn't know how to react.

The next time I heard from him, he sent me a letter, postmarked Liberia. I didn't write him back, because I wasn't sure how to proceed. I needed to know the truth about the way he lived his life, but he wouldn't tell me. I didn't see him again until Christmas when he took me to Paris and showered me with presents. He acted like himself and even apologized for being so angry in New York. I was probably just trying to check my social media? That was the moment I learned that in order to stay with him, I needed to refrain from asking questions, or lifting one finger to find out the truth. I loved him unconditionally and I needed to give him the freedom to handle whatever he had to handle without my interference. I cried like a baby to have him back… even if he lied to me constantly.

Since then, I learned to be discreet when I heard him referred to by another name. I let him think I hadn't heard. It was easy. He wanted to believe I was ignorant. Both of us knew the truth would separate us. I had to play dumb if I wanted to stay with him.

So far, I'd heard him referred to as Christian Henderson, Damen Cross, Riley Fulks, and William Farris.

Trinity interrupted my thoughts. "Look," she said, "my parents just walked in."

"They look pissed."

"They are."

I glanced at her. "Are you getting expelled this time?"

"Probably not. It looks like dad came carrying his extra-heavy checkbook. See the bulge in his pocket? He's gonna pay them off."

"Didn't he already pay for the gazebo in the park?"

"And the stone gardens," Trinity admitted. "Those knuckleheads just don't get the message. I don't want to go to school here. I've said it a million times, but they'd rather go on holiday in the Mediterranean ten months of the year than play house with me. Why aren't they worried about me going astray? I could get addicted to meth or crack, get an STI, or get an abortion. Pissy parents!"

"I still think you're lucky. At least, they're not dead," I said absently, my conversation playing on repeat. I was on repeat because I was thinking about what I needed to do to get Christian's attention. "Trinity, what do you think a girl would have to do to get booted out of this school on her first try?"

"What?"

"I have never been to the disciplinary office. What do you think I'd have to do to get expelled—no negotiation—first try?"

"Well," Trinity said, rubbing her hands together. "The difficulty is hitting that magic number between really annoying the school board and involving the police. You could get thrown out if you made a bomb threat or set a fire in one of the chemistry labs, but do you really want to toy with getting a criminal record? Those old bats on the school board have dealt with so many wild ones that hardly any scam turns their heads. Believe me, I know." She paused and looked at me with shrewd eyes. "But Beth-baby, if you wanted to get Christian's attention by acting up, shouldn't you have started already? We only have one year of high school left."

"Yeah. It's just that for some reason I always thought that once I graduated I'd get to live with him. Tonight, I realized that's never going to happen. Once I finish here, he'll ship me off to a university and phase me out of his life. I'm never going to get to spend any time with him."

Trinity nodded. "I understand. There isn't a girl in this school who doesn't faint every time he picks you up. You should have called in a bomb threat when you were fourteen. They would have gone way easier on you."

I rolled my eyes. "That's the best advice you have?"

"No," she said, grabbing my arm. "You could do the very first prank I ever pulled."

I thought back. "That naked picture you painted of the chairman of the board? No, thanks! I don't know how you kept your gag reflex down."

It stung when she flicked my ear. "No, idiot. That was my first prank in high school. I'm talking about my very first, please-pay-attention-to-me, act of defiance. I pulled it so many times, my parents stopped reacting, but the first time I did it they were wetting themselves and I bet Christian would, too."

"What?" I asked curiously.

"I ran away from school."

"Now, that's an idea," I said nodding.

"Do you have money? How far away could you get?"

"I have money," I hedged.

After I woke up healed in Mexico, consequences started mattering again, and the truth about my parents' finances came forward. They were oceans deep in debt. After everyone was paid in full, there was a little money for me, but it was nowhere near the amount I would have needed if I was going to live in the luxury they had provided for me. Christian put that money away, and I wasn't to touch it until I was an adult, but it was peanuts compared to the money he spent on me regularly. All the same, I did have Christian's money in the form of a credit card. If I used it to pay for flights and accommodations, he would undoubtedly be able to trace me in a jiffy, but the idea wasn't to run away to a place where he couldn't find me. The idea was to run away to a place where he would come after me.

"You could give it a try." Trinity winked and started down the stairs that would lead her to the reception. We were students and weren't exactly invited, but Trinity didn't let that bother her. She wasn't going to miss the chance to see her parents, no matter the consequences.

I breathed in through my nose and out through my mouth to steady my nerves. I hoped I could revert to the little girl I always played when I was with Christian. If I couldn't be his woman, I had to settle for being his little girl. After one more breath, I was ready and followed Trinity down the grand staircase.

In my school uniform, I sauntered up carefully behind him. He was drinking a glass of champagne and talking to a nondescript parent. I put my fingers over his eyes and said, "Guess who."

He put his hand on mine and asked, "Is my girl out of bed without permission?"

"Maybe."

"Is she in her pajamas?"

"No!"

He took my hand off his eyes and turned around to see what I was wearing. "Darling, you look quite respectable. I thought you'd dress up if you decided to crash the 'adult' party. It's like you aren't even trying to blend in."

I put my arms around the crook of his arm, pulled his elbow against my chest, and rested my head on his shoulder. If it had been my first time doing that, I doubted he would have allowed it, but I had been doing that since Mexico. It was one of the rare forms of physical contact he allowed. We didn't hug the way families did. He tolerated my arm clamp with an easy smile and placed a teensy kiss on the corner of my forehead.

The parent beside us started talking, like that level of clinginess in a seventeen-year-old was normal. Nothing was amiss to him. "This must be Beth." He put out his hand for me to shake and I momentarily had to relinquish my hold on Christian. "Good job sneaking in," the nameless parent praised. "I don't know why they don't allow students to come to these functions. I hardly ever see my boy." Then his cell phone interrupted him and he excused himself to take the call.

Workaholic, I thought as the man walked away. No wonder he never got to see his son.

Christian turned his head forty-five degrees and whispered. "Beth, if you keep hanging on to me like this, people will think we're a couple."

I chuckled and gave him a bit of space, though I kept my hand in the crook of his arm. "That would be so embarrassing... for me. It couldn't possibly be embarrassing for you. I mean, you're so old that being seen with a cute young thing like me could only raise your reputation. I can hear them now, whispering about the adorable little woman you have on your arm. When they look at me, they wonder how I could have let my standards fall so totally when I clearly have so much to offer." This was said to gently mock him. He always spoke of himself like he was so hilariously grand. "The last few times we've gone away together, the hotel clerks wondered why we got separate rooms, so it wouldn't be the first time someone thought we were together."

Christian glanced at me. "Your school uniform ruins the effect."

"Too true," I replied.

His lips parted like he was about to say something, but no words came out. He had been growing more and more distant. He was putting space between us. It was in dark contrast to how we used to talk when we were together. We had conversations like bubbles in the bath, you weren't sure if they were doing anything until there were none. Like bubbles, his words were often meaningless, as if he was afraid to give himself to me. Even though he used evasive words, there had been thousands of them. Now there were dozens.

He was going to dump me and he wanted it to look natural.

Instead of giving me words, he placed a kiss on the side of my head, like I was a child. When he finally did speak, his words were light and meaningless. "What have you been up to? Slip anything good into the punch? I hate to break it to you, but it was already spiked when I arrived and not with anything tasteful, I might add."

"I didn't. That's more Trinity's game. I think the adults are plenty capable of getting themselves smashed without my help. Besides, it's not like alcohol would improve their personalities."

He laughed. "Probably not." Then he dumped the rest of his champagne into a plant. He never overdid it with drinks.

"Can I ask you something?" I asked, trying to wheedle out the reason for the distance between us.

"Of course," he drawled.

"Do you have a girlfriend these days?"

"Are you worried I wouldn't tell you if such a thing happened?"

"Yes," I admitted.

"What, exactly, do you think would change between us if such a person existed?" he asked. His eyes darted around my person to see if there was something about me that he had missed, and then his gaze returned to my eyes, where the challenge in his question lingered.

I should have handled his direct gaze better. Unfortunately, I involuntarily averted my eyes and swallowed everything that had been waiting on my tongue.

"Besides," he continued, "I would never refer to a woman I was seeing as my girlfriend. Girlfriends are for young men. You should be someone's girlfriend."

"Why would I want a boyfriend? You make being single look so charming."

Again, he looked me over to see if he had missed something. His eyebrows lifted and dropped quickly as he dismissed whatever he had been thinking. I realized he was looking for signs of maturity as he discarded his empty goblet on a waiter's tray. "To change the subject," he began slyly. "I was going to ask you where you wanted to go this summer. I was thinking about Sydney or maybe Okinawa. Want to go swimming?"

"What about your place? I know you have a flat in London I haven't seen."

He shrugged his immaculate, elegant shoulders. "It's boring, and I only stay there for work. It's nothing but a bed and a window."

"Yes, but I haven't seen out that window," I persisted, showering myself in innocent enthusiasm.

"It's an alley-way, darling. An alley-way. I'd much rather take you scuba diving."

I sighed and tried a different tack. "Christian, do you realize that I don't have a home? I may not have visited my parents' home more than twice a year when they were alive, but at least that was a place filled with pictures of us, books we had read, music we chose instead of elevator music, motel art, and old magazines. I haven't had anything like that in years and I'm so lonesome for it I could die. Can't you give me a place that could be my home?"

While I was speaking, he looked worried, but he calmed down considerably by the time I finished and answered smoothly. "Is that all? Why didn't you say something sooner? I hate being in the same place. I can't put down roots, but I can understand it if you want to hang your Christmas stocking on the same hearth every year. I'm sure we could arrange for you to visit one of your aunts."

"No," I interrupted. "I don't want to see them. They're still disgruntled that my parents didn't have enough money to spread around. Don't try to fob me off on them. I want a home with *you*."

He shook his hand dismissively. "You know my work has me hopping planes every other day. I would never be there."

"Fine. I bet I'd see you more in London than I do now."

Christian looked like he was tired of talking to me and I knew from his expression that he had no intention of giving in to my demand.

After that, he danced with me twice and Trinity once. Then he faked a yawn, patted me on the head and said his good-nights.

I stared at the pristine lines of his back and shoulders and felt like clawing my heart out. He was about to get a shock. I was going to run away from school.

***

20

Running away from school was too easy. Maybe it was because I was seventeen instead of eight like Trinity had been, but I felt like it should have been harder. I made flight reservations online and then I faked a headache to get out of class. I picked up my bag and slipped over the fence by the pool. That was how Trinity always snuck out and, for some reason, no one ever clued in that she just hopped over the fence by standing on the crates of salt. Once outside, I called for a ride and went to the airport.

It was hard for me to decide where to run away to. In the end, I decided to stay in Canada, but the farther away from Toronto, the better. There was a stable outside Calgary that I was quite fond of, so I decided to go there.

The trip was uneventful, as was checking into the hotel.

Day one: I hoped to make myself as much of a nuisance as possible, so I stayed in the hotel room and racked up the bill.

Day two: I took a taxi to the stable and went riding all afternoon. Except that I hadn't been riding in ages and my thighs and backside ached like murder by the time I dismounted and went back to the city. At the hotel, there was no sign of Christian.

Day three: After the bruises from the day before, I didn't want to go riding again. Instead, I lounged in the tub for most of the morning and then went shopping in the afternoon. I wished Christian would somehow meet me in the mall. Shopping without his opinion was a waste of time. In the evening, I had supper by myself in the hotel restaurant. I drove myself crazy staring at the door. Impatient, I thought that no matter where Christian was in the world when he found out I was missing, he should have been able to make it to Calgary by then.

Day four: Sick of Calgary and depressed that Christian hadn't shown up, I decided to take a train to Vancouver and made plans to be on the next one. The journey would take a day and a night, so he would have to meet me in Vancouver if he showed up at my hotel after I left. Whatever. I went to the dining room and ordered four lobster tails without any sides to feed my sorrows.

Day five: I didn't leave the room. I sulked and watched day-time TV until nightfall and then I watched late-night TV, which wasn't any better.

Day six: I packed up and paid my bill. My credit card still worked, which seemed like a bad sign, showing that I hadn't got his attention at all.

I went to the train station.

I got there an hour before boarding, so I sat down to wait. The place was littered with people but gave the impression of being empty since there were so many unoccupied chairs. Which was why it seemed unusual that the seat next to me was immediately occupied by one of the mustiest people I had ever smelled.

It was a man, swarthy and unwashed, wearing cheap cologne. He hadn't shaved in days and his loud hibiscus printed shirt was only buttoned halfway up his chest. For pity sake, we were in Canada! Who did he think he was? And why did he keep looking at me?

I tried to ignore him by burying my face in my magazine, but he was getting so close to me that I could feel his breath on my neck.

"Do you mind?" I said in my snottiest, rich-girl, voice.

He didn't move. "You like the fashion magazine, yes? Yet, you dress so boring. You need more style," he said in a thick French accent. "Do you know what I mean by style?"

I moved over into the next seat.

He slipped into the chair I had just emptied and kept talking. "You should let me teach you. I can turn you into a star."

At this point, I turned and looked directly into the sleazy loser's eyes. Color didn't matter. Shapes were all that mattered and I saw them at once. The nose was wrong, but everything else checked out. I took a chance. "Stop teasing me, Christian. It really hurts my feelings when I don't look good in the clothes you like the most. I look fine in this. Not everyone has the shape to dress like a supermodel."

He had been smiling, but he stopped when I said my lines. He leaned back in his chair and his shirt fell even more open as he placed his hands behind his head. "How did you know it was me?"

"Because it is you," I said, like calling his bluff was nothing. I stuck my nose back in my magazine and pretended to read.

22

He scratched his head and lifted himself out of his chair. "Whatever. The fun part of our meeting is over. Get up."

"My train isn't boarding yet."

"Doesn't matter," he said with zero humor in his voice. "You aren't getting on that train. We're done with pleasantries. Get up."

I did.

He grabbed my arm and ushered me out the front doors. "I look like crap and I need to change. I have a room down a few streets." He pushed me into one of the waiting cabs and told the driver where to go.

Sitting next to him, I got a better look at his face. He had to be wearing pounds of makeup to make his skin look so dark. Well, even if it was a tan, that still didn't explain why he was wearing a rubber extension on the end of his nose. As I looked closer, I saw he was wearing phony eyebrows, too. What was he up to?

"Christian?" I asked softly.

His glare could have killed me, but he seemed to check himself before the daggers got to me. "Did you forget my name already?" he asked flippantly in his French accent. "It's Louis."

"I'll remember," I said, excitement igniting inside me.

We stopped in front of a dingy hotel. I had only seen such shabby establishments from car windows and I'd certainly never been inside one of them. Christian took me past the check-in desk and up the stairs to a room on the second floor. He pushed me in and locked the door behind us. I watched as he stooped to put an electronic device under the door. Then he tugged his shirt over his head, flashing me a view of his bare back before he disappeared into the bathroom. The door closed and I heard the water running.

The room was the sorriest excuse for lodging I'd ever seen in my life. I wanted to sit on the bed, but the covers looked stained, and the whole place smelled funny. Instead, there was a plain wooden chair that I settled into while I waited for him to get cleaned up. It was then that I made the miserable realization that we had left my luggage at the train station.

When Christian came out of the bathroom, I didn't recognize him at first, because a red-haired teenage boy opened the door. I stared at him, trying to piece together what had just happened. He had been trying to disguise himself when he was dressed as Louis, but as far as I was concerned, it wasn't a very good disguise. When he came out of the bathroom, he looked like a completely different person. The beautiful angles of his face had been replaced with curves like he hadn't already lost his baby fat. His eyes that were normally a sweet murky color were now a pale blue, transforming the look of his entire face.

"What's going on?" I asked.

"My room here is under the name Charles Lewis," he said simply as he dropped his bag on the floor. "From here, the story is that I helped you run away from school because we're in love."

"Can we talk about why I actually ran away from school?"

"There isn't time," he said as he circled the room picking up oddities he had left scattered. "The story goes that after we spent a few days on the lam, we ran out of money and I convinced you to return to school. I'll fly back to Toronto with you. The plane leaves in an hour and a half."

"Can we go back to the train station?"

"Why?"

"I left my bag there."

He snorted. "Then you left your bag there. Honestly, I'm willing to put up with all kinds of crap from you, but taking the time to go back to the station—that's a no-go. Look, Beth, seriously—I understand. You want attention. I wish I could give it to you, but I don't have more time to give you than I already do. The truth is you are the only normal thing I have in my life, so please, don't wreck it." He looked at me with appealing eyes that somehow still looked like his even though so much had changed.

I shook my head. Once I had processed what he said, I knew his made-up story about us being in love wasn't important. He was using that story as a tool to lure me back to school. He hadn't disguised himself to be my boyfriend. He was disguising himself to hide himself. It wasn't a real offer, and I hadn't gone to all the trouble of running away so that he could ship me back without a shot being fired.

"You think I want attention? Yes, but that's not all I want." I said without batting an eyelash.

"You're not going to tell me, are you?"

I crossed my legs and mentally glued my bottom to the chair. I wasn't going without a fight.

He zipped up his bag. "Time to go." He picked up the phone and asked the front desk to have a car waiting for him downstairs. He was about to pick up the device from under the door when he saw I wasn't moving. "Beth, get up."

"I don't see why I should come with you. I haven't got what I want."

"What do you want?" he asked as he retrieved the thing on the floor.

"Back at your school, didn't you say something about a home?"

His offhanded way of describing my most crucial desire made my blood boil. I didn't answer him.

He came over to the chair and grabbed my arm. "Get up," he ordered again.

"I want attention, but I also want a place that connects us, not just a random resort where we made some memories," I said, looking up into his face, humiliating tears forming in my eyes. "I know you're keeping secrets and I won't ask you about them. You're worried I'll wreck the balance of your carefully crafted life. I promise I won't wreck it. I want to make our relationship better. You can never be my dad and I don't want you to try, but I want you to be my... there isn't a word for what I want."

"All right," he said, tightening his hold on my arm. "I'll give you what you want, but you've got to give me what I want right now."

"What, exactly, will you give me?" I muttered, grasping the armrests of the chair with white-knuckles.

He frowned darkly. "I'll give you a key to one of my places and you can go there this summer, whether I'm there or not."

"Done," I said, uncurling my fingers from the chair and allowing myself to be led out of the room without the necessity of being man-handled.

After we left the room, we had to walk down a long hallway to the stairs that led to the hotel lobby. When we first started down, the stretch was empty, but as we continued, two men in suits appeared in the exit. Suddenly, Christian put his arm around my shoulder and, holding me like a teenage boyfriend, he cuddled up behind me. Then without warning, he began nuzzling my ear with his nose. I involuntarily pulled back, because I was completely unprepared for him to touch me like that.

"Smile," he whispered in a seductive tone as he buried his face in my hair. "Look natural until we get to the end of the hall."

I bit my cheek.

It had to have something to do with the men we were passing. He was hiding his face in my neck. They went by without noticing us at all. When we got to the end of the hallway, I peeked over Christian's shoulder to see which room they were going to. Sure enough, they knocked at the room we had just vacated.

Heat flooded my face. If I had made Christian wait any longer there, we would have been caught by those thugs.

In the lobby, as Christian finished paying his bill, we heard a crash from upstairs. It sounded like the door of our room had been broken down. Christian acted like the sound didn't have anything to do with us and got us out of the hotel and into a taxi in record time.

My heart was beating like a drum machine as he stuffed me into the car and told the driver to go to the airport in a cultured British accent.

I wanted to ask him all kinds of questions about what he had done to land himself in such trouble. Was it me? Was it a consequence of helping me with my heart? I couldn't ask. I had promised I wouldn't ask and wouldn't try to find out.

On the plane back to Toronto, we didn't talk, but Christian held my hand. There were freckles painted on his ordinarily brown forearms. It looked natural. His fingers lazily tangled with mine and it felt like the stuff my dreams were made of. I had to calm down. He was only doing it to keep up the charade. Charade or no, it felt real.

***

Back at the school, he dropped me off in front of the gates and ripped a page from a book in his pocket. He scrawled on it and, keeping the accent, he said, "This is my address—one of them anyway. You can use this as a home and if you ever decide to run away again, please run here." He produced a keyring and unhooked a key for me. "This opens the door. Don't get lost." He looked around. "I think that's everything. Is anyone watching us?"

I peeked around. "I don't see anyone, but probably."

"Yeah, teenagers could be hiding anywhere. Better make it real, just in case."

With that, he bent, wrapped one arm around my waist, and pulled me to him. With no more warning than that, he kissed me on the mouth and my senses blotted out everything else. There may have been teachers yelling, or high school students hooting. I didn't care. I put my arms out and twisted my fingers in his fake red hair.

If it wasn't real for him, it was thoroughly real for me and my reality changed forever. Whatever had been 'wrong' for him about our secret kiss in the hospital, was now shaping into a real future for me. Sure, he hadn't wanted to kiss a fourteen-year-old, but I did not make him kiss me in front of my school. Finally, I saw a tiny part of him that wanted me.

***

The aftermath of the incident was boring. I didn't get expelled, but I got suspended from class for two weeks. The principal called Christian and he had a meeting with the administration. Then he gave me a lecture on how I was too precious to run away from school with a boy no matter how *attractive* he might be. It was amazing how straight he kept his face while he lectured me about my romance with 'Charles'.

When I was alone with Trinity, she asked me what happened. "I still can't figure out how the heck you managed it. You were supposed to run away to get Christian's attention and instead you turn up back here with some amazing new boyfriend?"

"It's simple really. Christian never came to get me," I lied. "He could have looked up my Visa bill online and tracked me down, but he didn't have the time. After spending almost a week in a hotel room in Calgary, you meet a few people. His name is Charles Lewis."

"So, what's going to happen next?"

I smiled. "He's invited me to his home in Scotland for the summer and Christian says I can go, just so long as I don't run away from school in the meantime. Cool, eh?"

That wasn't exactly what Christian said, but whatever. Two could play his game.

CHAPTER TWO

The House that was like a Mask

Flying to Scotland by myself was more stressful than I imagined. Christian had taken me all over the world, but never to Scotland, and he never allowed me to fly on my own. He considered taking flights with me as part of the service of being my guardian, but since I had been assertive enough to go off on my own once, he was letting me go off on my own again.

As the plane took off, I started to worry I might get bored at his house by myself. He did say he wouldn't be around much, but I could count on having the seven days he usually spent with me during summer vacation. Even if he wasn't around, Christian undoubtedly decorated his house with things that would tell me more about him than his mouth ever had.

Aside from that, I thought of all the things I never got the chance to do at school. I could go to the market and prepare my own food. Granted, I had never taken a cooking class in my life. My school offered culinary courses, but no one with an ounce of academic potential attended. "Planning to be a housewife, are we?" I could hear Trinity's goading voice in my head. All that was behind me. Once I was on my own, I could do whatever I wanted. All with the delicious flavor of Christian in the air. I'd be using his dishes, reading his books, borrowing his razor, and maybe even sleeping in his bed.

On top of everything else, I would be in Scotland.

When the plane landed, I stopped under the arrival sign to find a man holding a sign that read 'Beth Coldwell'. He was a chauffeur. Other than the flight, Christian wasn't going to let me do things by myself.

I sighed and glanced at the driver expectantly, while he scouted over my shoulder for someone flashier. I really didn't want to go with him. It cut down on the adventure, but if I didn't go with him and got lost… which was clearly what Christian had on his mind when he arranged for him.

"Hi," I said suddenly. "I'm Beth."

The guy jumped, unable to hide his shock. "Of course you are. Let's get your luggage."

I wasn't like his usual clientele.

Half an hour later, I was sitting in the back of an extremely glossy black car, with my purse on one side and a picnic basket on the other side. "Compliments of Mr. Henderson."

I waited a full minute before I started interrogating Douglas, the driver. "Does Christian usually order picnic baskets?"

"This is the first time I have been hired by him. I had orders to pick it up right before I got you at the airport."

It was obvious what the driver thought of me. I could see myself in the rearview mirror because I sat in the middle of the backseat. I had hazel eyes and a round face. There were freckles on my nose and a dimple in my left cheek. My hair was light brown, frizzy and untamable. The color barely contrasted with my honey shaded tan. It all sounds adorable, and it was. The problem was that I still looked like a child, and I wondered when I would stop.

Christian made me feel awkward about my body all the time. He didn't mean to. At least, he didn't offer me cosmetic surgery, but he was always trying to doll me up and turn me into someone... shiny. For instance, we might be on vacation together. He would buy me clothes that made me stylish and elegant, but he would also try to buy me impractical, fashionable clothes I didn't know what to do with. I couldn't wear them to school. They looked like red carpet ball gowns. What was I going to do with a sequined gown that didn't hide my surgery scars?

His behavior made more sense after our little adventure in Calgary where he dressed up like a sweaty Frenchmen and then like a redheaded teenager. I was starting to think that costume changes were more of an interest to him than I had imagined. Maybe he wasn't trying to make me over because he was dissatisfied with who I was, but instead, because he liked seeing how a costume changed someone.

I opened the picnic basket and I fell in love with him all over again! He sent me cheese, sliced baguette, butternut squash soup, and ripe pears. How could a guy who was hardly ever around know so much about how to please me? I opened the thermos first and drank in the smell of spicy soup.

I settled back into my seat and watched the rain fall against the car windows. It was raining that day. He must have known, but that didn't mean he was in Glasgow. We headed north and I thought about how going to his house was going to be like opening a present.

***

Truth be told, I fell asleep before we got there. Via alternative transportation, it would have taken hours to get to his house from the airport. With the car, I hoped it would be less. Christian's home was north of Glasgow, into the wilds by Loch Lamond, in a place called Balfron.

When the car came to a stop in front of the house, I was a little baffled as Douglas woke me and helped me out of the car.

It was dark, but all the lights were on. The house looked like a castle though it was finished with pale stucco. It resembled a castle because parts of the house showed visible block-style formations. There were fine square pillars guarding the driveway, and the grounds were kept immaculately. The lights from the closest house were quite distant. Wasn't there supposed to be a town?

Douglas got my luggage and walked with me to the front door. He rang the bell.

"Where's my picnic basket?" I suddenly asked.

"I'll take care of it for you," Douglas replied. He sounded like he thought the basket was garbage.

"Get it, please. I want it."

He grumbled that he would.

I could hear movement behind the door and a second later, it was answered by a woman. I blinked. It was supposed to be Christian.

"You must be Beth. Welcome to Cross Winds," she said formally in her Scottish brogue.

I giggled as she let me in the house. "Did Christian seriously name his house like something out of a Gothic romance?"

31

The woman looked less than amused as her forehead furrowed. "Cross Winds has been the name of this house since the late nineteenth century. I assure you, Mr. Henderson did not name it, but it's a tradition we like to keep. I am Mrs. MacGavin and I'm both the housekeeper and the maid." She opened a wallet, gave Douglas appropriate payment and a tip.

"I'll just be back with the young lady's basket," he said as he took the money.

"Basket?" Mrs. MacGavin asked curiously.

"It's mine," I said tonelessly. If she wanted to preserve the distinction in our ranks, I could be equally cold to her.

The truth was, I kept everything Christian gave me. I kept old theater tickets, odd bits of paper, receipts, and anything else. I even kept an old bagel in my trunk for six months before Trinity found it and threatened she would tip the administration that my room needed to be searched for drugs if I didn't throw it away.

Douglas returned with my basket and ducked out.

Mrs. MacGavin shut the door behind him. "I know it's late and you probably want to get to bed, but I've been instructed you must receive a tour of the house before I leave."

"You're leaving?" What I wanted to say was *thank goodness*, but I managed to keep it down.

"Yes. Normally, I come and give the house a thorough cleaning only before Mr. Henderson is set to arrive. Otherwise, the house remains empty. Would you like some tea?"

I shook my head. "Water will be fine."

She led me into the kitchen which was an incredibly spiffy affair. I sat at the marble-topped bar, while she poured me a glass of water and continued her discourse.

"Cross Winds has a gardener who comes every day, dead of winter or heat of summer. His name is Henry Brandon. There are two conservatories in this house as well as a greenhouse in the yard. Mr. Henderson has hired a temporary cook for you. Mable will cook you breakfast, lunch, and dinner. Unless you cancel your meal. There will be a menu for you to approve for the next day at every dinner meal. Here is the menu for tomorrow."

32

She handed me a piece of paper with the meals printed on fancy card stock with crinkled edges. Breakfast was scrambled eggs with fried tomatoes and toast. For lunch, I was eating smoked haddock and tomatoes and chives. Then for dinner, I was being fed a full venison meal with potatoes and gravy.

I ran a hand over my stomach. Christian didn't know I was practically a vegetarian, because I ate like him when I was with him. I'd have to talk to Mable about the food when I met her.

"Looks good," I said to Mrs. MacGavin, giving her back the menu.

"I should also tell you that I'll be stopping by every morning to tidy up. I'll show you your room."

As we climbed the staircase, I suddenly realized that since Christian had hired a maid, I would not have the pleasure of cleaning his house (it wouldn't have been a pleasure for any other person). He had also hired a cook, so I wouldn't be going to the market or fixing my own meals. Part of what I wanted was ruined with these extra people around, because he didn't think I could take care of myself.

I lingered behind as Mrs. MacGavin hurried up the stairs. "You wouldn't know to look at the place, but Mr. Henderson had quite a bit of renovating done to prepare for your stay."

"Why would he do that?" I wondered.

"Well, your bedroom didn't connect to the bathroom at first, but he made a door."

Mrs. MacGavin led me into my bedroom with a flourish. Christian had been shopping I could see. It had probably been an ordinary room once, but now he'd made it into something extraordinary. I ought to have been grateful. He thought it was what I wanted, a place for myself, when I wanted to be in his place.

The room had originally been brown and cream to match the rest of the house, but was now white as white with college dorm room fashion. Meaning there were pillows in the shape of clouds with faces on them and beads hanging from the walls intertwined with fairy lights. The bed was brand new, comfortable-looking and puffy. There was a tiny pear tree by the window with a note for me on how to care for it while it was 'visiting' me from the conservatory. It was all kinds of adorable and yet sort of wretched at the same time. Christian really knew how to give gifts while withholding what I really wanted.

I read the note and turned to Mrs. MacGavin. "Is that all?"

For a moment, it looked like she couldn't think of anything else to tell me, but then she remembered one last thing. "You *need* to tell me if you decide to go back to Toronto. Here's my card."

"You don't think I'll stay long?"

"No. Not unless you fall in love with Henry Brandon."

I scoffed. "Why would I fall in love with Henry Brandon?"

"I'm just saying it will be lonely here if you don't make a friend. Goodnight, Beth. I'll lock the doors on my way out."

It wasn't soon enough. I couldn't snoop with her around. As soon as I heard the click of the front door, I charged around searching for Christian's bedroom. Aside from my room, the bathroom and a linen closet, every other door on the top floor was locked. The knobs weren't just sissy bathroom locks either, but fancy outdoor locks that required keys.

Furious, I went downstairs to explore.

Remarkably, yes, there were two conservatories. I almost didn't get any further than the first one. It was round and had beautiful plants that circled the whole outside edge. An ornate fountain trickled water by a padded sofa. In the center of the room was a tiny round table with two chairs. I wanted to eat breakfast there with Christian.

The second conservatory had a pool in it. It was very long and narrow with crystal blue water, no stairs in and no diving board. Very obviously, it was for swimming laps. The edges were garnished with beautiful plants. I even figured out where my little pear tree had come from.

I found the library. It ran right through the center of the house. It had once been a ballroom, but Christian had it converted. I could have screamed when I saw it, but not because I was pleased. Most of the bookshelves had glass doors installed over them that could only be opened with keys. I was outraged. He had gone through a lot of trouble to lock me out of his life. I found one bookshelf that was left unlocked, but it looked bizarre next to the old hardbacks because the spines were a rainbow of color. It didn't take me long to figure out Christian had bought out the entire young adult inventory of a bookstore and arranged the books here, without bothering to put them up differently than how they came off the shelf.

After that, I found a formal dining room, another bathroom, a door down to the cellar which was so tiny, it didn't cover the whole base of the house.

I had almost lost hope that I would find a speck of Christian's personality when I saw a door that branched off the back entry. It was a little room that contained a battered couch (that had probably once been a dog's favorite spot), an old bicycle, and a pile of dogeared fashion magazines. Christian was too classy to place his magazines next to his finely bound books. Did he ride the bicycle? The tires were flat. There was an old quilt on the back of the couch. I went upstairs, got my pear tree, and slept in that strange little room. It was easy. I was so tired I could have fallen asleep on the stairs on my way down.

***

In the morning, I didn't wake up on time for breakfast. I waddled into the kitchen with the blanket wrapped around my shoulders. Mable was long gone. Instead, there was a plate with a little cover over it on the dining room table. It was stone cold and I had to warm it up in the microwave.

I took the plate into the room I slept in and cuddled up on the couch to eat the food. It was pretty good aside from the tomatoes. I should have been up on time if I wanted those to taste good.

I sat and ate, all the while composing a scathing email to Christian. Since I was alone in the house, I said my attempts out loud between bites.

"Dear Christian, your house in Balfron is lovely. It's especially lovely that you locked up all the books..." My tone wasn't right. I had to quit and try again. "Dear Christian, thanks for letting me come to stay at your home in Balfron. You didn't need to go through all that trouble to renovate. I..." Stuck again. How could I complain that he'd renovated his house for me so I'd be more comfortable? Third time's the charm. "Dear Christian... When are you coming? I want to see you."

Then suddenly, there was a tap at the door.

I nearly jumped out of my skin. "Who is it?" I asked timidly.

"It's the gardener," came a British accent.

I put down my plate and answered the door. Then I stood back, completely stunned. Red hair, freckles across the nose. "You CAME!" I shouted and threw myself into his arms. For maybe three glorious seconds, I thought my wildest dreams had come true. I thought that I wasn't the only one who wanted our relationship to be romantic and he had concocted a fake identity so he could be the teenage boyfriend he insisted I needed.

Then it all came crashing down.

"Wait. Wait. Little girl, get off me!"

He essentially threw me off. I stared at him in bewilderment. Surely, this was Christian dressed up as Charles Lewis.

"Now I don't know who you think I am," he said, leading me back into the room and keeping me at arm's length. "But you're making a mistake."

I didn't answer him. Instead, I looked at him very carefully. He was right. I was making a mistake. I had looked at color rather than shape. You can imitate someone's look, but you can't look exactly like someone else. This guy was not Christian. Christian's shoulders were very square and so were the knuckles in his hands. Christian's hands were bony. This guy's hands were meaty and his shoulders sloped. The biggest difference of all was that he was at least ten centimeters shorter than Christian. How could I have thought he was the same person?

"My name is Charles Lewis," the boy continued. "Who do you think I am?"

"Charles Lewis," I answered in a dispirited monotone. "It's just that Christian told me so much about you, I felt like I knew you." I looked away and turned my back to him. "Sorry for coming on so strong. It won't happen again."

Charles' expression was perplexed. He thought I was crazy. Except it didn't matter in the face of my disappointment.

"All right," he said in a slow voice.

"Where's Henry Brandon? I thought he was the gardener," I said, trying to move away from the fact that I had hugged a stranger in yesterday's travel clothes.

"I'm helping him with his work this summer. You'll probably see me a lot. I'm in charge of the plants in the house."

"That's good to hear. If I were doing it, all of them would be dead by September. I'm Beth. I won't get in your way."

I got up, wrapped the blanket around my shoulders and drooped out of the room, leaving my dirty dishes on the arm of the couch.

Charles followed me. "Did I do something wrong?"

I didn't bother to look back at him. "No. You didn't." But suddenly an idea smacked into my head. I turned around and asked Charles. "I have a question though. Were you always going to come here for the summer? Did you come here last summer?"

"Yes."

I drooped further. "Well, that explains it. Nice to have met you."

"Wait a second. What did Christian tell you about me?"

I sighed. "I'm sorry. I can't talk right now. I need to get changed. I'm very embarrassed that I met you in these clothes and that I jumped to hug you. See you later."

I left Charles looking like a 3D puzzle gone to pieces, but I didn't care. I got my things and went into the bathroom to have a shower.

What had Christian done? I couldn't think. He had dressed up like a boy he knew on the fly and then invited me to spend the summer with the real boy instead of himself? This was worse than the servants, worse than the books, worse than the bedroom, and in fact, it was worse than anything. How far would he go to make sure I was never a part of his life?

CHAPTER THREE

Red Haired Replacement

I met Mable at lunch. She was a beautiful piece of work. Her hair was brown like mine, but it had been touched up with way more highlights. She wore an extremely messy bun, navy nail polish, smoky eye shadow, and even though she worked as a cook, she drove a yellow Mercedes. I met her in the kitchen.

"You're Beth?" she asked when I came in.

"And you're Mable?"

She nodded and continued chopping chives.

"Nice car," I said pleasantly.

I expected her to say something curt like, 'It's my husband's', or 'Christian lets me use it when I have to go back and forth from the house three times a day', or 'It costs a fortune to maintain', but she didn't say those things. What really came out of her mouth was, "It was my birthday present to me three weeks ago. You've got to take care of yourself sometimes."

She placed the haddock in front of me with a flourish and packed up the leftovers to take home with her. "If you want anything special in the fridge, just write it on the back of the menu and I'll get it when I go shopping tomorrow."

I saw she had left a menu for me to approve on the table and heard the front door click. She was already gone. I got up and looked out the window. She was walking down the front steps, pulling her sunglasses over her eyes.

I ate up, but I wasn't two bites in before the house phone rang.

With one word, "Hi," I knew it was Christian.

"Hi."

"How are you settling in?" he asked pleasantly.

"Fine."

"And your trip went well?"

"Yep. Thanks for the basket. The food you picked was fantastic."

"Good. And how do you like your room?"

38

No sense lying. "I wouldn't know. I slept in your dog room."

"My dog room? What dog room?" He laughed.

"You know, that little room with the old couch, the bike, and the ancient wool blanket." I left out mentioning the fashion magazines.

He groaned. "You shouldn't sleep in there. Why aren't you sleeping upstairs?"

"It was really nice of you to have a room prepared for me, but you could have asked me what I like."

He sounded surprised. "You don't like it?"

"I like it fine. That's not the problem. I wanted to make up the room myself. You've already done everything."

"Well, feel free to change anything you like," he said obligingly.

"You won't feel hurt if I rip the whole thing out and change every last detail?"

"Uh..." he said.

That was the first time I ever heard him say the word 'uh'. He always knew exactly what to say. He never stuttered.

"I'll leave it alone," I suddenly decided. "You made it for me and I'll leave it alone."

"Not perfectly alone, Beth. It needs to be lived in."

"Yeah, I want to live in your house," I said, my words heavy with an internal meaning that didn't come through in my voice. "Why are your books locked up?"

"Because they're valuable. Each volume is a collector's item worth thousands of pounds. They are not for reading. Many of them are first editions and if you touch even one of them I'll send you to public school next semester," he quipped.

"You sell them to pay my tuition?" I gasped.

"Don't assume, but the sale of a few of them would pay for an entire year of your schooling—eighty thousand dollars or so. Anyway, I'm teasing. Enjoy your lunch and I'll see you this weekend."

I withered when he hung up the phone.

The rest of the day bordered on boring. I kept 'almost' running into Charles. After lunch, I tried to tour the yard, but he was working in the flower beds. It looked like I was trying to bump into him when I didn't want to see him at all. Hiding in the library wasn't much better. He kept coming in. I didn't realize there were plants in the library until he came in to water them. In the end, I went back to the dog room and didn't leave until it was time for dinner, which I ate completely alone.

The next day ran nearly the same, except by that point I had decided on a strategy to avoid Charles—pick a spot and stay in it. Charles came in to water the plants in the library three times before I figured it out. I wasn't accidentally running into him; he was the one who was stalking me. I hoped I was imagining his interest. Maybe I was wrong and house plants in Scotland needed to be watered carefully, drop by drop, with an extra small watering can.

The next day, he finally chirped up. "Are you really this reclusive? Is that why you came here?"

"Huh?"

"Why did you come here?" he blurted. "There has to be a reason why a promising young woman such as yourself came to the middle of nowhere to read. Are you getting over a painful love affair? Did you come here so you could lick your wounds privately?"

I ran my tongue along the outside of my bottom teeth. "Not exactly. I'm not 'getting over it'. I'm experiencing that painful relationship right now."

"And being here makes it less painful?" he asked anxiously.

"No. Being here makes it *more* painful," I said, surprised at my own forthrightness. I sighed. "It's just that sometimes it's better to feel what you feel, don't you think?"

"You sound like a soppy singer."

I flicked my hair out of my face and went back to reading. My book was trite by the way, but everything is when you're essentially stuck in the waiting room.

"Why don't we become friends?" Charles asked, carefully approaching and reading the cover of my book.

"Christian would *love* that," I said coldly.

"If you're so against the idea, why did you hug me the other day?"

"Can we pretend that didn't happen?" I asked, feeling heat assail my cheeks.

"No."

I glared at him. I never hated a person for having freckles before. I had freckles, but every spot on his face, every curve on his body that didn't belong to Christian was hateful. I wanted to be with the Christian who was faking being Charles Lewis so he could be with me—so he could be a teenage boy and kiss me in front of everyone. How come he couldn't be Christian? I wilted. The clueless loser in front of me didn't deserve to be despised.

I bit my lip and went back to reading. I had to tolerate him until I could get an explanation from Christian.

"So, what did Christian tell you about me?" Charles persisted.

"Please ask him yourself," I said in a small voice. "I'm not good at explaining and I've already made a fool of myself in front of you. He's coming this weekend. You can talk to him then."

After I said that, Charles stopped trying to talk to me and went back to his work. I should have been lonely, but I wasn't. With Charles gone, I got to thinking and hoping. I felt blind about the masquerade unfolding before me. I just needed a hint. What could I find out if I could unlock the master bedroom on the second floor? I wasn't good at picking locks or intrigue by myself. I needed Trinity.

I picked up the house phone. That was where I made my first mistake. My cell phone was upstairs, but I knew there was nothing wrong with charging Christian with a long-distance call. He paid all my bills anyway, so I picked up a phone on a side table and dialed her number.

Trinity was spending the first month of her vacation in Muskoka at one of her parents' vacation homes. She was planning to spend the second month in Paris brushing up on her French. You'd think that would be a dream vacation, but her parents were going to be in Rome for both months. Her step-sister lived in Paris and she only was taking her out of pity. When I called Trinity, she was sitting on the back porch looking down on the unbelievable beauty of the lake country, all the while swatting mosquitoes. She was never without her cell phone.

"I can't believe I'm only hearing from you today, Beth-the-bum. Your phone has been dead since you took off. Did you know?"

41

I frowned. Actually, I didn't know because I found my cell phone boring. It had plenty of juice the last time I tried it, but I didn't have internet access and without it, the phone quickly lost its appeal.

"Sorry," I said, "but now you've got the house number here and it's not like I'll be going anywhere."

"I've been thinking of coming to see you for a weekend when I'm in Paris. Do you think Charles would mind?"

I nearly bit my tongue out. That was right. She thought that this house belonged to Charles. I had to think of a lie. Half-truths and half-lies made great cover-ups. "Trinity, my life is so screwed up. I didn't meet a random guy in Calgary."

"What?"

"Charles is Christian's gardener. He sent him to get me because he couldn't get away. I'm staying in Christian's house. That's why he let me come here."

Trinity loudly popped her bubblegum. "That man is so skewed. So, he left you there to fool around with his gardener? I love it. I wish my parents would die and leave me to some sexy businessman."

"Except, aren't you eighteen in six months? What good will it do you then?"

"Touché. Anyway, how are things going with Charles? Still romantic? Is he good with his tongue?"

"As of this moment, my plans surrounding him are off. It's safe to say that we won't make a good couple no matter what Christian thinks. I'm mad at him for even suggesting it."

There was a weird sound almost like a cough on the other end of the line.

"Trinity?"

"That wasn't me," she defended.

Then there was a click.

"Crap. Someone has been listening on my end of the line," I said hotly.

"Who?"

"Charles. He's the only one here, except I thought he was outside. I'll have to call you back."

42

I hung up the phone, just as Charles burst into the library. "What's going on?" he demanded.

"You like listening in on private phone conversations?" I asked smoothly. That rich, snobby voice was so handy. My disdain could always cover up all my other emotions, including embarrassment.

"What? I picked up to make a phone call." His face was as red as his freckles.

"Well, when you heard the line was in use, you obviously should have hung up immediately. What's your excuse?"

"You were talking about me! I had a right to hear what you said."

"No. You didn't. We could have been talking about anyone. Just because we were talking about a man named Charles, it was ridiculous of you to assume it *was* you."

"Were you talking about some other Charles then?"

I shrugged indifferently.

"You little liar!" he said without hesitation.

That took my breath away. I had never been called a liar in my whole life, even when I lied outright. I was so angry, it felt like my ability to talk was lost in my fury.

"You were too talking about me," he said forcefully, putting his face close to mine. "You just won't admit it."

I hated him. His cheeks were pudgy and the muscle in his jaw looked weak. I wanted to slap his face. I almost did, but he moved away from me and headed toward one of the conservatories saying horrible things all the way.

"You're just angry that I didn't fall for you when you threw yourself at me the other day," his voice echoed across the room as he walked out.

I couldn't let him go like that. I got off the couch. I had to make him understand how wrong he was, but even though my feet stomped across the library carpet, I couldn't think of what to yell at him.

"I don't like you," was all I managed to come up with by the time I caught up with him by the pool.

"Of course, you don't. Not after I called you by your right name—a liar. Why would you tell your friend you met me in Calgary? I've never even been to Canada. What are you covering up, little liar?"

I snapped. I picked up his watering can and dumped the whole thing out on his head in one splash. Not that it had much water in it. It was a small watering can.

"I'm not a liar," I said coldly, as water ran down the end of his nose in a stream. "You heard the wrong part of the conversation. Don't assume you know what's going on. It's rude." I dropped the watering can while he stood there stupefied.

I turned around and tried to make a dignified exit back into the library. No such luck. Charles came up behind me and hefted me up off the ground.

"What are you doing?" I squealed.

"Just so there's no mistaking—I didn't accidentally push you into the pool," he said as I fought him. "I picked you up and threw you in deliberately."

"No!" I screamed.

And just as Charles was about to dump me bottom-first into the pool, a smooth voice at the door interrupted him. "Perhaps I should have expected this."

Charles didn't drop me, but instead turned his whole body, so both of us could see Christian standing in the door frame.

"What are you doing?" he asked Charles.

"Uh?" Charles sputtered.

"Put me down, you groundhog!" I practically spat.

Charles lowered my feet to the concrete. As soon as I got traction, I rushed to Christian. His expression was concerned as he took in the details: my flushed face, Charles' wet shirt, the redhead's heaving chest.

Christian, himself, looked collected. He was the adult in the room, and I felt it as he said, "Why don't you head upstairs, Beth? I'll be up to talk to you in a minute. I just want to have a quick word with the gardener."

I stepped past him, and Christian closed the door to the conservatory behind me with a slap. I didn't hear what he said to Charles. I was in too big of a hurry to do exactly what Christian told me to do. I was halfway up the stairs before I remembered that I wasn't doing that anymore. I paused and thought of returning, but the sound of an outside door closing stopped me. He had already finished talking to Charles.

CHAPTER FOUR

The Bugs were Sprawling

Things felt normal when I sat down to dinner with Christian. He gave Mable the night off and took me to a polished restaurant. He sat on the other side of the table wearing a navy suit jacket and a white collared shirt. I wore a dress that was worth a small fortune, with the idiotic notion that if he saw me in the right dress, our relationship would change. It wasn't working. No matter what I was wearing, I still felt fourteen years old again.

"I don't like Charles," I said after we ordered.

"Should I let him go?" Christian asked, turning his eyes on me.

I looked at him very closely. He was wearing contact lenses, but they looked clear. Naturally, Christian would not condescend to wear some cheesy colored lenses where you could see the pixels. His eyes were probably naturally hazel I decided as I picked up my water glass.

"It's a pity it hasn't worked as well as I envisioned," Christian continued. "I thought you might have a memorable summer with him. That was why I asked Brandon to invite him up. Have you met Brandon yet?"

With my worst fears confirmed, all I could mutter was a quiet, "No."

"Well, hold onto your heart. Brandon is a surprise."

I frowned. "Why are you setting me up with these guys?"

"Beth, I'm not setting you up with anyone. I know you don't like your family, and I can't be your family in the future. The only thing to do is to make a new family for you. I'm not telling you to fall in love with Charles or Brandon any more than I'm telling you to fall in love with Hilary or Mable."

"Who's Hilary?"

"The housekeeper, Mrs. MacGavin. Ha! She didn't even tell you her first name? She's a cold one. In any case, I can't have you jumping around from house to house, so make friends with these people. Although if you want me to, I will dismiss Charles."

I leaned back in my chair and felt the poison swirling on my pallet. "You must really want me out of your life."

He instantly retreated. "It's not that, Beth. You must know why I can't be around."

"I don't know," I said quietly. "I wish you would tell me clearly rather than make me guess."

His hand came across the table and he placed it slowly over mine. "My brave girl. I'm sure you have been able to come up with a very good guess."

With his hand on mine, I ventured to say, "My best guess is something so wonderful, not even I am foolish enough to believe it."

He took his hand from mine. It was a gesture meant to keep my hopes down.

"I did not choose these people by pulling their names out of a hat. I chose them specifically. Please understand, I am giving you people rather than a place. People make homes."

"All right. Did Charles explain what happened this afternoon? Did he say why he was going to drop me in the pool?"

"I asked him. He said it was a mild flirtation and he thought you were having as good a time as he was."

I shook my head in disgust. "Did you believe him?"

"You didn't look the feeling was mutual when I came in. I've thrown you into pools before, but you always seem to like it. I sent him home. You're the one I wanted to talk to."

"He heard me talking on the phone," I admitted. "I was talking to Trinity. He listened in on our conversation. You can't know how surprised I was to meet the real Charles Lewis when I came here. I had to come up with a weird story to cover up all our lies. He heard everything. What I said to Trinity made sense in the end, but for Charles to hear it... He thinks I came here in the first place because I wanted to... be his girlfriend, hang out with him, s-something." I was breathless and stuttering by the end.

Christian glanced sideways at me, a chuckle on his lips. "Do you want me to give you a chance to clean it up, or do you want me to send him away?"

I didn't like it, but that sealed it. I rolled my eyes. "I'll fix it then."

46

That daredevil, let's-go-play, expression lit up his features. His eyebrows bounced once and matched the smug set of his mouth. "That's my girl."

I felt stupid. I was doing what he wanted again. I needed to make a bigger effort to go against him.

When we left the restaurant, Christian's hand lingered on my waist as he led me out. He was still touching me when we reached the car. For just those few seconds, it felt like he might be rewarding me for trying to play his game.

***

That night, I slept in the room Christian renovated for me. It wasn't as bad as I originally imagined. He had thoughtfully put little comfort items all over the room. For instance, there was a picture of the two of us at a restaurant in San Francisco. Aside from the books he had purchased for me in the library, there were editions of my favorite books lined up in a row. There was a jewelry box on the dresser with a collection of new pieces for me. He was really kind. I just hadn't been able to appreciate it, because in my heart I wanted so much more.

That night, I slipped out of bed and tapped on his bedroom door. When there was no answer, I peeked inside. The bed was empty. Where was he?

I padded down the hallway and all the way to the bottom of the stairs. I found him in the library. All the lights were on and there was music playing from a stereo system in the corner. Christian was on a ladder that was attached to the bookshelf to help someone reach the higher books. He was dressed for bed, wearing a pair of sweatpants and a black sleeveless undershirt. Even though he was listening to music over the speakers, he had earphones over his ears. His mouth was moving softly to the music as he moved an electronic wand over his books.

"What are you doing?" I asked, pulling my dressing-gown closer around me.

He looked at me and pulled his headset off. "Did I wake you?"

"No," I said, peering up at him curiously. "What are you doing?"

47

Christian shook his head to show he wouldn't answer me and put a finger to his lips to show that maybe I shouldn't ask too many questions either. "The music is a little quiet, isn't it? Why don't you turn up the volume?"

I went to the receiver and found the volume dial. We were alone in the house, so I kept turning it up as Christian indicated until it was louder than I thought was necessary.

He dropped the wand in his hand like he was caught in the act, so he may as well fess up. "I'm looking for bugs."

"Normally, don't the maids just use a vacuum?" I quipped.

"Okay… I'm looking for tiny audio recording devices. This is why I don't like staying in the same place all the time. Fresh hotel rooms are almost always clean."

"Have you found any?"

He pointed to the sofa table with his chin. He had a gavel there with a sound block, and he had pounded a few of the tiny devices to nothing but broken parts. I picked up a few of them and pulled on the red wires.

He slid down the ladder and stood beside me. "Still want to call this place your home? Any place I am will always have these disadvantages."

"You don't want to pull me into this?"

"Obviously not."

I glanced at the wand. "How does that thing work?"

"It's simple," he said, pulling the headphones off and placing them on my head.

They were still warm from the contact they'd had with his skin. I loved it, but like always, I couldn't let him see that I loved it.

"Turn it on, and point it to the place you want to examine. If it lights up and beeps then you've got a hit and you've got something to find. This room is enormous and I got three off that wall. Why don't you start by checking the furniture and the lamps?"

The machine clicked softly through the headset as I ran the black wand over a side table. The machine beeped just as Christian said it would. I bent down and felt the underside of the table. I couldn't feel anything.

"Sometimes, you have to get really involved to find it. I often turn the furniture upside down when I'm doing this."

I got on my back and stuck my head under the table. Setting the wand down, I felt the rough wood with my fingers. Once I did that, the bug was easy to find. It was stuck to the middle of the table with a glob of adhesive. With effort, I pulled it free. When I saw it in the light, it had taken a small part of the table with it.

"Good job," Christian said with an easy smile. "You're a natural."

"Stop it," I said with a good-humored grin. He always complimented everything I did, even though he said at the beginning that using the wand was easy.

"Sometimes, they hide the bugs in the furniture in such a way that you can't find them unless you rip the joints apart. When I realize that's what has happened, I put the piece of furniture up for auction. It's worse when they hide them under carpets or floorboards. That's when all of this gets really discouraging. I have gone through rooms smaller than this and found twenty pieces of surveillance equipment. They think that you'll have a pile of ten of them and think that there's no more. What we're seeing now is a rush job. Someone did this recently and on the fly. Do you want to break it with the gavel?"

I said yes and he placed it on the sound block for me. I expected it to make more noise than it did. If I had been hammering the gavel it should have sounded like a judge in court. Instead, it was just the sound of the plastic and metal changing shape and breaking. That was why I hadn't heard him breaking the other bugs when I was upstairs.

It was funny though. I had seen the gavel in the room many times and it never occurred to me that it was anything other than decorative.

"Seriously, Christian. Who could have done this?"

He pulled a face. "It's best not to think about it. I know that sounds counter-intuitive, but you could drive yourself crazy trying to figure out who in your circle is betraying you when someone was breaking in and replacing the devices daily. In my experience, being a gentleman is a better tactic."

"Why?"

"In being kind to the person betraying you, they start to question what they're doing. Sometimes, I've pulled bugs out of offices every day for a month. Then, after a sincere conversation with the lady who cleans the toilets, there are no more bugs. On the other hand, ruthless people will find a way no matter how nice you are or how tight your security is. Try to feel secure. I've known Brandon, Mable and Hilary for a long time and I feel safe having them totter around the house while you're here."

My head jerked up. "You mean, they're here for security?"

He tapped my forehead with his finger. "What do you think 'safety in numbers' means? What do you think family means? Just that those around you are familiar? No."

"Sorry, I didn't understand," I mumbled.

He flicked up the music playing on the speaker, so the sound filled the whole house. "Now that you've seen what I'm doing, we're going to quit this room and do your bedroom."

"Why?"

"Because that was the room I had renovated, thus it is the most likely to be littered in bugs and cameras. I had planned to do it before you arrived, but something got in the way. Normally, I don't have to do this because we're in a fresh, clean room in Jamaica or something." He picked up his gear and I followed him out of the library.

There was something special about walking behind him up the stairs. When Christian walked, he walked with purpose. I didn't walk like that. Never. I rushed, but I never considered myself a force for change.

He took the wand and did the closet. Soon he came back with a device. "This has a camera as well as a microphone," he said drably.

My eyes opened wide on the implication.

"Change your clothes by the closet?" he asked in a hesitant voice.

Someone had been recording me as I changed my clothes?

"I should have been here ahead of time. I should have cleaned this out," Christian said, dropping it on the floor. Then he placed a hard-cover book over it and jumped on it until it snapped.

"It's not your fault," I muttered, scanning the room like I could see the cameras if I looked hard enough. "I wanted a home with you. This is part of that, isn't it?"

He frowned. "I didn't want this for you, Beth." Angry sweat was forming at the base of his neck.

"It's okay," I said, sliding my hand into his. "I'm not a regular teenager. Do you know how many people saw my body when I was in the hospital all those years ago? If we made a list of everyone who has seen my breasts, it would be a pretty long list."

He grasped my hand and suddenly kissed the back of my knuckles. For a second, I thought he might have wanted to do more, touch me more, kiss me more, but that was all he did. "You are such a resilient girl," he said, casting his eyes about the room wearily rather than look in my face.

After that, he returned to his own room and retrieved a second set of tools. He placed the headphones on my head and put the black wand in my hand. "This is my back-up set. Do this with me," he said, not like it was a request. "The work will go faster with two, and if you still want to have a home with me, this is the price of admission."

I flipped the switch to turn it on and we got started.

***

My room turned out to have the most surveillance equipment in it, which I thought was odd. Shouldn't his room have had more?

All of the bugs and cameras were in fairly superficial locations, so he didn't think the builders he used for my renovations were to blame.

"They could have done it in such a way that we would have had to saw your room into swiss cheese to find them."

"Do you think the house is clean now?" I asked as we consolidated our piles of broken devices into one box.

"I don't know. The main point now is to continue checking the rooms daily. Noticing when a new piece shows up will be crucial to discovering who is planting them."

"Why don't we set up a camera?" I suggested. It seemed like the obvious solution.

"Their camera? Our camera? There is no difference. They can get information from our camera just as easily as we can. In my opinion, cameras make people stupid. Something looks one way on the camera's footage, so it must be true. Besides, I don't want either of us to turn into the sort of people who spend their day sorting through video footage."

51

***

He left Sunday night with a promise that he would visit the next weekend. He said I could invite Trinity over in August and made arrangements for Charles Lewis to be elsewhere during her visit, so at least I could enjoy my time with her. He said smoothing things over with Charles was up to me.

On Monday morning, I slept in Christian's bed until noon. He hadn't given me permission, but he also hadn't locked the door. Mable found me in his room and brought me lunch in bed since breakfast was untouched.

"I wish I were Christian's daughter," I heard her whisper under her breath as she left the room.

On Monday afternoon, I met Mr. Brandon. His name was Henry Brandon, but just Brandon seemed to work just fine for him, so I called him that. Everyone had been right about him. He was a total show stopper. He was a full-grown man with dark hair, thick eyebrows, stubble on his chin and a bone structure designed to make girls melt. To top it off, he had the one devastating charm Christian had to leave out of his long list of male attributes—an intoxicating Scottish accent.

It was much nicer having him around rather than Charles. When I came around to meet him, he gave me a little lesson on how to care for the plants.

The first day I asked him, "Why are you telling me this?"

"Well, hen, someday I might not be here and it would be better if someone knew. These gardens are fussy for a house no one lives in. Two conservatories? If I were Henderson, I'd have chucked all the plants outside ages ago and replaced them with silk ones. But then again, if he didn't need a gardener all year long, where would I be?"

"Is this your only job?"

"Not all the time, but sometimes it is." He winked at me.

I blushed. Really, the guys I knew were nothing like him. "Are you really busy right now? With other gardens, I mean?"

"Next week, I'll be doing some landscaping elsewhere. Charles will take care of the plants here."

I groaned. "Really, I don't mind learning. Why don't you teach me how to take care of the house plants so that he doesn't have to come?"

Brandon's eyebrows popped up. "Is there a reason you don't want him to get paid?"

"Okay, I didn't mean to deprive him of a paycheck. Can't he get paid while I do the work?"

"What have you got against him anyway? He told me about the tiff you two had. Something about the swimming pool?" Brandon stood expectantly, waiting for me to fill in the blank.

"I've never been so embarrassed in my life," I managed to spit after a minute.

"Really? He didn't even get you in the pool from what I heard. Charmed life," he commented and went back to his work.

I watched him cart a wheelbarrow full of additions to the compost heap. His clothes were shabby. Both the knees in his trousers were patched and his cuffs were frayed. His boots looked ancient, like someone had once worn them to war, and his shirt had more stains than I could count.

I liked him.

***

I didn't get out Christian's bug detector until after everyone had gone for the night. It was time to check to see if any replacement bugs had been planted. I went around the house and made sure all the doors and windows were locked with their curtains pulled closed. Then I started by scanning Christian's bedroom. It was empty. I scanned the room twice, just to make sure, but it had stayed clean.

In my second solitary sweep of the house, I found a few devices Christian and I hadn't found on the first night we went looking.

Then, because I had grown suspicious of Charles, I checked the conservatories. Christian had not named him when he spoke of the people he trusted. Well, I didn't trust Charles, and he was always in the conservatories.

I looked carefully, but there was nothing new. Even so, I didn't think that meant Charles wasn't spying on Christian and I. He was in and out of the house so often, he didn't need electronic eyes and ears to observe what was going on.

After I smashed the devices on the sound block, I went up to Christian's room. From his bed, I made a map of the house and listed the exact location of every bug and camera Christian and I had found.

I fell asleep breathing in the scent he left on his pillow. I thought it made it feel softer.

CHAPTER FIVE

When the House was Empty

Even though Christian had told me not to waste my energy thinking about who could have planted the surveillance equipment, I was alone in a house with nothing particular to do or think about. I agreed with Christian that it didn't seem like anyone on his payroll was likely to have planted the bugs. Besides, if any of them had wanted to spy on us, it would have been more effective to simply hang around with their ears open. By that logic, the cameras were more likely to be placed by someone who only visited the house occasionally.

Mable had taken to cooking my food at her house and bringing it over on a covered plate. She was so in and out, she seemed like the most likely person to be planting bugs, except I didn't find any new bugs after that first night I looked alone.

Mrs. MacGavin came to the house every day to tidy up. She was at the house more than made sense. It wasn't like I was a snail that tracked a trail of slime wherever I went, but to hear her tell it—I was the worst snail she'd ever met. I got a glass of milk in the morning, took it with me to the library, used a coaster, drank the rest of it, went to the bathroom, came back and she had snapped up my cup like I was a total burden. Well, it was an awfully good thing she was around to clean up after me. She also changed my sheets every day. They didn't even do that at posh hotels. She held out a trash can for me two bites before I finished my candy bar. Sometimes she even waited for me to finish eating, hovering behind me like she was the next person in line at the airport. It was unnerving.

If someone wanted to spy on me, why bother setting up equipment? Just send in Mrs. MacGavin and tell her to clean up after me. She'd have a thorough report by the end of the day.

Charles stuck his tongue out at me when our paths crossed. I pretended I hadn't seen him. He gave me the creeps. I had made absolutely no effort to try to clear up the misunderstanding. I had told Christian I would fix it, but I couldn't remember clearly what I had said to Trinity, and I worried I wouldn't be able to untangle the lies. If I just kept my head down long enough, he would forget exactly what happened.

The one person I never suspected was Brandon. He never came in the house and something about finicky electrical equipment just didn't seem like part of his personality. He was more of a shovel and pitchfork kind of man. His raw masculinity made it seem like no part of him ever spied on teenage girls. With very little effort, he could have been a model or an actor and seduced any woman he desired. He had to be a gardener because he liked it. It seemed unthinkable that he was interested in anything that wasn't growing under his care. He was pleasant in an unconcerned, mellow way. He was not a suspect.

"You must love being a gardener," I exclaimed, watching him work.

"It's the only job in the world that's worth doing... at least for me," he drawled.

"It's great you have something you love to do."

He stopped and looked at me. "You must have something you love too?"

I shrugged. "I almost died of heart disease, and let me tell you, what's important in life gets very narrow when you're about to die."

His eyes traveled to my neckline, where a portion of my surgery scars showed. It had been so long since someone noticed them with any concern that I opened the flap of my shirt further, so he could see a bit more.

"Does your heart bother you anymore?"

"No. It hasn't for years."

He smiled broadly. "Your family must be very relieved you are healed."

"I suppose they are, but they're not fun. My father's people only think about money. I won't be a mentionable member of our family unless I have a house the size of a hospital, an apartment in New York, and a cabin on the Canadian Shield."

Brandon regarded me gravely during my speech, but he did not interrupt, so I went on.

"I don't hate them, but nor do I want anything to do with them. I'm not going to give them what they want, which is a connection. They want to be connected to powerful people, so if I decide to live like a hermit on the edge of a very cold beach in Iceland, I'll be a failure to them. I have no value, except what I can give them. I don't have complicated needs by myself," I finished.

"I bet you don't," Brandon said so softly that I wasn't sure if I heard him right.

"What did you just say?"

"Nothing," he said as he scratched his nose.

I looked at him twice, but it didn't seem like he was making a joke, so I continued. "Anyway, I'm distancing myself from them, so that one day, they'll forget I ever was."

"Problem solved," he said, and his tone struck me as unusual. Wasn't the sweet-natured gardener supposed to tell me to get along with my family and be sure to make them a part of my life? In those two words, and the way he said them, he left me with the feeling that he thought I was better off without them. His clear blue eyes were free from maliciousness. It was a very different message than the one Christian gave me.

"Do you have a family?" I suddenly asked, wondering if he'd had a hard time with them, which might be the reason for his advice.

Brandon dropped to his knees in front of his crumbling rock wall. "I never think about them. I chose something else."

He patted my head with his gloved hand, leaving specks of dirt in my curls, before he took the handles of his wheelbarrow in both hands and lifted all those heavy rocks like they were light.

With Brandon gone, I was bored and Charles was in the garden. I thought some friendliness might go a long way in helping him forget anything ever happened.

He was watering the roses when I approached him. I sat down on one of the stone walls that wasn't crumbling and started, "Hey Charles, do you mind if I ask you a couple of questions?"

He glanced at me. "Only a couple."

"What's your birthday?"

"December second."

He was nineteen, so to save my questions, I did the math in my head and figured out his birth year.

"You said before that you've never been to Canada?"

"I haven't been."

"Do you have a passport?"

"No."

"Have you ever tried to get one?"

"No." He was getting huffy now.

My brain was whirring. Why had Christian had all the stuff with him to turn him into Charles Lewis? At the airport, I saw Christian had a British passport with Charles' information. Had that thing been government-issued, or faked? Christian had also said his hotel room was in Charles' name. Why? What was special about him that Christian was impersonating him?

"What's your family like? Are they in business?" My questions were risky because I didn't like it when I was quizzed about my family.

He set down his hose and gave me a sideways glance. "Why are you suddenly so interested?"

"I just was wondering if you're playing at being a gardener when actually, you're something more," I said, hoping he would think I was being the snotty rich girl I was and interviewing him to see if he was good enough for me. I hoped it was a shortcut in getting him to spill his secrets.

"I don't have much family," he said slowly. "Brandon was a friend of my mum's."

"Okay..." I said slowly, thinking that had not been what I had been hoping for.

He looked like he wanted to say more, but couldn't. Then I realized that what he had just admitted to was a lie. What he was saying was a rehearsed excuse designed to give a plausible explanation. He'd been told to say that, and he was saying it.

"Okay. Next question—"

He interrupted. "I don't know if I want to answer any more questions."

"It won't take long."

"It's not the length of the questions," he rebutted. "It's the content. Why are you asking me about my passport? Shouldn't you be asking me questions like, what's your favorite film? What kind of music do you listen to? What are you doing Saturday night? Stuff like that?"

I paused. I did not want to ask him out on a date. I leaned back on my elbows. "Okay. Do I need to ask you about your favorite film? Do you need me to ask you a collection of random questions to hide the question I really want an answer to?"

He glared at me. "Maybe you do."

I smiled. "Or maybe I could bribe you by telling you things about me? What do you want to know?"

"Do you want to date me?" he asked without flinching.

"No."

"No?" he gasped in surprise. "After all the flirting you've done?"

My gaze flicked around nervously. "I haven't been flirting with you intentionally."

"You've been making eyes at me," Charles insisted.

Just like when I was with Christian, I tried to make myself look innocent by crossing my ankles. "I don't know much about dating," I admitted.

"Really?"

"I'm only seventeen."

His expression read that he thought he was the man-of-the-hour since I'd never dated before. "Then ask your questions. I have this place I want to take you—"

"I don't want to leave the house. Besides, I only have one more question for you. Do you know Damen Cross?"

"I hate you," he said shortly as he turned on his heel and left me there.

I watched him go and wondered what had made him so angry. Damen Cross was one of Christian's aliases. Sometimes I did Google searches on him just to see his face. Damen was gorgeous beyond understanding. There were three pictures I liked the best. The first one was of him on the red carpet at a movie premiere with a famous actress. The second one was supposed to be a casual picture of him on a pier by a lake, but it came off as a glamor shot. It was for a financial magazine about big money makers in investment banking. The last one was of him cutting the ribbon at the grand opening of a bank.

He had dark wavy hair and penetrating brown eyes. His jaw bone was the same, the eye shape was the same, but his eyebrows were bushier, and his chin looked rounder than that of the Christian I knew. Like it or not—it was definitely him—adding extra pieces or perhaps taking them away. It had never occurred to me that he might be wearing foam on his face when he played Christian, but if he didn't, why had he been forced to escort me back to my school made up like Charles Lewis?

Brandon came around the corner. His wheelbarrow was empty. "What bee got in his bonnet?" he asked, pointing his chin in Charles' direction.

"I asked him if he knew Damen Cross and he flipped out and walked away."

Brandon smiled and his kind eyes turned up at the corners. He took off his work gloves, smacked the dust from them and threw them in the wheelbarrow. "I have no idea."

I growled and began biting my thumb.

"But…" he said tantalizingly, "if I were to venture a guess, I would say that he wouldn't like to be asked about another man. He fancies you, so it might make him jealous."

"But this guy is a millionaire and many years older than me, so why would he be a threat?" I whined.

"You're not the only person who's here for the summer with no friends and no one to talk to," Brandon reminded me.

"I have people to talk to."

"Mable says you don't talk to her. Hilary says you don't talk to her. Apparently, you talk to me and the big man and that's it. Aren't you lonely? Isn't Charles better than no one?"

I sat cross-legged in the well-trimmed grass. "I don't want to date Charles. The idea is oppressive."

"Then why did ye tell your friend ye were winching him outside your school?"

"I was what?" I cried in misguided outrage.

"Kissing him. Kissing him," Brandon amended.

"Oh…" I said, cooling. "Argh! Seriously, this is a misunderstanding that is not my fault. You're just as bad as Christian. I think half the reason he sent me here for the summer was to set me up with Charles, but I don't want to be set up."

"I am not suggesting to ye that you date him," Brandon said. "I just thought there wouldn't be much harm in befriending him."

"Do you think he could befriend me? I have never been able to be 'just friends' with a man I liked. Why would he be able to just be friends with me if he likes me so much?"

Brandon didn't reply but instead smiled at me as if he understood my little ploy to insert myself into Christian's life. The thing that was the most charming about it was that his expression did not smack of disapproval or ridicule. Unless I was mistaken, it seemed like he was rooting for me.

I looked at the gardener. "You know, you're really easy to talk to."

"Am I?" Brandon said. Even those two words were inviting.

"Yeah. I feel like I could tell you anything."

But when I admitted to feeling that way, something in his countenance fell. Something in his eyes barred me from telling him anything more. He was warning me with the set of his lips and the shards in his eyes that he and I were not to become close. I might have suspected him as the person who was bugging the house, except that he was such an easy confidant for me that he couldn't have been. I would have told him anything, but he was begging me not to.

***

It was late. Christian was supposed to be back from London. I knew he wasn't working his supposed job as a communications director, and I was very curious about what he did with his weekday.

I didn't hear him come in, but I heard him splash in the pool. As quietly as I could, I hurried out of bed and down the stairs. I was half-way through the dining room when I heard voices. The door between the dining room and the conservatory was open and I could hear Brandon's voice. A few steps closer and I could make out what they were saying. Christian was in the pool and Brandon squatted on the deck, bending low to speak to him.

"No!" Christian exclaimed, failing at keeping his voice down.

Brandon's Scottish accent faded completely as he said clearly, "You think you can make it not true by denying it? Have you looked at her? Did you look at her all those years ago? That's not baby fat coming off her cheeks."

Through the crack in the door, I watched Christian stand up and thump the water with his palm angrily. The splash did not hit Brandon. "I need more proof."

"You need to tell her the truth and get her away from here," Brandon insisted.

"And if you're wrong? What then? What will happen then? What if I tell her what you've told me and you're wrong?"

"I am not wrong!" Brandon said bitingly.

Christian shook his head. "This is too big. If you're wrong and I have to repent and turn her loose, she won't be able to keep the secret. No one can keep the secret and I'll have a whole new group of devils biting at my heels."

"Not with her," Brandon maintained steadily. "I am not wrong and you have nothing to fear from her. She'll be able to keep the secret."

"It won't be up to her," Christian retorted, getting more heated and more contradictory.

"Someone will put her and me together in an equation, they'll think she knows something, and suddenly she'll go missing. You know what will happen then?"

Brandon looked away. "You don't have to keep rubbing it in my face that I don't have as much experience with these things. I can imagine all sorts of grizzly situations if you ask me to."

"She deserves to have another chance at the life she has. If you're right, waiting a few years won't change anything," Christian said, using the reasonable voice he sometimes used with me.

"Yes, but can *you* wait?"

Christian scoffed. "Why wouldn't I be able to wait?"

Brandon looked at him meaningfully.

"We don't talk about that. I don't even think about that."

Brandon chuckled. "You know what might be the most beautiful thing in the world? A beautiful woman who is not an object. She never thinks of herself as an object. She knows she is actually the only thing worth living for, worth dying for, and yet she's not a trophy. She's an actual force for change, like a queen on a chess board. If you're the king, your hands are tied, but she's going to wage war for you."

Christian stared at him with his lips parted in disbelief. "What nonsense are you talking about?"

"Your girl. Even if you dress her like she's a princess with a petal skirt, eventually she is going to get blood on her face and you will think you've never seen a woman so finely attired."

Christian frowned. "You don't know that."

"I do know that. Mark my words. I warned you how this was going to unravel. Send her back to Canada at the end of the summer if you must, but you're fighting against this unnecessarily. She's ready. You're the one who's not ready."

Christian turned toward me in the water so his chest was visible, and I felt the familiar tightening of my chest as he did so. He lifted himself effortlessly out of the water and reached for his towel. He dried his face and wrapped the towel around his neck as he stood to face Brandon. He was taller and looked down on him.

"What did she say to you that supports that conclusion?" Christian asked.

"It's not what you think. She doesn't understand what's going on yet. She's still asking questions about Damen Cross." He left the conservatory through the door that led outside into the summer night, and Christian followed him.

I sank against the wall. The only thing that was clear to me was that I needed to get out of the dining room and upstairs to my room before anyone found me. What they said needed dissecting, but not just then. I scurried down the hall and up the stairs.

CHAPTER SIX

The Kiss that Broke Heaven

The next day was hot and I went into the library to cool down. The first thing I was going to do involved hitting the switch to turn on the overhead fans, but as I came in I saw they were already going. I put on some music. Not loudly, but loud enough that I could still hear it through my headgear. I slid my headphones over my ears and began sweeping the room for bugs with my wand.

I checked a few of the tables before I saw something move out of the corner of my eye. Looking up, I saw Christian, perfectly still, sleeping on a sofa. I hadn't woken him. As stealthily as I could, I prowled around until I was leaning against an end table behind his head.

"Darling," I said softly, mimicking the way he always called me darling. It was his way of putting space between us, by making me sound young and reminding me I was under his care. "Darling, darling," I whispered. "Sometimes I think you want me to grow up so I won't be your problem anymore, and sometimes I think you want me to grow up so you can kiss me without censure. Will sleepy Christian tell me which one it is?"

"How did you do looking for the bugs? Did you find any more?" he muttered through set sleepy teeth.

"I found three more, but they were in completely different places than where we found the first batch," I affirmed when he opened his eyes. "Whoever is watching us is a real sicko. Have you figured out who it is?"

"It's hard to tell, darling."

I dropped down a bit and whispered in his ear, "Do you think my dorm room has cameras installed in it too?"

He looked up into my eyes, giving me an upside-down view of his face. "It's a possibility."

I lightly smacked the side of his head with my palm. "Why didn't you say something sooner?"

"I check it every chance I get."

64

"You could have told me and let me make sure it's safe, since you're not around very often," I retorted.

"Be calm. It's better if you live your life without suspecting they're there, and up until now, that was possible. Lend me your wand," he ordered. "Let's see how good a job you did finding the little beasties."

I passed him my equipment and he took it in hand.

"There are superior places to make records from in the room. It's always wise to check those first." He gave the room a scan, checking the tables and the entryways. "Looks good, except you missed a second camera over the bookshelf there." He pointed.

"Then it's not good. I missed one."

"Yes, but that one is very high up and you would have to be... I don't know, at least six inches taller to have put it in range of the meter. I'd say you did a good job."

"Do you think we should find another place to live because there are still so many bugs?" I asked, discouraged that I couldn't get all of them.

He didn't answer me. Instead, he commented, "This is a new camera. I know this wasn't here when I did my sweep of the library last week. I'm going to have to start from scratch and do the whole house over again." He took it over to the sounding block and crushed it with a little more rage than before.

"Christian," I suddenly said, putting my hand on his tan forearm. "What kind of conversation are they trying to hear? What are they trying to find out?"

He looked at me like I was stupid.

I stared back at him and momentarily pursed my lips in frustration. "Are you and I likely to have a conversation they would want to listen to?"

"Beth, I'm not sure how to react to finding a new piece of surveillance. If there's a new piece, then I do know who put it here. If it was them, then on second thought, I'm not sure if it's worth it to scan for new bugs and remove them. As long as we keep your closet clean, so they aren't getting a free peep show, it might be better just to be ourselves. As long as you and I are what we usually are, then there won't be a problem for the rest of the summer."

65

"Isn't there a place we can talk for a minute?" I asked, feeling blocked.

He turned and led me into a conservatory. "This is a bad room for recording information," he said, pointing to a noisy fountain that was always running. Immediately, he began sweeping the room with the wand again anyway. "Seems okay," he said after a couple of minutes.

He pulled the headset off and joined me on the couch close to the fountain. "Is there something on your mind particularly?"

I glanced around the room nervously. "Would it be better to go out? Should we just go out for lunch?"

"Sometimes that makes it easier for people to spy on you. For this moment, I think we're safe. Go ahead."

I had been doing a lot of thinking, and I had decided to assert my independence. I was seventeen and only had a few months left before my birthday. He would never give me what I wanted if I didn't tell him what I wanted.

"I don't want you to be my guardian anymore," I said slowly, shyly meeting his eyes.

His expression was wounded, but only momentarily. His face immediately took on the mask of good-natured tolerance he sometimes used. "Only two weeks of this and you have already decided that this isn't the kind of 'home' you want? Well, I can't blame you," he said, averting his eyes and straightening the cuffs of his shirt.

I leaned closer to him, so his forehead and mine were almost touching. I was drawing him closer to me to make it seem like I wanted to whisper what I was going to say next in his ear. "The thing is," I said, "being your responsibility is getting in the way of what I really want."

"Which is?" He turned to look in my eyes accusingly.

"This," I said, right before I kissed him.

The moment my lips touched his he needed no further encouragement. It was like the moment in the hospital room, and the moment outside my school, except better. His lips moved like he had waited forever for that moment. Like he had stayed away from me all those years to stop himself from doing exactly what I had initiated. His fingers were in my hair and the armrest bit into my ribs and thighs.

There was too much between us, and I couldn't draw breath. Christian kissed me as if he would rather kiss me than breathe.

It was everything I dreamed of.

Suddenly light broke upon us. Charles had opened the door to the conservatory. As he glared at us, it was obvious he had already seen us through the windows, and he came in to stop us. Christian broke away from me, but it was too late. The redhead had already seen me kiss Christian instead of him, and all the taboos, all the reasons Christian and I were not allowed to be in love flooded the room.

Charles sneered at us and let the door fall shut.

Christian wiped his mouth delicately with his knuckles like he could wipe our kiss away, but didn't exactly want to. "Go pack your things," he said firmly and regretfully before he rose and went out into the garden.

***

As I stumbled down the hallway toward my room, I thought of running after Charles and getting him to promise me that he wouldn't tell anyone what he had just seen, but I didn't change my course. Christian told me what he wanted me to do and I would do anything for him if he loved me.

Maybe he had a way to sort it out.

In my room, I threw open my suitcase and packed as hurriedly as possible. Maybe Christian had an idea of where to take me. He did say that his first instinct was to change locations. Maybe he was going to take me somewhere else for the rest of the summer. Maybe everything wasn't ruined. It was just stupid Charles who had seen us. He wasn't a big deal, right?

From my window, I saw Brandon by the stone wall. Charles was with him, striding back and forth angrily while Brandon listened and leaned on his pitchfork. Brandon saw me from the window. His expression gave away nothing.

I turned away and finished my packing, suddenly wanting every last thing Christian had put in my room. I took the jewelry and the picture from the bookcase. I ripped the fairy lights from the wall and shoved them in my case. I hauled the whole thing down the stairs and met Christian and Mable in the front hall.

Christian looked nothing at all like a ruffled gentleman as he explained. "Mable will take you to Glasgow and stay in a hotel with you tonight. Then it's off to Muskoka to spend the rest of the summer with Trinity."

"I thought Trinity was going to Paris for August."

"Not anymore. I just got off the phone with her aunt in Ontario and plans have changed. They're so pleased you'll be able to join her." He actually sounded quite pleasant, like what just happened in the conservatory hadn't really happened and he wasn't reacting by sending me away.

"When will I see you again?" I breathed, suddenly terrified.

"Soon," he said, venturing a kiss on my forehead, then stopping himself midway.

"Will you call me?" I persisted.

"Of course I will, darling." When he said 'darling' my hope for a phone call evaporated. I couldn't even ask him why Charles seeing us together was the disaster he supposed. Wasn't Charles somehow a friend of his or Brandon's? Someone who wouldn't want to hurt him? Then I thought of the camera Christian had found that morning in the library. He said he knew who had planted it. My face fell. It could only have been Charles. He was the only one who Christian didn't trust who had full access.

Christian picked up my luggage and walked with Mable and me out to Mable's yellow Mercedes. He deposited my case in the back while Mable got behind the wheel.

"Can't we talk about what happened?" I whispered to Christian as he bid me farewell on the passenger side of the car.

"If things clear up, I'll be in contact. Be a good girl and let me sort this out. It may take some time."

Brandon came up at that moment and stood wordlessly next to Christian. I waved him a little good-bye wave and he saluted me. I thought his gesture was free of sarcasm, because he didn't think what had happened was scandalous. He didn't think I was gross for having made out with the closest thing I had to a father. Abruptly, I hugged him. The gardener patted me on the head.

"You were my favorite one," I confessed.

"Stop it, hen," he drawled pleasantly. "Now get in the car, while I'm the last one who's cradled ye."

I did. I watched Christian and Brandon cast glances between each other and wave to me as I drove away with Mable. The last thing I saw was Brandon scratch under his collar and tell Christian something under his breath. Unless I was mistaken, the one word I could make out was 'sloppy'.

CHAPTER SEVEN

The Blueberry of His Eye

His eyes were a really deep blue. It was almost like an electric shock, and I couldn't stop looking.

Three years had passed since the summer I had last seen Christian, and I had started a whole new life. Now I was starting my third year at the University of Alberta, and I knew I hadn't seen Mr. Blue Eyes during my first two years. The more I looked at him, the more I wanted to look at him. His name was Rogan Cormack, and I had never spoken to him. The first time I saw him, he probably passed under my radar. I didn't notice him until I heard him laugh. The sound made my heart take a dive and I took immediate, intense notice. He sounded exactly like Christian.

Then, I couldn't stop staring.

His hair was black and cut very short in the back. It grew longer on top. His hairline was completely hidden since his hair was always brushed forward, so I couldn't see if he had Christian's widow's peak. His eyebrows were extremely bushy and looked in need of Christian's usual trimming, but no university student was as stylish as Christian had been. Rogan wore hoodies and toques. He also wore thick rimmed glasses; their frames an intense indigo, which made his eyes look even bluer. His goatee was trimmed close to his face and the rest of his jawline was always so cleanly shaven it was as if he shaved right before class.

The thing was, I couldn't forget Christian's laugh. When I went on vacation with him, all those years ago, I took pictures. I took movies. I recorded his voice and his laugh. My memory of him couldn't fade, because I was reliving the time we had spent together by reviewing those photographs, watching those movies and listening to those sound bites.

When I started looking for hints that Rogan was Christian, I found them everywhere. His face looked different, everything about the way he styled his face was different. His eyelashes threw me at first. They

70

were unbelievably black, like his hair. It changed the whole mood of his face. He looked ten years younger dressed like a student. He was obviously hiding who he was, not from everyone, but from me. Christian had a distinct Adam's apple as an identifier. Rogan wore turtlenecks or scarves to ensure I never saw his neck. It was cold that fall, and he wore tight leather gloves, that he hoped hid the right angles of his hands. The gloves hugged his hands so tightly, they were practically liquid, so even though I couldn't see color, I could see shape and that hadn't changed.

After staring at Rogan for two months, I could swear an affidavit that it was Christian in disguise. I didn't question why he had chosen to appear in front of me as a different person. He had his reasons, both for being someone else and for not making contact with me. I hoped he had found an identity he could use that would allow us to be together, and was waiting for me to notice him, but I wasn't quite ready to introduce myself.

I had changed. The girl I had been three years ago was gone. When I ran into people I had once known at boarding school, they didn't recognize me. I had grown three and a half inches, and though I hadn't lost more than twenty pounds, the added height had changed the whole shape of my body. I still had my freckles, though I hid them under liquid foundation. I had also learned to work with my curls so that they became ringlets instead of a frizzy poof. My hair was still more brown than blond, but apparently, I was unrecognizable because I had learned how to contour around my nose to make it look more elfin. Occasionally, I got asked out on dates by men I had known as boys who could not believe the transformation. Their surprise was almost insulting.

I knew Christian wouldn't be fooled by makeup or weight loss. No matter how much I changed, he would know me.

***

The summer I spent with Trinity in Muskoka turned out to be life-changing. We had both been abandoned by our adults and together, with lit firecrackers under the starry sky, we decided to give up Paris.

71

Paris, we decided, was an idea. By that point in the summer, I had called Christian a hundred times, left him a hundred messages, texted him a hundred times, emailed him a hundred emails, and made myself annoying in every way I could imagine. At the hundredth one on each medium, I stopped. He knew where to find me just as easily as Trinity's parents knew where to find her. We were being hung out to dry by people who worshiped Paris.

The idea of Paris is the pursuit of glamor over substance. Trinity chose Paris as her symbol because her trip had been canceled before Christian called her aunt. She just hadn't had the nerve to tell me what had happened over the phone. Her step-sister (a woman who was the child of a union that had nothing to do with either of Trinity's parents) had seen a picture of Trinity on Instagram with her pierced tongue. She vowed she couldn't take a girl like that into her peaceful Parisian apartment and outright refused to take her. It was the first time Trinity had been refused entrance because of her antics and appearance.

Trinity was on the verge of an epiphany. That summer she decided that she needed to start looking out for herself and when she graduated from high school she was going to make herself an apartment. Not a Parisian apartment, but a place where anyone could come, no matter what they looked like. No more glamor.

That was Trinity's warcry and though I knew I had been dumped by Christian for other reasons, it didn't stop the pain. Since I had no banner to parade that explained my hurt, I allowed her to think that my problems were the same as hers. It was easy to fall in line. One thing that was clear to me was that Christian had been worried about what someone thought about us together. If public opinion meant that I couldn't couple with an incredibly handsome, charming man who happened to take responsibility for me when my parents passed away, then I didn't want anything to do with worldly wisdom.

What Trinity was saying aligned perfectly with what I wanted. I didn't want to be in the spotlight. I wanted to avoid my family in Toronto and Ottawa. I wanted to go somewhere quiet where no one had any expectations for me.

When the summer ended, we returned to boarding school and Trinity cracked the books like she was possessed. Her green hair grew out and when it finally had long enough roots, she went to the salon and had all the green cut out. She looked normal in her graduation pictures and normal again on convocation day. Her parents might have been pleasantly surprised if they had bothered to come.

Christian didn't come either. I kept my eye out for him, but that important day, like many others, passed without his presence.

The summer after high school was spent without parental consent. We moved to Edmonton. Trinity had wanted Calgary, but I wanted Edmonton. I won because the university in Edmonton was rumored to be better. It was the city where I had first known Christian. The university campus was spitting distance from the hospital where I had been treated. Trinity was taking a degree in biology in the fall, which basically amounted to premed. I was taking business because I had no ambition and I hoped I could do nothing but fall on my feet if I took a degree in business.

Trinity and I had both received our trust funds. Mine was the money my parents had left me when they passed. It was enough to pay for my degree if I was careful.

Trinity and I rented a beautiful studio apartment at the top of a building close to the university. We lived there for two months before school started. We went shopping and decorated. My contribution was the beds. I had two beds custom ordered for us to be like two private rooms. They were like cabinets with ceilings and cupboard doors that enclosed our mattresses. We made paper turn dials to show whether or not we were inside. At the end of August, when they were delivered, they ended up being the last things I paid for with Christian's credit card. I would have gone on using his money, as often as I could for as long as I could, but the next time I swiped his card, the waitress told me it had been canceled. It was a blow, not because I couldn't spend his money anymore, but because it suggested he wasn't doing well if there wasn't money for me to use.

Of course, the life Trinity and I lived in Edmonton had nothing in common with the life I had lived in Edmonton before. I went to the florist Christian had brought me flowers from, like he was going to be there, choosing roses. I went to the hospital and wandered the halls, but none of the doctors or nurses who had treated me all those years ago were around. I didn't bump into anyone I knew.

Trinity was a completely different person. She no longer did anything to impress or shock those around her. She did exactly what she thought was comfortable, so she took out her earrings and eventually her tongue ring. She wore sweaters and padded around the apartment in slippers with a cup of tea nestled in her cold hands. Suddenly, she had a lot of ideas on interior decorating and made our space one of the 'cool places to hang out'. That had been her ambition, to make her home a place that would take anybody. Except, it wasn't *just* anybody. Trinity ended up having a bunch of relatives that started taking note of her as soon as we arrived. She didn't even know she had snooty academic family members on her mother's side. That meant that the people who hung out at our apartment were not homeless people but fellow university students who had enough spare time to 'hang out'.

Since I was no longer being waited on hand and foot, I lost weight. I had to do my own laundry, pay for my own groceries and carry them. I got a job at the copy place on campus. I worked there because it gave me money and saved me from Trinity's constant flux of inane guests. It was a shame my university education didn't interest me much.

I didn't realize I was living like a zombie, merely going through the motions of life without really living. I let Trinity have whoever she wanted at the apartment for as long as she wanted. I'd wake up in the middle of the night to her talking quietly with a small knot of idealistic students discussing the dreams they'd had the night before. I didn't know what I had been thinking when I bought the beds that looked like cupboards, but it was a good thing I did. When inside, it muffled the ruckus. I wish I could have joined them, but I felt burned out.

I felt that way until I heard Rogan Cormack laugh. That probably wasn't Christian's real name either, but I had finally been brought back to life. My heart hammered at the sound of his voice. At the sight of him, the blood pounded into my ears and spread heat everywhere.

Finally, he had returned.

Except, I was failing myself. I didn't know how to approach him. I didn't know how to plan a strategy to get him into my life. The first time our eyes met, he stepped in the print center to get a copy of his driver's license.

Gibson, my boss, had been about to serve him when I interrupted. "The copier in the back is doing that thing again," I lied with a smack of my gum.

"Oh," Gibson said, looking at Rogan who was waiting.

"I'll take it from here," I said, finishing the copy. "You know," I said with a saucy wrinkle of my nose. "There's a copier on the second floor that's really good for quick jobs like this." No matter what, I couldn't let him know I recognized him.

Rogan leaned forward and whispered conspiratorially, "Someone's using it. I think they missed the memo about it being for quick jobs."

Gibson came back and said noisily, "Beth, there's nothing wrong with that copier." He saw me leaning forward on the counter and said, "Oh!" He turned around and on his way back said, "I'd better check again."

Rogan looked at me like he had seen that trick before, and was only vaguely amused by it. "How much do I owe you?"

"It's on the house," I said. "It's the least I can do since you had to walk all the way down here."

He cocked his head and gave a mock salute. "I'll be sure to come back."

He left and Gibson joined me at the counter. "What was that about?" he asked grouchily. "I've never seen you flirt with a customer before."

"I have a crush on him," I explained, enjoying the act of finally telling someone the truth about my feelings.

Gibson looked at me like I'd grown horns. "You don't have to ask me for permission."

***

Speaking to Rogan gave me the encouragement I needed. However, it was weeks before I saw an opportunity to talk to him. I was ready when I slid into the seat opposite Rogan in the food court. He was typing something on his laptop and didn't look up. I handed him a smoothie in a foam cup and asked pertly, "Do you like blueberry?"

He eyed me skeptically. "Who are you and why do you think I'm homeless?"

"Sorry, I must have made a mistake. I thought you were a university student." I looked at him meaningfully, like all university students must be poor. "So you're not homeless?"

He took the smoothie from me and popped open the lid. "There's not some weird drug in here, is there?"

I rolled my eyes. "Yeah, I knew there was a reason I picked you. Look, I know you're in my economics class and I wanted to ask you to be my partner on the next assignment. This is just my way of introducing myself. We were supposed to have our partners by the end of the day. I'm not slipping you the date rape drug or anything. I promise."

"That's good, because I have my whistle," he said.

I laughed. None of the men carried rape whistles. It was a girl thing. "I just couldn't remember anyone else in the class except you and when I saw you sitting here, I thought it was good luck," I lied.

"Sorry," he said before he took a strong drag on the straw. "I already have a partner. I got one before leaving class. You should have done that too."

I smiled at him. He was trying to make it as hard as possible. I didn't let it bother me. "Forget about the assignment," I said coolly. "How about a dinner date?"

"And your name is?"

"Beth."

He cocked an eyebrow. "Well, Beth, you're not really my type."

"Really? What's your type?"

"Her," he said, pointing at a girl on the couches with his smoothie straw.

I turned my head to get a better look. Oddly enough, I knew who she was. Socialite extraordinaire, she was a relative of Trinity's. Her name was Felicity-Ann, but she always got called Felix, or Feline, or something like that. Her hair was blonde and long. Pricing her outfit at a thousand dollars, excluding her coat, would have been low-balling it. She hadn't ditched her parents, so she didn't count her pennies.

Felicity-Ann noticed our interest and shook off her friends to come over.

I rolled my eyes and sipped on my beverage. I really loathed her type, if only because Christian had always liked it.

"Rogan!" she exclaimed pleasantly as she placed a hand possessively on his shoulder. "I haven't seen you in ages. Did you get your cell phone replaced?"

"Yeah, yesterday. I haven't had time to renew all my contacts."

"What took so long, anyway?" she pouted. "I've had *so* many things I've wanted to invite you to."

He adjusted the glasses on his face. "You know me. It's hard to find the time."

She shrugged her beautiful shoulders. "But there's a party tonight I want you to come to."

"I'm sorry. I can't," he interrupted. "You really should try to schedule me in advance like this girl here. She was just trying to squeeze her way onto my schedule."

I loved that man! Just sitting there listening to his ridiculous, condescending voice filled my heart with glee. That was just like Christian. The way he made it sound like both of us were a burden, and he was merely tolerating us because it amused him, was irresistible.

"Oh, Bethie, I didn't see you there," Felicity-Ann said snobbishly. Of course, she had seen me. We'd known each other since Trinity and I moved to Edmonton. She was just trying to lower my stock in front of Rogan.

I smiled at her like we were best friends. Never badmouth another girl in front of a man. It only makes you look bad and makes the other girl look more desirable. Christian taught me that.

"It's no problem. I didn't see you either," I said breezily with a flick of my hand.

That shut her up. Her shoulders slumped and she lowered herself into the chair beside Rogan. "When's your next free day?" she asked him with a flirtatious smack of her lips.

"I don't have free days. I'm actually driving down to Calgary tonight. Too bad you're busy with your party."

"I could ditch it and tag along," she offered immediately.

"And too bad I'm busy," he continued. "I'm on my way out now, so I'm going to have to shoo you along." He closed his laptop and started packing it up.

Felicity-Ann got up to give him room. "Okay, but I'd better get a text from you or something."

"Of course, you will," he said, giving her a little push back toward her spot on the couch.

Another girl would have been discouraged by the constant blow-off, but not me. To me, it only provided further evidence that he was Christian in disguise. What I was witnessing was a perfect example of how he treated women. Granted, he was less cordial than gentleman Christian, but the message was the same.

He slid a toque over his hair and seemed like he was going to leave without saying anything more to me, but he picked up his smoothie and drank some more of it.

I stood up and met his eyes. "What about our date?"

He took another long sip from the straw. Then he put the cup on the table with a slight echo. "I'm not likely to whore myself off for a smoothie." Then he winked at me and disappeared around a corner.

I shook his cup. It was empty. Did he drink that monster-sized smoothie in five minutes? And he left the cup for me to throw away, which was the reason for the wink.

Well, I was completely mesmerized.

***

Except that evening, I was hit with another blow. I knew something was off as soon as I entered the apartment and Trinity was home without a guest. For two years, we had had an odd rotation of visitors. Now the apartment was blank, and Trinity sat alone in the middle of the shag carpet, playing on her phone.

"Oh, you're home," she said when she saw me.

I looked around wearily. "Is Brighton in the bathroom?" I asked.

"No."

"Did you two break up?" I asked, looking around again like I'd see him behind a sofa. He practically lived at our place.

78

"No," she giggled, and that was when I saw it. She had a diamond ring on her finger. Since her personal makeover, she didn't wear rings unless she was going dancing. It was very noticeable.

For a second, I didn't know how to react. If Brighton had asked Trinity to marry him, then that was tremendous… for her. I didn't have any complaints against him, other than his considerable lack of flair. She'd been dating him for a year and a half. He was a law student who found time to work at the Campus Food Bank, where she worked. Their attraction had been instant. Though it was clear what his charms were, none of them were physical, but he was extraordinarily attentive to Trinity after the fashion of a guard dog. Trinity, who had never been cared for by a man in her life, was one hundred percent charmed and they started dating.

Stupidly, I hadn't seen marriage in their future. I had always taken it for granted that Trinity and I would live together for at least four years. But as I saw her seated on the rug with her legs crossed and her eyes shining, I saw at once that our time together was coming to an end. The question was: how soon?

"Nice ring," I said with a carefully chosen smile as I set down my bag.

"We're getting married," she said, sporting her engagement ring.

"Wow," I said, hiding my unease.

"I know the ring isn't worth that much," she justified. "It only cost about seven hundred dollars. Can you imagine the look on my father's face if he saw it? He would die of embarrassment at his daughter marrying a man who only spent seven hundred on an engagement ring. He would demand that I break it off until Brighton could afford to get me a ring that cost over eighty thousand. You don't think it matters how much it costs, do you?"

I clicked my tongue sharply. "No. We're not in Paris anymore."

She understood what the reference meant immediately, and looked at me as if to beg my forgiveness for backing out of our deal.

Without words to excuse her, I dropped on the rug next to her and put my arm around her. I had been her friend too long to dismiss what she was getting when she married Brighton. I was still in the league of people who remembered Trinity from her wild, attention-getting, days.

Everything was perfect as long as she wasn't dumped on the sidewalk in front of an emergency room by friends who didn't want to get arrested. She was a long way from that and marrying Brighton would take her even further away.

"Congratulations!" I exclaimed. "Have you set a date?"

"We were thinking this summer," she said dreamily. "That way, he'll be done law school and I can move with him wherever he goes to do his articling. I might not have to give up on my degree if we move within a certain radius of a decent university."

I nodded. "I'm happy for you."

"The only thing I'm sad about is leaving you alone here after the wedding," she said mournfully.

"It's all right," I said, picking up her left hand and making a show of looking at her ring. "I'll put some effort into finding another roommate... or maybe I'll just live here by myself."

"I don't want to leave you alone," she protested. "I'll help you find somebody if you have trouble." She winced.

Then I winced.

She wasn't finished giving me the bad news. "And there's something else. Brighton wants to take me home for Christmas."

I nearly choked. As it turned out, I had already taken all the bad news I could stand for one evening, and this final bit was going to make me cry.

"He doesn't want to take me for the whole holiday," she adjusted quickly. "Just for Christmas Eve, and then we'll be back by the twenty-seventh. I'll be able to spend New Year's Eve with you."

I nodded slowly. I had never spent Christmas one hundred percent alone.

"I'm sorry," she said, "it's just..."

I blew her off. "There's no need to apologize," I began. "We're friends, not life partners. Go. Have fun. I'm sure I'll be able to think of something to do. I'm not helpless."

Trinity dropped her head apologetically. "I'm so sorry. I'll see if I can help."

I sighed. "Really, don't worry about me. I'll think of something."

I didn't have a bedroom to stomp off to, so I went to the bathroom and started the shower. Even though all I did was lean against the counter with my knuckles against my mouth while the water ran. I didn't cry. I breathed and got a grip. There was nothing to be afraid of. Christian was back, and this time, he wasn't my guardian. He was Rogan, my contemporary. All I had to do was let him know what was happening with Trinity. Everything would be fine. Even if Trinity moved to the moon, everything would be fine. I just needed to find a way to tell him how scared I was to be alone, and how I had never got over the hurt I felt when he left me.

***

I was having trouble making my battle plan. I couldn't tell if my first attempt with the smoothie had been a success or not. I decided he was probably at the university to get a sense of what my life was like and once he was satisfied I was living well without him, he might be on his way. Maybe. Maybe not.

I only knew one person who was a mutual acquaintance, and I really did not want to talk to Felicity-Ann. I saw her that afternoon in one of the student lounges drinking a bottle of water that was too expensive for the pop machines.

I stood in the doorway and thought about approaching her.

Nah. It wasn't worth it. I went out the other way and tried to think of something else.

In the end, the weeks leading up to exams ticked by and I didn't manage to do anything more than say hi to Rogan in economics. He said, "Hi," back, but the way he said it made me think he was really saying, "Don't expect anything from me... ever." It discouraged me.

I was on the verge of becoming a zombie again, but an opportunity presented itself two days before my final exams. I was walking through one of the lounge areas when I saw his shoulder blades protruding from one of the couches. Many of the campus buildings were open all night around exam time and many students slept on the couches, but I had never expected to see him, of all people, take advantage of that. It seemed out of character, especially for the Christian I had known.

I had taken a nap there a time or two myself, but usually in the afternoon, and not at night. It was better than sleeping on the floor, but the experience would have been greatly improved by a blanket and a pillow. He was lying on his stomach, using his backpack as a pillow to prop him up. There was probably a laptop in there, a far cry from comfort. So, I went about conjuring a pillow and blanket for him. It was easy. The University Bookstore sold so much UofA swag that finding a pillow and a fleece blanket was easy. I was lucky I popped in two minutes before they closed for the night.

I sat in one of the chairs, pulled the tags off the blanket, and spread it across him. It barely covered him, he was so long. I was less sure how to maneuver the pillow in. I put my hand under his head and he immediately stirred.

"What are you doing?" he asked groggily.

"Quiet. I'm just lending you a pillow, and then I'll go, okay?"

"What?" he repeated like he was too disoriented to understand what I was saying.

"I know," I breathed cynically. "You aren't the kind of guy who would whore himself off for a blanket and a pillow, even in December. It's okay. Don't feel like I'm trying to get anything from you," I lied. "I just felt a little sorry for you, so don't feel obligated." I didn't bother moving his backpack and shoved the pillow under his head.

He shifted onto his back, put the pillow on his backpack and rested on it. "Actually, that's much better," he sighed, and he sounded exactly like Christian. "Thank you. I was getting a crick in my neck."

"My pleasure." I threw the plastic bookstore bag in the garbage and got up to leave.

"Wait a second," he said.

I turned around. "What?"

"Well, maybe I will whore myself off for a minute. Let's talk. I wanted to ask you. Do you normally ask men out on dates in that abrupt, crazy, way?"

I sat down in the armchair next to him. For him to open a conversation like that was an extremely good sign, even if it meant he was checking up on me like he was still my guardian. "No."

"Then why did you do that?"

I decided to start slowly and move the conversation with purpose. I had to convince him I was *not* living well. That way, he might try to involve himself in my life so he could save me. I started talking. "I used to know this man who always did things like that. He hardly ever showed up without a present of some kind. Often he would send presents before he arrived. Sometimes they were really overwhelming because of how much they cost or how much trouble they represented. I thought a smoothie was small enough that it wouldn't make anyone feel burdened. I'm sorry if I offended you. I'm not sure if I even know how to meet someone without at least offering them a stick of gum."

"Who was this guy? Your daddy? Your boyfriend?" He looked more like Christian without his heavy rimmed glasses.

I shook my head. "He was neither of those things… and both those things. Long story short—my parents are dead and he was assigned to look after me. When he realized I was falling for him, he gave me the boot and I haven't seen him since."

"Have you had a boyfriend since then?"

"No," I said with a snap of my tongue. "One guy is nice to me and my vision is so small that I can't see anyone but him. Pathetic, right?"

Rogan nodded like he did think it was very pathetic. "Are you doing anything fun for Christmas?" he asked, changing the subject.

"Nope. My roommate, Trinity, is going to visit her new in-laws, and I don't have any family, so I'm home… in my apartment… alone for the holidays."

Saying that truly shocked him. "Don't you have any other friends besides your roommate?"

"Sure, I do. But I'm not close enough to any of them to butt in on their Christmas morning plans. Besides, you shouldn't be confused about how that man I mentioned treated me. Even if I loved him with all my little-girl heart and he was the only person in the world I could see, he still left me alone in boarding schools and hotel rooms an awful lot. I'm used to being alone. You know, he could hardly spare four weeks a year to spend with me. You know, before I made things awkward."

Rogan's reaction during this speech was strange. He tightened his jaw and felt beside him for his glasses. A second later, they were on his face.

83

"I'll tell you what I'm going to do on Christmas morning," I said briskly. "I'm going to get up, make myself breakfast with everything I like in it. I'm going to play music. I'm going to bake cookies, and anything else I feel like. You know why? Because it's very obvious I'll be alone for the rest of my life, so I may as well get used to it." I felt very close to crying as I said those words, but I gritted my teeth visibly and almost growled rather than cry. I managed to say, "When he left me, it was worse than when my parents died. He was the one person I trusted. I was rejected, cast away, and I still don't know exactly why. For months, my hope was dashed in pieces every night before I went to sleep. He didn't call me today. Even though three and a half years have passed and hope is dead, it still feels like it happened recently. The blood is still fresh. I'm still bawling, and honestly… I don't think I'll ever heal."

"Don't you live in a party flat?" he asked. "Are you feeling this way while you live in a party flat with Trinity Powell?"

"And if I am?" I growled.

"Have you seen a counselor?"

"She moved her office and didn't tell me," I admitted. "I haven't had the stamina to try therapy again."

That got him. I'd cracked him. That was the pathetic cherry on the pathetic cherry cake. The regret and sorrow on his face were perfect. It wasn't Christian's face, but the expression was perfect. That was the expression Christian would wear if I ever truly got the chance to tell him what he had done to me when he broke contact. He thought I would get help from somewhere. He thought someone would be there for me. I had shown him I was alone.

"Trinity has been lovely to me," I said. "Our apartment may look like a party apartment on the outside. On the inside, Trinity cradles lost souls and tries to point them in productive directions. She's not throwing keggers. She has healing crystals hanging from fairy lights. She has textbooks on psychology. And yes, she wants to heal me. I'm the one she wants to heal the most, but the person she's actually healed is herself. When she brings these people into our home, she tells them positive things. She tells people they're strong, that they can do what needs to be done. She encourages them to be responsible and to take pride in that accomplishment. She tells them all the things she wishes her mother told her."

"And that's not what's wrong with you?" Rogan interjected quietly.

"No. I'm responsible and respectable. Regardless, my mother would be very proud of me."

"Why?"

"Because I'm finally pretty after the type of beauty she admired most."

Rogan moved to open his mouth and then closed it again without saying what he thought.

"Did I tell you I almost died when I was fourteen?"

"No," he whispered like he was very sorry he had started this conversation with me.

"Yeah. I wanted to live because of him, and he disappeared from my life without a word. I must be the worst person."

I was ready to leave that as my final thought, so I let the silence stretch.

"Well," he said casually, patting the pillow. "You're definitely not the worst person. I'll remember that you were my Santa this year. Amazingly, you can still think about other people, especially when I was so rude to you when you invited me to dinner."

I shrugged. "Don't mention it. You already said I'm not your type. I can't argue with that." I stood up.

"What? I'm *your* type?" he asked.

I bent over him and looked him straight in the eye. "You are exactly my type. Everything about you turns me on. Listen, don't worry about returning the blanket or the pillow. I'd like to be remembered as your Santa and Santa doesn't lend out presents." I straightened my back. "I feel like a fool for having told you all that. I don't think I even told my therapist all that before she decamped. Let's meet up again sometime and you can tell me your story."

"I don't have a story," he said slowly.

I laughed bitterly. "Of course you don't. My type never has a story. I like faceless men whose strongest desire is always to dump me. Merry Christmas!"

"Yeah, Merry Christmas," he called after me, but I was already gone.

CHAPTER EIGHT

Christmas Knight

I waved goodbye to Trinity. Brighton's parents only lived forty-five minutes out of the city, so her coming and going didn't have any drama. I didn't even have to drive her to the airport. It was the afternoon of Christmas Eve and I had finished my shift at the print center. The university was empty. The semester was over. Trinity had invited me to a party Felicity-Ann's parents were throwing on New Year's Eve, so I did have something on my calendar to look forward to, but every moment felt like a hollow tooth I still had to chew on.

I cleaned the apartment. I didn't know it about myself, but after all those years of maids picking up after me, I couldn't live in a dirty place. If I cleaned, I felt important. You didn't think maids were important until they didn't come. The cleanliness stopped me from wallowing in self-pity.

At least our apartment wasn't ugly around Christmas. Trinity set up a merry little Christmas tree and garland all over the place. She even bought little goodies and put them around the living room to remind me that she still loved me even though she wasn't around. There was one present under the tree. It was from her. She had taken the present I got for her with her to open on Christmas morning.

After the place was tidy, I sat down and opened one of the bags of cookies she had left. I tried to read. The sun went down early as I pawed through the freezer looking for something to cook. I had just decided to order a pizza when there was a knock on my door.

When I opened it, there was Christian. I took a step back. He was standing in the hall by the elevator with a stack of packages in his arms like nothing had changed.

"Well, if it isn't Santa Claus in the flesh," I exclaimed, giving my voice an edge. "And they said you weren't real."

He blinked. "Was I mistaken? I thought you might be pleased to see me."

"Oh, I am, darling. I am." I accented the 'darling' with poison. "Come in."

He looked around nervously, which was a bit satisfying considering how cool he was in unfamiliar situations. He paused before coming through the door frame.

"There isn't a water bucket balanced on top of the door," I said. "There isn't a knife hanging from the ceiling either. Trinity decorated and had veto power over my ideas, so the place is basically baby proofed."

He glanced at me from under his perfectly groomed eyebrows and came through the door.

He set his packages next to the Christmas tree and turned to look at me. I suggested he sit on a bean bag chair that was filled with rice and watched with evil satisfaction as he spoiled the flatness of his ironed trousers by taking a seat.

"You look different," he said, as awkward as any father figure visiting his daughter's dormitory.

"If you're going to talk to me like that, you can leave now," I said.

He did a double-take. "Sorry. It's been a while since we last saw one another. How should I speak to you?"

"You threw me out after I kissed you. Perhaps we could talk about that."

He leaned back. "Unbelievable. To get here, to get this far to see you, you have no idea how much trouble it has been, and you want to talk about that?"

"Yes. You can start with that and then you can tell me why you never got in touch with me. You can say why you ignored four or five hundred of my requests to speak, and after you've apologized four or five hundred times, then I'll think about whether or not it's appropriate to accept gifts from you."

"I am sorry I did that. I felt like I had to," he said quietly.

"Why did you have to? Why did you have to break my heart? If I shouldn't have kissed you, you could have just said. We could have worked it out. If I wasn't supposed to love you, you could have told me that instead of kissing me back."

"It's not that simple," he said painfully.

"Why?"

"Why?" he repeated. "Because I can't live a normal life. Beth, surely you know there are serious things wrong with wanting me."

"The only thing I'm aware of is that you screen my calls."

He put his hand over his face and looked at me between his fingers, all the while shaking his head like he couldn't stand to reply. "Beth, you have to know I am on the run. You wanted a home, I tried to give you one and I failed. It was always safer for us to live apart and to see each other only occasionally. I tried to make something more permanent and it took me three and a half years to get back to you, just for tonight. Just for this visit."

I ground my teeth together. He was going to pretend he wasn't Rogan.

"These people don't want my money," he continued. "They want me."

"What does that mean?"

"It means I have secrets, and if anyone thinks, even for a second, that you have my secret too, you won't be safe. If I'm away from you, if I'm not part of your life, then you're safe. You being safe is more important to me than whether or not I get to see you. I don't want them to do to you what they've done to me."

"Yes, an email would have thrown everything off balance. A text would have made the world explode. When you explain it like that, it makes perfect sense," I fumed.

"Beth," he said, deepening his voice. "I can't let anything bad happen to you. Even though a normal life is fraught with its own kind of peril, it's what is natural, and what I was trying to give you all those years ago when you had your heart problems. I can't go back on what I wished for you."

"And what if," I said, looking at the ceiling, "what I wanted was not life when you held me in the hospital room? What if what I wanted was not even a kiss? What if what I wanted was you?"

"What?" he gasped, finally the same heartbreak I felt manifested on his features.

"I only ever wanted you. I'm not even sure I cared when my parents died, because you are what love looks like to me, and a thousand times more comforting than they had ever been. What if I would welcome whatever horrid future you see for me if I could stay with you? What if I didn't mind scanning for bugs, changing my face, and lying until my tongue fell off?"

He interrupted me. "You don't know what you're saying. You've never been tortured."

"I was three and a half years ago," I said steadily.

"What?" he gaped.

"When you sent me away with no explanation, and deliberately and purposefully cut me out of your life. I was left answering the question of what I had done wrong! I was in hell. I must have replayed those last few days we spent together over and over. Obviously, I should not have kissed you, but I tried to make sure we were alone and even though most people would condemn us because I was a minor under your care, I never once got the sense that you didn't want to kiss me. It felt like you did."

He let his thumb graze his bottom lip as he listened to what I was saying, then he sighed. "That was without a doubt the most expensive kiss I have ever had to pay for. Not just me, and I'm still paying for it."

"Why?"

"Because Charles had dirt on me, and if he had not been inflamed with jealousy that day, I probably would have been able to convince him not to give what he knew to the wrong people." He shook his head impatiently. "I still haven't sorted it out."

"What does that mean for you and me?" I asked, briskly.

"Beth, you don't know what's happened, what's going on, who I am, or anything. It's the only way to keep you safe. I can give you tonight. Can't we just have tonight?"

It was tempting to ask him what tonight could entail, but I had to play the long game. "No. You can't. You have to come clean. You have to tell me who you are, what you've done, why people chase you and invite me to come along." I crossed my arms and uttered the most difficult words I had ever spoken. "I think you want me too. I think the years we spent together were hard on you and me because we weren't supposed to love each other, but I'm twenty-one years old now and I think it's okay if we stopped worrying about how we look."

Heated, he stood up and removed his coat. The shirt under clung to his shape beautifully as he turned to face me. "I think you're under a very grave misconception, Beth," he said intently.

"Oh?"

"Yes," he said, looking me in the eye. "You seem to think that the reason you and I have not been lovers is that I was worried about what people might think of us. I let you think it was."

"It wasn't?" I challenged.

"No. You see, I am not free to be in love," he said, making a triangle by putting a hand on his hip. "I haven't been for years."

"Why?"

"Can't your fervent little imagination come up with a grand host of reasons why I wouldn't be free to love you?"

"Your lips say you can and your tongue says you can't?"

"I just wanted you to have a nice Christmas," he said quietly. "I used to come and go so often in your life that I thought tonight might be possible."

"I want more."

"I've already said, I can't give you more. I tried and it didn't work."

My mouth hung open. I had nothing left to lose. This might be my only chance to have it out with him. I had to say everything until there was nothing left to say. "I want you too much to let you leave it at that. Why can't we be together? It seems impossible to me that you would kiss me on the doorstep of my school with that intensity just to put on a show for my classmates. That was why I ventured to kiss you that morning in Scotland and you kissed me like I was heaven itself. You want me. Why can't you have me?"

He shook his head. "It doesn't matter what I want. There are bigger things at stake than what I want."

I shook my head. "I can handle the truth. You opted to have an abnormal life and I'll do anything you're willing to do."

"Can't it be enough that I *want* to tell you?"

"Sure, if it means you come back tomorrow and we go out for dinner. If it means we have the sort of relationship where I know you'll be back, I know you love me, your mouth is on mine, and I know you'll be in touch as soon as possible."

91

The gut-wrenching pain I had felt for years was on his face. "I can't."

"Then you have to go," I said, rising from my chair. I picked up the parcels he'd brought with him and carried them to the outer hallway, where I threw them on the floor.

"Beth, what are you doing?"

"I'm putting an end to all this," I said returning to the room to find him striding toward me. "Trust me enough to tell me what's going on, or leave me alone! I can't stand the evasion. You want me and you won't admit it. Instead, you say you can't love when there are literally a hundred reasons why people can't feel love or have love. I don't want to make guesses about what is wrong. I want you to trust me enough with your pain that you can tell me anything. You're deliberately putting up a wall between us when I want everything! Not just the pretty parts of you, the parts you shine up, but the dirty parts that you would never show anyone. I want you. All of you."

He looked vaguely exhilarated by my declaration. One of his hands rested on his heart. "No matter how fine a woman you are, there are things I can't change."

"Then go," I said, starting to weep.

He put his hand on my shoulder and I slapped it away.

Christian straightened his body. "You're right. I won't come back, but I want to say one more thing before I leave, since it's the last time." He sought my eyes with his and with his beautiful eyes looking into mine, he said, "I thought your kiss was worth dying for, but I can't let you die for it." For a moment, I thought he was going to kiss me again. Instead, he looked away and said, "Be well and if you can… think of me sometimes."

I wiped the tears that came fast and covered my cheeks. "I won't. I will never think of you."

His expression was excruciating. Finally, I was convinced he suffered as much as me.

"Change your mind," I whispered. "Change your mind and trust me."

For a second, he looked like he might. Then he clenched his jaw and loosened it, only to say, "I can't." He picked up his coat, stepped past me and out the door.

I heard his steps echo all the way to the elevator. He had not stopped to retrieve the packages. I felt my knees crumple beneath me and I fell to the floor. I held my breath until I heard the elevator doors close. Then, I let loose.

I cried. I sobbed. I wept so bitterly that my tears ran down my neck and soaked my clothes. How could he have done that? How could he have come only to leave again? How could he have dangled himself in front of me so callously? I shouldn't have let him in. I shouldn't have opened the door.

As long as I was doing things I shouldn't, I got up and went into the hall. I gathered the gifts Christian had brought me with my foot by mildly kicking them across the floor. By doing this, I kicked each of them into the apartment and closed the door with them on the inside.

I didn't have the desire to open them on Christmas Eve, and as it turned out, I didn't have the urge on Christmas Day either. They sat unopened, just inside the apartment until Trinity came home and when she asked me what they were, I told her Christian had sent them.

"Do you want me to open them for you? Find out if they're anything interesting?" she offered.

"No," I said lifelessly. "I've had many presents from Christian. I can imagine what's in them. I don't want them, but I'm not ready to throw them away."

"Yeah?"

"Trinity," I said slowly, looking at her with eyes like moons on water, because I was about to cry again. "I have to tell you something."

"What?" she said, dropping to her knees.

"I've never told you this... but I'm in love with him."

She refrained from looking at me as though I was stupid, and instead gazed at me with compassion in her eyes. "I know."

"No," I said, grabbing her hand. "I mean, I love him in a way that is completely crazy. Like I'm obsessed with him, like every time I close my eyes, he's with me and if I let myself just feel without thinking, it feels like he loves me too. Like he loves me so much he would die for me. Like I would die for him, like I did die and he somehow made me live again. Like the bond between us is so strong that him leaving me makes me feel like death has come. I feel like I live in a world that doesn't have anything in it but him, and I don't know what he has done."

"What do you mean?"

I didn't mention the unforgivable thing he did to save my life when I was dying, even though I thought that was what he was skirting around when he said he couldn't love me. Instead, I said, "What has he done to make me love him like this?"

Now Trinity looked at me like I was stupid. "He's an eleven out of ten. Did you miss that?"

"How he looks isn't important," I muttered.

"Isn't it?"

Trinity didn't know that his look as Christian Henderson was a lie, and I wasn't about to tell her. It wasn't important. Whatever face he wore, he'd always be attractive in a superior way.

"The reason I'm telling you this, is because soon… Very, very soon, I'm going to start chasing Rogan Cormack. I've decided that there's wisdom in that incredibly vulgar saying."

Trinity raised an eyebrow. "Which incredibly vulgar saying?"

"That the only way to get over one man is to get under another one?"

"And you've decided on Rogan?"

"I want him," I said unapologetically.

"Why? He's nothing like Christian."

"Exactly," I said fiercely.

Trinity sighed. "You're going to have competition. Felix likes him."

"Yes, well, most guys like Felicity-Ann and in return she likes most of them. You have to stop the train somewhere."

Trinity put up her hands in surrender. "Okay."

94

CHAPTER NINE

Behind the Blindfold

The New Year's Eve party was at Felicity-Ann's parents' mansion. It was a monstrosity of brick that rose a whole story above every other building on the street. The first time I saw it, I mistook it for a church. Felicity-Ann's mother was a professor at the university, and her father was some sort of eccentric millionaire who also happened to be Trinity's uncle. Trinity's parents were coming to the party and to say Trinity was shaken by their forthcoming arrival was an understatement.

Coming unglued was the order of the day everyday between Boxing Day and New Year's Eve. She was only calm when Brighton was around. The rest of the time she was like a lapsed lunatic. She went to the drug store to buy shampoo and came back with three different kinds of temporary hair dye, black fishnet stockings, and a spiked dog collar.

I picked up the dog collar and said, "I didn't even know they sold these at Cousins Drug Mart."

"Yeah. It's amazing what they keep beside the till."

"What are you gonna do with those boxes of dye? Do you plan to keep your reformation a secret from your parents? You said it before. They already know and they don't care."

Trinity straightened her back and looked at her reflection in the mirror. "You're right. I don't have to keep my brown hair a secret from them, but I do have to keep Brighton a secret."

I scoffed. "You're not going to tell them you're getting married?"

"Felix doesn't know... unless you told her." Trinity eyed me suspiciously.

"No. I didn't tell her. I try to avoid standing too close. Well, now you have to explain to upright Brighton why he can't ask your father for your hand in marriage."

Her face went so white she lost her nose. "I can't let them meet. You think my father would go so far as to refuse our marriage? If he knew I was seeing a guy whose family isn't in the top one percent, he would flip out. Actually, just knowing that Brighton worked at the Campus Food Bank would give my father a heart attack."

"He wouldn't even let you two date?"

"No. Brighton can't come to the party," she said, pacing frantically. "But I have to be there. How can I get him to not come? I already invited him!" Her voice was becoming higher and higher pitched. By the time she said 'him' I could only guess what she was saying.

"How are you going to do that?"

She flapped her hands like broken bird wings. "I don't know. What if I fake sick?"

"What if you're *so* sick you can't go anywhere and neither can he because he has to nurse you better?" I suggested.

"He'd take me to the emergency room, and the doctors would know I was lying. I've done that sort of thing before."

"And he can't be convinced not to mention anything to your parents?" I persisted.

"No," she fumed. "That man has never told a lie in his life. He can't even pretend to be something different than he is. Do you remember his costume for Halloween?"

"No. Did he dress up?"

"He did. He dressed up as a food bank volunteer, which he isn't, because he's the director. He wore one of the volunteer T-shirts and that was his costume."

I gawked at her. That was so lame. Christian would have dressed up as the Phantom of the Opera, complete with a horribly disfigured face under his mask, except he wouldn't have gotten shot at the end of his performance. How could Trinity like a guy who was the opposite of that? "And you fell in love with this guy?"

The color came back to her face. "He's the best. If he says he's going to pick me up, then he picks me up. If he's late, he texts. He says he's going to be in class, I swing by, and he's there. Not that I have been jerked around by very many boyfriends. It was my parents who were always standing me up."

I did agree that those qualities were extraordinarily appealing in a man. For a moment, I was jealous. I shook it off and reminded her reasonably, "You've already told them off dozens of times. Why are you nervous about doing it one more time?"

"I don't want to ruin Auntie's party. I've already ruined so many things. I ruin everything. Brighton wouldn't like me to ruin the party or cause a big scene. At his parents' house, everything was so sweet. His parents love me so much. It's such a bummer I can't give him wonderful in-laws. You've met my parents. They hate everyone who doesn't have as much money as them, but not quite as much as they hate people who have *more* money than them. I don't know. My parents hate everything decent."

"I don't know what you should do," I admitted when she looked to me for advice.

"Will you stay home from the party with me?" she asked.

"No."

"What the heck? Why would you go to their party? I thought you hated Felix."

I threw my hair over my shoulder. "I want to see if Rogan goes. I'm sure Felicity-Ann invited him."

"Your interest in him is weird. He likes Felix. A guy who likes Felix could never like you."

I shrugged.

"Well, you can be stupid if you want. You've given me the luxury enough times, I can reciprocate the favor. What are you going to wear? They're millionaires and we're poor relatives."

"I'm going to buy a new dress and I'm going to get my hair done," I said with a little hand flourish.

"If he likes Felix, you're *not* woman enough for him," she said honestly, pinching both my thin cheeks at once. "That girl has curves that make Coke bottles jealous."

She was trying to protect me and I appreciated it. I loved honesty even when it was too honest. "It's cool," I said positively, brushing her hands away. "I may not be the Bond girl Felicity-Ann is, but I get asked what ballet I'm in when I'm in the auditorium."

"Go get him, tiger," Trinity growled supportively. She still thought it was a bad idea.

***

On New Year's Eve, I stopped in at my apartment to get dressed before Felicity-Ann's party. Even if everyone called her Felix, I couldn't bring myself to do it, not even in my head.

That night, I felt particularly stung by what I knew Felicity-Ann would be wearing. She sent Trinity a picture of her dress and dared Trinity to show up in something better. So I'd seen it. It was a short red dress with black flowers on it. When I went shopping, I tried to find something that would beat it. I fought the throngs at West Edmonton Mall for three days straight. Finding something incredible was easy. Finding something that made me look incredible was a different story. In the end, the dress I bought cost over six hundred dollars, but that was okay if Rogan would be at the party.

It was wine purple with a high neck and a bustle in the back. The bustle was the best part, which was made of black transparent fluff that looked like a ballerina's tutu. My coloring was great for purple.

I went to a salon and got my hair done in loose ringlets and curious braids done up at the crown.

When Trinity saw me all dressed up, she almost fell on the floor. She had decided to bite the bullet and was taking Brighton to the party—rage or no rage. She was leaving everything in his hands. But she was stunned when she saw me.

"I should have gone shopping with you," she said, glowing. "I have to take you with me when I buy my wedding dress. Beth, I never knew you had so much style. Where have you been hiding it?"

I frowned. "This is what Christian would have bought for me if I had taken him with me. He always has the best taste and buys the most expensive thing."

"When do I get to meet this Christian?" Brighton asked.

I glanced at Trinity and got my coat. The awkward silence got deeper as I grabbed my purple scarf. She'd explain to him sometime when I wasn't around.

***

98

At the party, the first person I saw was Felicity-Ann. She had discarded the dress she sent Trinity a picture of and was now wearing a violet low-cut gown with a tiny purple scarf knotted around her wrist. I knew we looked similar and even if my dress was better than hers, no one would ever say I looked better. I just didn't have the face, the figure, or the hair for it.

Felicity-Ann's parents were all smiles as they welcomed us to their party. Trinity immediately scanned the room for her parents. I stayed beside her for moral support.

"I don't see them," I whispered over the hum of the band.

"Neither do I, but that doesn't mean I'm in the clear. They could be late or out of sight."

I silently agreed with her and glanced around the room again.

"If I don't see them in an hour, do you think it would be rude to slip out?" she asked.

I suddenly remembered a verse from the book of Christian and recited it for her. "If you leave a New Year's Eve party early, you have to tell everyone afterward, including the host, that you stayed until the end."

She hissed back at me, "Brighton doesn't lie."

"Whatever. The person you need to please is him. I've been to a million of these things. He's not going to want to stay, so you can leave whenever he wants to go."

"What are you going to do?"

"Depends on whether or not Rogan shows up."

"It might not make what Christian did to you hurt any less," Trinity suggested tensely.

I smiled and showed my teeth, half smiling, half snarling. "I think it will."

Then I saw him. He was leaning against a wall next to one of the escape routes. He was wearing a dark blue collared shirt, with the sleeves rolled up to the elbow, and a light blue tie. In his hand was a glass of something bubbly. He was talking to someone, but the second his friend's attention was distracted, he dumped half his drink into a planter.

It was *him*.

It had to be him. Other men didn't do that. I ran back to the front entry, leaving Trinity in the middle of a sentence and asked the butler to give me my scarf. At my request, he gave me instructions on how I could enter the room by the door beside Rogan without passing through the party. He was a really useful fellow as he took me around the back way.

In the hallway, I peeked around the corner to make sure Rogan was still there. He was. I put my back against a wall and tried to calm down. What I was about to do was normal. Everyone did this sort of thing at parties. I'd seen something like it happen a dozen times before. I had just never been part of a prank like this. I needed to chill out. Beauty was all about confidence. All I had to do was act like I wasn't scared.

I took my scarf and looped it around Rogan's head so that it covered his eyes like a blindfold. I didn't keep my face hidden from the man he had been talking to and gave him a little playful nose crinkle before gently pulling Rogan around the corner into the semi-darkness of the hall.

"What's going on?" he asked clearly in the quiet corridor.

I didn't answer him. I kissed him and it was like getting transported back to that moment in the conservatory before everything was spoiled. I opened my mouth and was so ecstatic when he opened his that I trembled. This was the man I loved. His taste, his breath, his charm, and the feeling I had spent years waiting for. I felt his hands on my upper arms, not to move them, but to feel them. His hands moved down to my elbows, then to my waist and back. I felt him crush the fabric of my dress between his fingers, pulling me against him so hard that it was no longer me pushing him up against a wall. I heard a seam break, and he immediately let go of my dress to hold my face gently in his hands.

Then he reached up with one hand to tug off the blindfold. I pinned his bicep to the wall and breathed out the last of our kisses.

When I finally had to come up for air, I leaned forward and whispered in his ear. "Count to ten and come find me."

I let go of him, leaving my scarf behind as the only clue to my identity and nearly tripped on my heels as I came down a few steps into the main room. I stumbled over to Trinity, my face on fire and my feet faltering.

"What did you just do?" she asked when I finally arrived behind her. I didn't answer her. "Is Rogan behind me?"

"No."

"Can you see him?"

"No."

I bit my lip in frustration. "There's a hallway to your eleven o'clock. I was just in there with him. Has he come out?"

Trinity found the spot with her eyes. "No."

"Keep looking. Tell me when you see him. This is really important to me."

She kept staring and I kept waiting. It was a full two heart-pounding minutes before she said, "There he is."

"Is he alone? What is he doing?"

"He's holding your scarf. Yeah, he's alone. He looks super puzzled. He's fixing one of the lenses in his glasses."

"Crap! I broke his glasses. I shouldn't have tied it so tight."

Trinity gasped. "What did you do?"

"What I came here to do. Is he coming over? I can't look."

"He's smelling the scarf. Did you put something on it, like perfume?"

"No. Dang it. I should have. Is he coming over here?"

"Nope. I hate to break your spirit, but he's standing beside Felix."

"He's what?" I spun around.

Trinity wasn't joking. He had his hand on her wrist where her purple scarf sat and he was spinning her around like he was dancing with her. Even from across the room I thought I could read his lips when he pulled away from her and said, "Found you."

I couldn't bear it. He was going to *her*? Didn't he know my kiss? Didn't he know my taste? Didn't he think I could do something like that? Why did he go to *her*?

"I have to go," I said, panicking. "I have to go right now. I can't stay and watch this." I turned around and made for the front hall. I had to find that butler, get my coat and get away from the worst party I had ever been to.

"What's going on?" Trinity said, following me. "I thought you were going to stay and help me weather the storm."

"I can't," I said. "I wish I could, but I'm in no condition to stay. I thought he would find me. I thought he would know it was me. Instead, he thought it was Felicity-Ann with her little purple scarf wrapped around her wrist. He thought my scarf was a present from her. That it was a couples' scarf and she was already wearing hers."

"Honey, I don't understand what's happening. Didn't he see you give it to him?"

"No. No, he didn't. I was playing a game. I never thought it would backfire like this. I thought Felicity-Ann was going to wear red. I have to go."

"Well, I'll come with you. I don't want to be here anyway. Just give me two seconds and I'll grab Brighton."

I stood in the arch between the hall and the party wishing she would hurry. My knees were shaking so badly, I thought I might fall on my face, and what if Trinity's parents arrived at that very moment?

Across the room, I saw something very different from what I was expecting. Trinity had not gone to get Brighton. She had walked clear across the room to where Felicity-Ann and Rogan were dancing. My scarf was around his neck. It almost stopped my heart to see her tap on Rogan's shoulder. He stopped and looked at Trinity. She unceremoniously snatched my scarf from around his neck.

"This is not her scarf," she said loudly pointing at Felicity-Ann.

"Then who—"

Trinity strode away but turned around to spit at him, "And it's not mine either, you idiot."

I slipped around the corner, only to see the butler standing there with my coat stretched out between his hands. His face looked pained. Even he knew I wasn't having a good night.

Trinity picked up Brighton before she made it back to the door. She stuffed my scarf into her bag and said briskly, "I'll give it back to you after we're home. No need to make this any more humiliating than it already was."

"You always know what to do," I said as I buttoned my coat and stepped out into the cold. She wouldn't cause a scene for her own sake, but she had no problem causing one for mine. That must be why Brighton and I loved her so much.

CHAPTER TEN

Voice on the Line

It was January. My shift at the print shop was over, but I couldn't seem to pry my lazy butt off the stool. I hooked my oversized boots around the metal legs and pouted.

Gibson saw me over his computer screen and said, "Go home, Beth."

The print shop had been really busy that day. The new semester was starting in two days, so we'd been flocked by newcomers, not to mention the regular riffraff. The rush had ended and evening had come. The shop didn't close for another couple of hours, but my shift was over and for the moment, it was empty.

My boss, Gibson, was a cozy guy who was old enough to have finished his Ph.D., but instead, he was tidying up his masters at a leisurely pace. He was one of those people who loved university life and was in no hurry to leave it. He was also a person who could not possibly have been Christian in disguise. His lack of height disqualified him.

"I don't want to go home," I whined.

He wiped his glasses on the underside of his T-shirt. "Why not?"

"Felicity-Ann will be nesting in my apartment."

"Nesting?" he asked curiously.

"You know. What girl chickens do, as to equal what male roosters do—roosting."

Gibson gave me a funny look.

"She'll be talking to Trinity about the wedding and I'd rather put a hole in my head than go back there."

"Ah," he said.

I had already explained the whole New Year's Eve fiasco to him while the printing machines hummed away.

I let my head loll back. "You're judging me, Gibson. Stop it."

"Yes, I'm judging you," he said flatly, as he began typing on the computer.

Gibson was not my friend, even though we talked a lot. He thought I was a spoiled brat. I was and I couldn't hide it. When he was interviewing me for the job, he told me how much I would be getting paid and I laughed. It seemed like such a paltry amount, but I sucked in my breath and apologized quickly. Even if I was used to bigger bucks, I needed a job. Behind my back, I knew he called me 'The Rich Witch.' Instead of being insulted, I was rather pleased. He could have been much more insulting and besides, everything he accused me of was true. We'd be talking and I'd drop something into the conversation like, "When I was in Cairo, I…" And he'd roll his eyes.

He only had a speckle of sympathy for me because I was an orphan and I had been abandoned by Christian, who I missed very much. I wasn't sure which thing made him tolerate me.

"I don't see why you want to avoid Feline so badly," he said, using one of her nick-names. She was *that* famous. "She's not as evil as you make her out to be. She's been in here a few times and I gotta say, she has better manners than you."

"That's because you're a man and she knows if she leans over a little and gives you a little smile, it'll be far more pleasant for everyone," I countered.

He pulled his shaggy eyebrows together angrily. "She's not a slut."

"I didn't say she was a slut. I implied she was flirty." I stuck my tongue out at him.

"Not with me," he amended quickly. "She was intelligent and well-spoken. You're jealous. The guys look at her instead of you."

"Is that a crime? She's blonde and—"

"So dye your hair."

I could never explain it to him. Though I did find her annoying before the New Year's Eve party, the fact that Rogan/Christian had gone to her instead of me killed all the love I had for her.

Gibson seemed to realize he had struck a nerve with me and continued gentler, "If she's so awful then why does your girl, Trinity, hang out with her?"

Gibson thought the universe of Trinity. The campus food bank and the print center were on the same floor. It wasn't difficult to see why he had a good opinion of her. She beguiled everyone except her parents into loving her with her frankness and her open heart. I could never be like her.

I took a deep breath. "She says that what happened on New Year's Eve wasn't Felicity-Ann's fault. It wasn't like she deliberately tried to sabotage me, so Trinity won't tolerate me being mad at her."

"Take lessons from her," he advised darkly. "Now, I told you to go home, so go."

"I don't want to!" I whined.

I looked at him. He was about three seconds from having the man equivalent of a hissy fit.

"Fine," I said, hopping off the stool. "I'll go, but if blood gets splattered, it's on your head."

"You'd better not hurt her," he cautioned with a pointed finger. "It's not her fault that guy preferred her."

I put my coat on and as I was buttoning it up, I bawled, "Why do you care if I get along with her or not?" I had hardly finished my sentence when I realized what was going on. Gibson had a teensy crush on Felicity-Ann. She was completely out of his league, so he never mentioned it to anyone, but obviously, he did. That was why he called her Feline and defended her so hotly when I said bad things about her.

"I just don't like you being mean to her. She didn't do anything wrong. You said so yourself."

I nodded meekly, wound my brown scarf around my neck and headed out. So, Gibson was suffering from a hopeless, one-sided, love... just like me. That was what won me his meager sympathy.

***

Three months later.

"Go home, Beth," Gibson said unemotionally.

I twirled around in an office chair and stalled going home.

It was the end of March and everything was exactly the same as it had been at the beginning of January. In three months, nothing had changed. I had not seen nor heard from Christian. No one had seen Rogan. Felicity-Ann, who basically haunted my apartment, said she thought he had transferred schools. Trinity was not married yet. Her wedding was scheduled for the middle of May. I almost wished it was over, just to get Felicity-Ann out of my life. Aside from Rogan, she did not have a steady love interest, and so she was more available than ever to help Trinity plan the wedding. Trinity didn't even need me. I wasn't even a bridesmaid. Not that I especially wanted to be a bridesmaid. She wasn't having bridesmaids. She said she didn't want to pay for the dress and the hairdo and whatever else, so they weren't having any of that. I rolled my eyes and wondered what Trinity's mother would think if she knew about all the tradition-breaking details of her daughter's wedding.

Gibson was turning into my only friend, except he was glaring at me.

"What?" I grumbled as I stopped spinning.

"I heard a rumor," he said.

"Tell me! I love rumors."

He was hesitant. "I heard that Felicity is looking for a place to live closer to campus."

I batted my eyelashes at him in a mock expression of disbelief. "Doesn't her mommy practically live on campus as it is? How much closer has she got to get? Isn't she almost finished her degree by now anyway?"

"Never mind. You're so catty."

"I am not generally catty! I just don't like *her*. Why are you mentioning this to me like it's any of my business?"

At least he had the decency to look slightly awkward as he dropped his bomb. "I thought that you might let her room with you since Trinity is leaving in a month."

I narrowed my eyes at him. "In case you didn't realize this, Trinity and I live in a studio apartment. We sleep in enclosed beds, so they're almost like separate bedrooms, but not quite. If Felicity-Ann took Trinity's place that would mean that I would not even be able to go into my own bedroom and shut the door. She would be in my face constantly. I would suffocate from..."

"Jealousy?" he supplied.

"Whatever. I don't want to live with her."

"Do you have any other prospects?"

"You know I don't. Not unless you want to come live with me."

"Thanks for the offer, but I'd suffocate from..." he paused to let me supply his fault.

I stayed silent and didn't supply anything for him. I didn't want to live with Gibson either, even if he was becoming my only friend. I'd die from his dry humor that didn't taste one bit like Christian's. I didn't know what he'd die from.

He didn't finish his sentence when I left him hanging and went on. "I just thought I should warn you that she might ask you herself."

"Why?"

His ears turned slightly redder. "Because I suggested it to her."

I nodded. "No harm done. I just have to tell her no."

"As long as you're not mad."

"I'm not mad, but Gibson, I've got to tell you, she is not as sweet and generous as you think she is."

"Yes, she is. You just can't see it because you're competing with her for some guy who never would have looked at you in a thousand years. Not that he's around anymore."

Reminding me of that fact hurt, especially because it was a fact. I got up and got my coat.

Gibson knew he hit a nerve. He did it often enough. "I'm sorry," he said, letting his voice follow me as I left the print center behind me.

When I got back to my apartment, I found that I had won the lottery—Felicity-Ann was not there. Trinity was on the computer looking at her email.

"Is there an angry email from your mom," I asked.

"No. You know she doesn't email me."

"I just wondered if Felicity-Ann had ratted on you yet."

Trinity rolled her eyes. "Stop it. She's not going to tell on me."

I rolled my eyes and went into the kitchen. I was convinced Felicity-Ann was going to leak Trinity's wedding plans. It was only a matter of time and there were only six weeks left.

At that exact moment, my phone vibrated in my hoodie pocket. I didn't recognize the number, but I didn't get many spam calls, so I answered it. "Hi," I said.

"Hello, I'm calling for Beth Coldwell," the voice on the other end of the line intoned.

"That's me."

"Hello," she said again. "My name is Pricina Waldorf. I represent an organization known as the NS. I've been told to contact you in regards to your relationship with Henry Brandon and Christian Henderson."

My breath caught in my throat and I listened while she spoke.

"No need to confirm or deny it. We know who you are, and we're here to offer you an opportunity."

I tried to keep steady as my voice threatened to warble. "What sort of opportunity?"

"It's come to our attention that Henry Brandon is being held involuntarily at a compound northwest of Edmonton. We have reason to believe that you would be the best operative to extract him."

I went into the bathroom and turned on the shower to mute any bugs if our conversation was being recorded. "I'm not an operative," I said, leaning against the counter.

"We can use a different term if that suits you," she said in a crisp professional voice. "Due to your family connections, you are the ideal candidate for executing a rescue operation."

I didn't know if she was talking about my father's family, who I had abandoned, my mother's family, who had abandoned me, or my connection with Christian. "Does Christian work for you?" I asked when Princina paused to breathe.

"Not as such. Henry Brandon is our employee. As he is the one incarcerated, he has the best available intelligence regarding his extraction. He has asked us to secure your help. He believes that if you were to work together with Christian, his release would be possible. Apparently, Christian is aware of your value on this project but has refused to allow your involvement. He has been working solo on this project for months, without success. He needs your help specifically."

"He would never ask me," I agreed.

"Indeed. If you decide to help, I can give you the address of Christian's cottage and tell you what you need to say to him in order to gain access to the confidential information required in order to help free Henry Brandon." Princina's voice sounded mechanical, like an actress who had rehearsed her lines in order to sound as credible as possible. It discredited her.

"This sounds fishy."

"It does," Princina agreed. "I realize this call could sound like a prank or a trap. Unfortunately, there isn't a way to deliver this kind of message without it sounding fake. I am not available to meet you in person. If we did meet, it has about the same likelihood of convincing you as not. The reason we want you is that Brandon's captors know you, even if you don't know them, and they will not want to hurt you. Christian will be able to supply you with a plan that, as long as it is not executed by him, will succeed."

"And if I refuse? I mean, you haven't even offered me any money yet."

"Do you need money?" Princina asked condescendingly.

I realized my mistake. Even mentioning money was crass when dealing with the very rich.

"Beth," she said, sounding like one of my aunts. "From what Brandon has told me about you and your relationship with Christian, it appears he is blocking you because he wishes for nothing more than your safety. If you want to tear that wall down, you're going to have to do something that violates that wish in such a way that you might not be able to go back to the life you lead now. I'm not making you do this, nor am I making you an offer you can't refuse by adding an unreasonable sum of money to the mix. I'm offering you a choice. You can choose to live the life he wishes for you, full of safety, or you can choose to live the life that opened for you the moment Christian Henderson became your guardian."

"Why are you doing this?"

"Because Brandon told me this is what you want. If it's not, hang up the phone." She stopped talking and waited.

I didn't hang up.

"The address is range road 275-1."

I wrote it on my palm with my eyeliner.

Princina continued, "When you meet Christian, you must tell him that you know the secret he's been hiding and you are there to help Brandon. If he tries to get you to tell him the secret without showing you the situation, say that you wouldn't be there if you weren't prepared to help. After that, no matter what you see, you must lie forever afterward saying you already knew, you just weren't prepared for the situation to be so dire. Can you do that, Beth?"

"Can't you tell me the secret before I go?" I asked.

"No. I'm not cutting open the fruit for you so you can see how rotten it is before you take a bite. I'm telling you it's rotten. You can decide if you want to move forward knowing that. If you have not made your way out to Christian's safe house before nightfall on Friday night, the offer will be rescinded and another plan of action will be made. You will not be able to contact me at this number after I cut the connection. Repeat the address to me, so I can be confident I sent you to the right location."

I read it back.

"Let me give you a second address as well, as it might help Christian resolve to help you." She read another range road address to me. "That's where Brandon is being kept. Tell Christian if he won't help you, you'll go there alone to rescue Brandon."

"Should I do that?"

"I think it would be wiser to merely use it as a threat to help persuade Christian." The way she said the word 'persuade' was completely menacing. "I don't believe it will come to that." She paused. "Remember, the fruit is rotten. Nothing good is going to happen, except that Brandon will be free and you will no longer be a child in the eyes of Christian Henderson."

I scratched my head. Who was she that she knew so much about what I wanted? It gave me the shivers. "Isn't there something more you can tell me? About you? About your organization?"

"No. Follow my instructions perfectly or don't follow them at all. Good-bye, Beth Coldwell."

The call ended.

CHAPTER ELEVEN

The Place Between His World and Mine

An annoyingly insistent voice from my phone's GPS directed me to Christian's cottage. I gave my phone a good charge and took a bus to a car rental place. I got the cheapest economy car they had and drove clean out of the city. I drove west into the late afternoon sun. I hadn't thought to bring sunglasses, so I was half-blind as I made my way to the address Princina had given me.

My first turn off led into a collection of pine trees. The sun made long shadows across the road. The second turn took me on a gravel road heading north. This was when my heart stopped beating like a snare drum because I was excited and started chiming like a triangle because I was afraid.

What if I was wrong and I was putting myself at terrible risk isolating myself in the country? That woman had said there was no way to bring me into his world without risking my old life. Suddenly, everything felt wrong. What if it was a trick and I had just brought myself to the house of an ax murderer and Christian was already dead and… I had to stop thinking.

At the last turn, I went west again into a dense forest on a road so narrow, it could only be a driveway. In the curve between the trees, I saw a house and a little barn. The house was one level with dark brown siding and a porch with an overhanging roof. It was cozy as it almost grew into a hill.

I got out of the car and locked it. I clenched my phone in my hand and approached the front door. I knocked. No one answered. I knocked again and again. When no one answered the door, I took a few steps back and looked at the house. What should I do? It was Friday and the sun was already setting. Was I too late?

Having absolutely nothing to lose, I decided to walk around the house and look in the windows. I stepped onto snowdrifts that clung to the side of the house. They were almost strong enough to hold my weight and gave me an extra boost to see inside the windows. I cupped my hands around my eyes to block the receding sun.

Someone was inside. Had they seen me?

I rushed back to the front door and pulled it open at the exact moment the person on the other side reached for it. I was a second quicker and the door flew open.

Rogan stood in front of me. He was sans his glasses, and his beard was coming in, but otherwise, it was him.

"Hello, Christian," I said saucily, and the look on his face was priceless.

"I think you have me mistaken..." he started saying.

I interrupted him. "Whatever, Damen. Whatever, Louis. Whatever, Charles. Whatever, Rogan. Whatever, Christian. Let me in."

I didn't see his exact expression as I pushed by him on my way into the house. The moment I was in, he closed the door hurriedly behind me. I didn't get further than the entryway when he grabbed my hand and spun me around to face him.

Face to face with him was startling. Not only was he incredibly handsome (made up like Rogan), but also showing volumes of unconcealed rage. He was not going to yell at me. The way he clenched his jaw made it clear he was too angry to think straight and thus had not said anything for fear of saying something he couldn't take back.

"Where did I fail, Beth?" he finally said, spitting the words.

"What?"

"Where did I fail? I have been trying to teach you that I am in constant danger and you will be in danger too if you chase me. Did I fail to make myself clear?"

"No. I just don't care anymore," I said, turning my head unconcernedly on its side.

He glared at me, unable to form words.

I took advantage of his hesitation and dove in. "I know your secret."

The blood ran out of his face and he looked white as the dead. He still held my arm but he took a step backward. "You can't know everything."

"I know enough, so now there is no way to leave me out of it. I'm here to help you rescue Brandon."

He stumbled against the wall. "Are you?"

"Yes."

"It only figures you'd show up here. He's been asking for you. He's been saying for weeks that he thinks you can save him." Rogan let go of me and leaned his back against the wall completely. He let his hand travel painfully across his eyes and at that moment, I realized that something irreparable had happened.

His left hand was gone. Lopped off at the wrist, he had his stub covered with bandages that were hidden by the sleeve of his sweater.

The blood pounded in my ears and my eyes. I was seeing red. "What happened?" I begged, leaning forward and reaching for his injury.

He glanced at it like he had forgotten his hand was gone. "It was cut off by an incredibly spiteful man," he explained. Then he frowned and shooed me off. "It doesn't matter."

His shoulders sagged and he stepped away from the entry to allow me room to enter. The house was warm and inviting. It didn't look much like the hideout of a secret agent, but then, I imagined nothing did.

He brought me into the living room without helping me with my coat. There was a fireplace at the end of the room and he sat me on the edge of the couch closest to it. I was so engrossed in his presence that I couldn't even focus on the room. With his good hand, he picked up the remote control for the gas fireplace and started it with an annoyed flick of his wrist. He lounged in the armchair the way the man I knew always did.

The look in his eyes was my paycheck for all the suffering I had done in between my conversation with Pricina and this moment. The indecision had been murder. Mostly, I was afraid she had lied to me. I stayed up most nights, thinking. I paced. I wrote pro and con lists. In the end, if I meant any of the things I had said to Christian when he came to see me on Christmas Eve, then coming here was the only path open to me. The anonymous woman had not lied. Christian was in front of me, and for once I felt that he couldn't slide me into the child slot he always relegated me to. He looked at me, with his undoubtedly fake blue eyes, like I was finally a woman. He was angry and it was beautiful.

"Who told you to come here?" he asked quietly, a dangerous edge to his voice.

"A lady sent me a message from Brandon," I replied, not choosing my words carefully. His hand was gone. None of this was a game.

"So you came here on the advice of someone you didn't know?" he asked scathingly.

"Yes."

He looked horrified. "Why?"

"Look, you seem to think that I have a life outside of you. You think I'm leading a meaningful life that is worth protecting. All I have been doing is going to classes I hate and rooming with Trinity. She's going to marry Mr. Brighton Pudding Face and leave me." I paused. "The only time I have ever felt alive has been when I have been with you. I haven't made friends, and you should have seen the hordes of people Trinity welcomed to our place. I feel like the whole campus has been ushered into our apartment on rotation, like we were a safe house or a wellness clinic. If I could make friends with any of them, I would have done it already. It's been years. I haven't had a boyfriend. I don't want anything but you, and now it's time for you to let me help you... in any way I can." I purposefully glanced at his stub.

"Beth," he said, rolling the word around on his tongue. "I don't want you here. I don't want you to see these things." From his voice, he was not talking about his missing hand. "I can make a few guesses about who contacted you, but whoever she is, she is telling you the truth about Brandon. He has been asking for you. I have ignored him because... all of this is too horrible. I don't want you involved."

"Do you feel backed into a corner?" I whispered.

He nodded.

"Good. Then you'll let me help?"

"If it was just me and my missing hand, I wouldn't. I'd put you outside and lock the door. I'd sell this house and make sure that you never found me again, but since you're here and it's not me who needs you, I'll take your help. It will be dangerous."

"Obviously. How did you lose your hand?" I questioned softly.

"I tried to take something that a man named Dr. Laurence Hilliar was absolutely convinced was his. I managed to get what I was aiming for, even with the handicap of missing my left hand. He's fuming."

"You sound happy," I interjected. "What could you possibly have stolen that was worth your hand, you idiot?"

He regarded me carefully, still with that gleam of mischief in his eyes. "I love it when you talk that way. Trust me. It was *very* worth it."

I gawked at him. "What? Have you lost your mind? Going after something so hard that you're even willing to lose body parts?"

He rolled his eyes. "Darling, this is not as serious as you think. I was having problems before this happened."

"How could it not be as serious as I think?" I burst. "You are missing your hand!"

He cleared his throat and when he spoke his voice was grim. "You were lying when you said you knew my secret, weren't you?"

"Not at all," I said slowly.

"Yes, you are. If that woman told you my secret, you would be begging to see proof. She didn't tell you exactly what is going on and she is dangling me like a carrot in front of you to make you do what she wants."

I felt like choking. He was right.

"Beth, I promise you, that woman is not your friend. No one, who is your friend, would want you involved in any of this."

"Are you going to send me away?" I asked slowly.

"I should," he said dangerously. "But I'm not going to."

"Why?"

"I've been having problems, because I'm a man."

I stared at him, completely baffled. "I've always enjoyed that aspect of you."

He blinked in such a darling way, it was better than a wink. "I've always enjoyed that, too. And I'm such an impressive man at that: over six feet tall, broad shoulders, abs for days, strong bone structure."

I could almost mouth along with his statement. I'd heard it so many times.

"I'm fantastic. I know. I make all the women crazy." He mock-sighed and continued with a more serious inflection. "It's just that my stunning skeletal structure makes it impossible for me to disguise myself as a woman. And now, with my hand missing, I am branded. I have too many unique identifiers to perform a covert mission with these people. If I try to sneak back onto that wacko's territory, everyone will know instantly it's me."

"So..."

"We can disguise you. If we make you look like anyone other than yourself, you'll have a better chance of success than I ever had. That's why Brandon wants you to go in my place," he said, his voice smooth until the end of his speech where it warbled.

He sat silently as he waited for my reaction. Frankly, I couldn't react. His whole system of escape had always been based on disguises. It should have been easy for him to come up with a disguise for me, but he looked upset.

"What's wrong?"

"I have to tell you the secret. If you're going to help me, you're going to need to know the secret and I... I can't tell you. If what we're doing is going to be a success, I have to tell you, but now that it's come to this... I can't. I need some time."

"More time than you've already had?"

"Yes. It's just that everything sounds so crazy—like it's not real. How can I tell you the secret, let you into my world, without making a fool of myself? It's impossible."

"I bet it's going to be hard."

"Extremely," he said confidently. Tapping his right fingers against his chin, he suddenly perked up. "All right, I think I've got it. Let's start this way. I am alive when I shouldn't be. Thus, everywhere I go and everyone I speak to soon wants to know my secret. Why am I alive when I should be dead?"

"Well, why are you?"

"I don't know, but no one will ever take that as an answer. I can say it over and over again, but those who get bitten by the snake of curiosity won't leave me alone. Everywhere I go, there is someone out to get me, hoping they will figure out my secret and be able to reproduce it for their own benefit."

"Which means?"

"Which means these obsessed people know about you. They would always try to snatch me right before meeting you or right after we said goodbye. You were my safe zone. But why? Why didn't they come after me when you were by my side? The whole thing made traveling a nightmare."

The hellishness was no exaggeration. Sometimes we would need to take later flights and let the tickets he had already bought go to waste because he said he was getting some trousers mended and he couldn't pick me up until they were done. He'd made up dozens of little lame excuses along those lines, and like an idiot, I'd believed him. I thought he was really that shallow.

"That's why you're chronically late?" I blurted.

He did a double-take. "You're thinking about that now? I thought at least that much would be clear by now." He breathed heavily. "I don't fake who I am every day of my life for no reason, Beth. The alias, Christian Henderson, is only for you. It's dangerous to play him because pretty much everyone knows I like to play him."

I nodded.

He continued pointedly, "Absolutely anyone who finds out about me wants to know why I'm still alive. Since I can never satisfy them, all I can do is run. Focus. So, if I was always being chased specifically when you were around, why do you think they didn't bust in on us and take me captive then? Do you have any ideas?"

I blinked. "No. Should I?"

"You are important to them. They would never confront me if you were with me."

I stared at him and remembered the additional cameras in my room in Scotland. "Why? Who are they?"

"This particular group has grown long arms and big teeth in the past few years. I have been calling them the Argonauts because I first became aware of them when I was in Toronto. They consist of Dr. Hilliar, his partner, financial supporters, and some younger thugs they use for surveillance. They have spent a great deal of time watching you."

I felt a shiver. The idea of being spied on made me sick.

"I had hoped that if I stayed away from you, they would lose interest in you. They backed off recently, but that doesn't mean they've forgotten you. Since they know your face, we're going to have to change a lot of things about you in order for you to slip under their radar."

"What are you going to do?" I questioned.

He smiled. "All the glamorous things I've always wanted to try. You have to look completely different—like someone they've never seen before. For that, I can't simply put a wig on your head. These guys are trained to look for stuff like that. You need to look authentic. A wig won't cut it. You'll need a dye job and a dozen other things, but don't worry, it will be a snap."

"I've never wanted to be blonde," I said caustically, thinking of the way Rogan had looked at Felicity-Ann.

He didn't catch my disdain or the reason for it and went on. "You can't get caught. Even though you are connected to them and they don't want to hurt you, you cannot get caught. If you're caught, they'll try to recruit you. You can't let them poison you with their greed."

I snapped, "What do you mean by that?"

"I mean that if your identity is uncovered, they will try to convince you to join their cause—hunting me down. They'll make it sound very grand, like the hunt for the elixir of life. That your assistance could bring long lives to thousands of people pegged for death." He paused and looked at me with an intensity generally unknown to his features. "You can't let them seduce you. What they want is barbaric. They want to commit crimes against humanity—my humanity—and use me as their guinea pig. As far as they are concerned, cutting my hand off was merely a starter."

"Shut up!" I interrupted. "I don't want to hear it. It's enough for me that they wanted to hurt you, and that they *are* hurting Brandon. You don't have to explain every detail. I still don't understand why anyone in my family would be especially interested in protecting me."

He frowned. "That's why it has to be you. That's why they didn't take me and you at the same time during any of the times we met. Somehow, you're family. If you're caught and identified, the worst thing that will happen is they'll try to recruit you."

"You're sure?"

He smacked his tongue against his front teeth unpleasantly. "I'd stake my life on it. Otherwise, I wouldn't let you try." He went to rub his hands together, but since he was missing one he ended up hitting the opposite arm of the chair. "I'm still not used to my hand being gone. Beth, there is so much more, but I'm afraid of overwhelming you. Today has been merely an introduction. Is Trinity expecting you back tonight?"

"Yes, but it's not a big deal. I'll just text her that I've gone for a little holiday by myself and I'm staying at a B&B tonight. She won't be suspicious. I've done that sort of thing before. Besides, she's probably hanging out with Felicity-Ann making plans for the wedding." I deliberately looked at Rogan to see if he had any reaction to my mentioning Felicity-Ann, but not a single muscle in his face tightened or relaxed.

CHAPTER TWELVE

Clumsy Confession

That evening, Rogan tried to make things pleasant between us. He made jokes and fed me the best food. Three things hindered it from being as pleasant as it might have been.

The first one was that his hand was gone. Actually, I was very impressed at how well he coped with not having a hand and I wondered repeatedly how long it had been missing. He cut mushrooms like a second hand would have made things harder for him. It was unbelievable how he got them to balance on their curved tops. He fed me grilled mushrooms with brie and toasted French bread. It wasn't that he acted incapable. It was that I felt that his mutilation was a crime against nature. Why disfigure the most perfect man? I felt sick thinking about it.

The second thing was that I wasn't sure if we were going to be together after we rescued Brandon. He hadn't promised me anything other than the weekend. He said we would finish the rescue operation before my classes on Monday, but what would happen afterward? Would we be together?

The third thing, and it was very disconcerting, was that he kept disappearing down the hall, unlocking a door, going in and coming out again. He'd lock the door, which he inevitably accomplished with considerable rattling, since he had to do it with only one hand. After a while, I was forced to conclude that a living thing was in that room and he didn't want me to see it. There was no noise from inside the room so whatever it was, human or animal, it was too ill to utter a sound. Sadly, I admired him for that, too. Whatever was behind that door, nurses in hospitals checked on patients less often.

As we sat at the table, I suddenly got the urge to tell him a secret. "I think I'm obsessed with you."

He glanced at me but kept chewing his dinner. "Oh?" He wasn't surprised in the least. "You must know, not only am I not Christian Henderson, but I'm not Rogan Cormack either." He outlined his face with his fingers. "The things that are me in this picture are few. When you discover what I really look like, how will you feel?"

"I've been preparing myself for it. Will you show me?"

He hesitated. The possibility of seeing what he really looked like hanging in the air between us like a lit firefly. "Not today," he said flatly. "There are already too many new things for you to accept today."

"Could you tell me what you're like when you're yourself?" I had ravaged the plate of food and there were not even crumbs left.

He glanced at me lovingly. I was wearing him down. Finally, he said, "I'm old."

"How old? Old enough to be my dad?"

He groaned. "If only."

"Then how old are you?"

"Old. I'm scared to give you a ballpark number. Not only that, but it's been so long since I've been myself, I can hardly remember. When I'm Christian, I have to seem like a playboy who isn't interested in taking care of my adoptive daughter. At the same time, I want her to have every comfort."

That was true.

"When I'm Louis, it's usually to get information from people and to meld into the crowd. No one remembers exactly what Louis looks like. I don't usually get on airplanes dressed like him."

"Charles?"

"When I played Charles I had this fierce little love for you. I say 'fierce' because a boy his age understands little about love beyond attraction, but that doesn't mean it's not real to him. I wasn't surprised in the least when he fell for you in Scotland. Of course, he did. I say 'little' because he loved you without understanding you. If he got to know you in-depth, he wouldn't like you."

"Why?"

"Because you love Christian. He would hate that above all things. He can't match Christian."

"Why?"

"Because he's scrawny with freckles and it only takes a droplet of doubt to disturb his pool of confidence."

"What about you?"

"I'm an ocean of confidence. A man as old as me doesn't have any use for doubt."

"So, when you were playing Charles, did you actually feel any of the things he was feeling?"

"Of course. That's what I'm saying. When I play a character, I use that opportunity to feel what they would feel to make my performance more convincing."

"So, as Charles, you really did love me?"

"Sure. If you like that juvenile kind of love and you might."

"You make it sound so small," I mumbled, disappointed.

"It is small. Especially when placed beside some of my other faces. A boy loves deeply enough to get into a fistfight. Some of the men I've played have loved so deeply, they would allow their heart to be cut out. And sometimes, I've happily played harder games of love than a one-time shot. I've spent years in hospitals cleaning the foulest messes the human mind can fathom out of pure love. If you stick with me through this adventure, you'll understand the difference between a childish infatuation and real love."

I felt like smacking him. "*If?* You think I won't?"

He shook his head. "I think you'll be tempted by these people when you come face to face with them, and that scares me. I want to send someone else, but involving someone else is more dangerous than involving you."

He wasn't going to tell me anything more about himself. He certainly wasn't going to tell me what he looked like without his makeup, and he wasn't going to tell me more about his personality. There was only one thing left. "What's in the room down the hall?"

He sputtered a bit of his drink, glanced at me, put his goblet down, and gracefully wiped his mouth with a white cloth napkin. "I don't think you're ready for that."

"Try me."

He frowned. "After you sleep. I'll tell you in the morning."

"Where will I sleep?"

"In my room."

I folded my napkin between my fingers nervously. "And where will you sleep?"

"In the locked room."

"Why would you sleep in there?"

"I don't want you to be scared and after I show you what has happened, you will be angry with me if I'm not either with you or behind that locked door. Try not to be afraid. It's a tragedy, not a horror movie."

I eyed him skeptically. "Since I'm staying in your room, can I wear your pajamas?"

He quietly groaned. "You might really be obsessed with me. It worries me and delights me."

"Which more?" I asked, bending forward.

He leaned in and met my eyes. "We'll see. You're about to join my little cat and mouse game where I play the prey. If the Argonauts find out your name, they will offer you what you want most—me. But I promise, you'll never get me that way. So, you can decide if you want my blood in a tube with the same amount of ardency as my trust in you."

"Are you saying you won't give me anything other than your good opinion of me if I manage to free Brandon?"

He stared. "Do you want payment?"

"Yes."

"What do you want?"

"You."

He smacked his lips together and looked away. "I should have seen that coming. Beth, if you ever get really close to me, you won't like it."

I piped up. "I don't know what you're thinking when I say I want you, but I am talking about time. Could you spend some time with me?"

"How much time?"

"A year?" I figured I needed that much time to make him fall in love with me.

He became thoughtful and started organizing the dishes into stacks. "I couldn't give it to you immediately, assuming everything goes well. I might be able to give you a year in sections. Like four months next April."

"You kill me," I said without a fleck of humor.

"If they stop hunting me, you can have me."

123

The offer hung invitingly in the air. "For how long?"

"For as long as you want me. I just don't want you to get hurt helping me, and the stakes are high."

"You don't have much confidence in my skills," I said swinging my hair over my shoulder.

He opened his mouth to answer me, but a crashing sound drew our attention down the hall to the locked room. Rogan jumped up from the table. "Wear whatever you want of my clothes. I'll see you tomorrow."

"What about the dishes?" I called after him.

"Do them or don't do them." Then I heard the clanking of his keychain.

***

Sleeping in his room wasn't as much fun as I had hoped. I realized he was trying to pace me and silence my fears, but in the end, he had just freaked me out by telling me there was something to fear without explaining what. I hardly slept at all. Any sound I heard in the house I imagined came from the locked room and then it would take a full five minutes to still my racing heart. By the time I'd chilled out, I heard another noise and started the cycle all over again.

In the middle of one of these moments where I was gripped by terror, I wandered out to the kitchen to calm down and met Rogan in the hallway. He didn't scare me or anything. I would know the shape of his body anywhere, even silhouetted against the window behind him. He touched my elbow and I touched his forearm like we couldn't stand to sleep under the same roof without restlessly leaving our beds to find each other. I wore the top of his pajamas and he wore the bottoms. It was completely by accident. Blue plaid pajamas. How had each of us found only one piece of the same set? He had on an undershirt, that put his triceps on display, which was something nice that never changed, no matter what his face looked like.

I opened the fridge and pulled out a jug of chocolate milk. Rogan met me at the table with a clear clamshell full of chocolate chunk cookies. Even with one hand, that man knew how to stock a pantry. I got the glasses and we sat at the table in near darkness.

"Tell me more," I whispered.

He broke his cookie in half and dipped it in the chocolate milk. After taking a bite, he began slowly, "Of all the people living in the world, I have only ever met one other person who is blocked from death."

"Who is it?"

"Brandon."

"He lives like you?"

"No. He hasn't needed to. He's less ostentatious, less interested in the world around him, and therefore, less involved with the world. He doesn't disguise himself, because most of the time, he lives as a hermit. Until lately that is, no one knew about him and no one chased him. I told you that people want to experiment on me. I've been experimented on so many times I've lost count, but he hasn't had to live like me. Charles betrayed us, and Brandon was captured for the first time. These guys who took him have been a bit more reckless than what I'm used to."

"What do you mean?" I asked edgily.

"I mean that what they did to him has never been done to me. Scientists are not usually this gutsy. It's unforgivable." Rogan's mouth was dry as he went on. "I keep saying this, but if having you here now was just for me, I wouldn't let you stay. If it was just me, or if their experiments were more normal, I wouldn't accept your help."

He was taking too long to explain what was going on. Each of his words was like a marble rolling down a two-degree angle.

"Okay," I said, trying to speed him along. "They hurt him. Did they cut anything off him?"

Rogan nodded.

I rolled my eyes. At the one juncture I would have liked him to be outspoken, he was stumbling. I was playing guess-the-body-part. "Was it a leg?" I asked, afraid to delve deeper on my first try.

The idiocy of the situation seemed to snap Rogan into some semblance of behavior. "You have to understand that what they removed from his body is unimaginable. No normal person could live."

"But you and Brandon are not normal?"

"No. We can't die. No matter how far you want to extend the violence, we can't die."

I stared at Rogan, into his deep blue eyes and my voice failed me. I bit into my cookie and looked away. I did not know how to react to his declaration. A part of me thought he was testing me to see how far down the crazy train I would go before I told him to shut up and stop spouting crap. Another part of my brain dared him to prove he couldn't die, but my mouth couldn't say those words. I didn't want him to hurt himself to satisfy some idiotic challenge.

Instead, I shoved all that aside and asked directly, "You're telling me that Brandon is the one in the locked room?"

"Yes."

"I thought he was kidnapped."

Rogan swallowed uncomfortably. "Some of him is still kidnapped."

I felt rotten, but so far the ideas were still abstract, so I was able to ask my next question without stuttering. "That means he's missing something vital, but he's still alive?"

Rogan nodded.

"What's he missing?" I asked, trying to keep the quiver out of my voice. I decided it was going to be an organ because it would have to be something that would take my faith to believe in. He was going to place me in a situation where I was just going to have to take his word for it. I didn't like that as I waited for him to do the unveiling.

"His head," Christian said slowly, gauging my reaction.

"That's not possible," I said firmly.

"For most people? No, it isn't. There is a loose scientific explanation, but it doesn't change that no one knows why we're blocked from death. What I do know is that this is possible. It's happening."

"Can I see him?"

He waved his hand. "Not yet. I need to explain a few things about his current condition."

"All right. Explain."

Rogan knew I didn't believe him. He didn't expect me to believe him, but like a school teacher who hates you with the same amount of venom with which you hate him, he was going to talk and I was going to listen.

"His neck was severed. I put tubing in his windpipe to keep him breathing. The rest of his neck bleeds, so I have it covered with gauze, but it needs changing regularly and he's leaking several other awful liquids at the same time. Just because he can't die doesn't mean he can't get an infection, so I'm feeding him antibiotics."

I stayed silent with my lower lip protruding. What sort of nonsense was he trying to pull? I had to make sure I didn't let him trick me because I was squeamish. "So you're squishing pills though his severed esophagus?"

He rubbed his eyes. "It's convenient. I'm feeding him painkillers and muscle relaxants too. Just because we don't die doesn't mean we don't feel pain."

"Well, I know I'd hate to be the test dummy for a guillotine," I said snottily.

His glare was like a whip. "Quiet, Beth. I know this is hard to accept, but try not to ridicule me too much. You'll scream when you see him. It's actually fine if you want to do that. There's nobody to hear. Not even him."

Rogan was so determined; I let him finish without any more smart remarks.

"I don't think his body is in a particular amount of pain other than the wound at his neck. It's his head that is suffering since all nerves lead to the brain. I'm feeding him so he's still passing waste, but his body is in shock. I have to keep him tied down. He keeps flailing around." Rogan shook his head like he was done talking to me. "And since his head is not with me, I don't find it peculiar that he was able to get a separate message to you."

"You mean, you think he's still talking with his severed head?" I gawked in revulsion.

"Sort of. Do you want to see him now?"

"No, but if you say I'm the only one who can help you, I guess I'll have to."

"Good girl."

127

CHAPTER THIRTEEN

Make Me into You

I stood in the middle of nowhere, on a deserted road with nothing but lines of trees on both sides. My car was in the ditch far behind me. It was dark. There were no street lamps and no moon that night. It was lucky the Milky Way was so bright or I would not have been able to see my way at all. I moved through snow that came up to my shins. The road had not been plowed. I had only been walking for five minutes and already my thighs were aching.

I took a deep breath and let it out slowly so I made a mini steam cloud.

Admission was the first step. I was freaked out. It wasn't treading through the snow in the dark that freaked me out. My freak out began when Rogan showed me headless Brandon. I had been expecting some parlor trick that was see-through to someone who didn't scare easily, so I got right in on the scene so I wouldn't be fooled. A decapitated person should not be alive and when I saw with my own eyes, felt with my own hands, that it was possible—I threw up in the garbage can. There were no strings on his fingers as he wrote the word HELP in my palm one letter at a time.

Once I was convinced Rogan wasn't a filthy liar (at least not on that occasion), he put all his efforts into telling me his plan and showing me what he wanted me to do. The disguise he had planned for me was... intense.

My hair was light brown and was usually a wavy, curly, mess. Fighting it with a hair straightener regularly wasn't on my timetable. Christian put a prosthetic hand on his stump and immediately dyed my whole head a light platinum blonde. When I saw it, I pretended to gag. He smiled wickedly and got out the hair straightener. Then he plucked and pencilled my eyebrows in.

Then he showed me what he'd done. My hair was stick-straight and I looked like a runway model... one of the pretty ones.

"I had no idea," I gasped, gaping at my reflection.

"If only that was enough," he said longingly. "Unfortunately, I have to go further."

"What do you mean?"

"I mean that these people have been watching you for years. They know what you look like. Luckily, you are a bit skinnier than you were in high school."

"I thought you didn't care to give me a complex about my weight."

"I don't," he said innocently. "If you'd gained forty pounds I would still have applauded you. The key is to look different. Either way is fine with me."

Then he put contact lenses in my eyes, which were unfamiliar and uncomfortable. My eyesight was perfect.

"Your eyes are green-hazel. I don't dare go blue. Blue contacts always look so phony on darker eyed people. We'll go darker. We'll go all the way to dark brown."

Again, he let me look at myself, but that was the kicker. By that point, I looked nothing like myself. He sprayed me with bronzer and showed himself to a master makeup artist.

Of the intimate activities he was willing to participate in, the makeover was very high up on the list. Every second, he was looking at me, touching me, asking me if I was comfortable, and generally showering me with attention. I should have let him do my makeup before.

He took me to West Edmonton Mall that afternoon, straight to the second floor and all the most expensive boutiques. The clothes he picked out were designed to make me look even skinnier and help me look like I had a different shape. He put me in the tightest black pants in the world and I had to object.

"I can't wear these," I complained. "They make my butt look enormous."

He shook his head haughtily. "You don't know how much I would rather they looked at your bottom than your face. I hope they won't look at anything else. You'll be much safer that way."

I frowned—deeply embarrassed. "But I can't look cute if I wear those."

"You will," he said confidently. "My face doesn't look anything like this. Trust me. This is what I do. You will look drop-dead sexy without showing off your skin. Satisfied?"

"Maybe I will be... when you're finished."

"Covering your skin is important. I can't let them see your moles."

"I don't have moles!"

"You have three." He pointed them out to me. One under my collarbone, on my back and my arm. "I know your body and if they've watched your footage, they'll know it too."

I blushed and allowed him to continue.

He was right about the clothes and by the time my look was complete, I wouldn't have known myself from surveillance footage.

We went back to his place and he drilled me on 'the plan'.

After that, he tucked me into bed and told me to sleep for a few hours. He said he had some work to do to get the car ready, and I needed my rest if I was going to work all night. I was so tired from my restlessness the night before that I slept undisturbed by the occasional noise from the other room.

That evening, I found myself walking pitifully in ridiculous girl-boots, any human being would freeze to death wearing, on a highway in Northern Alberta. I saw the lights from the building I was headed toward and prayed that I wouldn't screw up. I could do exactly what he instructed. I was spunky! I couldn't think about what these people had done to Brandon, or what they would do to me if I were discovered, but I could think about what I would get if I were successful—one whole year with Rogan... Christian... whatever his name was.

I trod through the thick icy-like-a-snow-cone snowdrifts until I got to the only door in sight. I knocked on it.

No one answered.

Feeling anticlimactic, I knocked again.

It wasn't until I started feeling desperate and crazy cold did someone finally come to the door. It was a young man with short spiky dark hair and a bit of winter stubble on his chin. In the reflection of his eyes, I saw what he saw. His whole face lit up like he'd chosen the right door on a game show.

"Hi," he said, dazzled.

"Hi," I said back, exactly the way Rogan coached me. "I had a car accident down the road. I'm alone. Can you help me? I'm really cold."

Actually, I wanted to die. It felt too stupid to put that expression on my face and to say those words. Rogan reassured me countless times that even though it felt like the opener to a horror movie or a porno flick, it wouldn't turn out to be either. These guys were animals, but not the way I thought. Besides, if I simply told them my name, he said they would heel like canines.

The guy opened the door wide and let me come in. The room inside was a break room where people had coffee and sandwiches. There was a fridge, a stove, a microwave, and about a zillion and one unused styrofoam cups. The place smelled like old rubber and motor oil. The guy in front of me wore heavy-duty brown overalls with a T-shirt with skulls on the shoulders.

"What happened?" Skull Boy asked. "Are you hurt?"

"No, I'm fine. But I'm lost. Is this anywhere near the Westgate Ski lodge?"

Skull Boy stifled a laugh. I was nowhere near it, but I had to act bewildered. He straightened his back. "No. You're on the wrong highway."

I let my shoulders droop and gave the impression of being completely defeated by the news. "Well, crap. My friends invited me up there to go skiing with them for one final ski of the season. Now I'm completely lost, and my car is broken. I went in the ditch and now it won't start. Do you know, I would have frozen to death if you hadn't opened the door. Thank you."

"Does your phone work?" he began. He was extremely pleasant. "Have you called a tow truck?"

"I tried, but I couldn't get my GPS to work. I don't know where I am. I can't tell them where to meet me if I don't know where I am!" I threw myself into one of the orange plastic chairs.

"So, I take it you have no idea what's wrong with your car?"

"None," I pouted.

He smiled. "I have a few minutes. Maybe I can figure it out. Did you go down near here?"

I sniffled. "I'm not sure how far I walked to get here."

131

"What's your name? I'm Steve."

"Jill," I lied.

"Well, let's find your car," he said as he grabbed his coat.

I recoiled with my back against the plastic. "No. I don't want to go back out there yet. I'm frozen solid. Can't I stay here for a bit? At least until I warm up?"

"Sure," he said brightly, dropping his coat and sitting next to me. He offered me a doughnut.

I accepted it. Taking off my gloves, I crushed my fingers together to get the warmth back into them.

"I'm sorry, we don't have a space heater or a fireplace to warm you up."

"Oh," I said vacantly. Rogan said that I mustn't act overly interested in where I was. My behavior must be patterned by the following priorities. First, I must be concerned about my own comfort. Thus I must eat everything they offer me. At that moment, I was cold, so I needed to act like it. Secondly, I must be anxious to be on my way. Thirdly, I must flirt. It should be fun for them to have me around. Christian said that these boys were girl-deprived, so I had to give them a reason to keep me around as long as possible.

Keeping my priorities in mind, I asked, "Do you know much about cars?"

Well, Skull Boy Steve knew a lot about cars. On my very first crack at it, I opened the floodgates of his automotive knowledge. I was trying to find out if he would be successful if he went out to try to fix my car (not even I knew what was broken in it). Perhaps if I had been dressed differently a different stream of car-related information might have sprung from his mouth, but since I was wearing a spotless white marshmallow coat with a fur trim hood, Prada sunglasses in my hair, and carrying a humongous designer bag on my lap, he couldn't stop talking about Lamborghinis. I acted impressed no matter what he said.

When he paused for breath, I got him back on target by telling him about the car I was using for this farce. "I've got a 2012 Camaro. Do you know much about those?"

"That's the vehicle you have outside?" he gawked.

"Yeah."

He glanced around for a second like he didn't know what to do. Then he asked, "Hey, are you warm yet?"

"I'm frozen. Really, really… frozen," I said in slow, serious tones. Things were going better than I imagined.

"Would you mind giving me your keys, so I can go have a look?" he asked with big puppy-dog eyes.

I hesitated, but only because I thought Rogan would want me to. He told me that I had to act cocky and protective about the vehicle, but there was no way they would be able to start it.

"Just give me a few more minutes," I begged.

"Do you want a cup of coffee?" he offered.

I shook my head, refusing because it was ready. I needed to make everything take as long as possible. "Do you have any idea how bad that stuff is for you? Besides, if I drink that, I won't be able to sleep until next week."

"But it's warm," Skull Boy Steve argued, lifting the pot.

I declined again and he started rooting around the cupboards to see if he had anything else he could feed me that would get me outside quicker. Actually, Christian warned me against sleeping, and he had given me a pack of stimulants to keep me awake if I should even think of losing consciousness. I had work to do.

A minute later, a package of ancient herbal tea was found and Skull Boy was boiling water in a kettle they never used.

"Are you from Edmonton?" he began.

"Yes."

"Going to school there?"

"U-huh."

"What are you taking?"

"I'm trying for my commercial pilot license at the inner-city airport."

"You've flown a plane?" he asked, staring at me.

I laughed at him. "Not yet. I'm starting the course this summer. It's all set up."

I tossed my super blonde locks over my shoulder. Rogan knew everything about men. That was what he told me to say and Skull Boy had stopped what he was doing and was practically salivating on the linoleum.

133

Finally, he said, "And you drive a Camaro? Will you marry me?"

I smiled a little flirty smile—again one that Rogan coached me on—and said bravely, "Get my car out of the ditch first. Then, we'll talk."

He popped his coat on and said cheerfully, "I'm on it." With that, he dashed out the door.

I couldn't guess what he was going to do. I still had the keys to the car in my coat pocket. This would be the perfect time to snoop, but I decided to wait. Undoubtedly, Skull Boy would be back once he realized he had forgotten to take the car keys and I didn't know who else was in the building.

A couple of minutes later, Skull Boy Steve was back. "I started my truck. The seats warm up. Soon it will be toastier in there than in here."

"Great," I said, acting pleased.

He finished making my tea and gave it to me in a travel cup since they had a ton of them. We went out the door and got into his humongous black Silverado truck. He had to give me a boost to get me in.

As his tires crunched down the packed snow, I showed him the way back to the car.

"Wow, you walked a long way," he commented as we pulled up behind the backend of my car.

"Yeah, I'm still cold," I said as I handed him the keys.

Skull Boy left the engine running and got out to assess the damage. From the comfort of his truck, I watched him get in the driver's seat, try a few things, get out, and go to the front to open the hood. It wouldn't open. He came back to the truck, got a brush and scraper. He was very enthusiastic.

"I think the hood might be frozen shut," he said before he went back over.

I watched him mess with the hood for twenty minutes. It wouldn't open and we were a two-hour drive from anywhere. By that point, I wouldn't have been surprised if Rogan had welded it shut.

But I was really warming up to Skull Boy Steve. I never imagined a guy would go to so much trouble for me in such cold weather. It was the end of March, but that didn't stop it from being unbearably cold at night in the Canadian Rockies.

He came back in and apologized. He was deeply embarrassed, offered to take me back to the compound and he'd come back with something to help get the ice off. "We should have headed back out here as soon as you showed up. Then it wouldn't have had the chance to ice over."

"Sorry," I apologized in a whiny voice.

"Not your fault," he replied lightly.

Back at the compound, there was another guy in the break room. His reaction to seeing me was almost as brilliant as Skull Boy Steve's had been. He was another dark-haired dude, except he was way shorter. He welcomed us by saying, "Is this your sister, Steve?"

"You wish! Her car broke down on the road. She came here for help."

"Hi, I'm Jill," I said with a wave.

"He's Conroy," Skull Boy said.

I sat back down at the break room table while Skull Boy explained the situation. I tried to think up a nickname for Conroy, but everything about him was too plain. He was wearing jeans and a black T-shirt. He had no piercings or visible tattoos and it looked like he'd shaved that morning.

"You should call a tow-truck," Conroy suggested tightly.

"She tried before she came here," Skull Boy gloated.

"Whatever. You should try again now, especially since you can't get the hood open."

"Nah, I can do this. It's probably something stupid like the wire disconnected from the battery. I can fix that."

Conroy frowned. "I guess that would be faster than having them drive all the way out here."

They talked for another minute about what to do and finally, they decided to tow it with the Silverado to the garage at the compound to have a better look. The Camaro aspect didn't do anything for Conroy. He was more interested in me. He kept glancing at me like a starved dog who smelled a fresh piece of meat. I never got treated like that. Men sucked if dolling up had such a strong effect on them.

"You should come with me in case I need a hand," Skull Boy was saying to Conroy.

135

"Fine, but…" His voice dropped to a low whisper. "We shouldn't leave her alone here."

"Call Chuck to watch her," Skull Boy hissed back.

"Chuck? Are you sure you want to leave him alone with her?"

"What? She won't like him. Have you seen Chuck lately? He looks like crap. She's probably got pepper spray in her purse and we'll be finished in like half an hour."

"Kay. I'll call him."

Conroy disappeared through one of the inner doors and Skull Boy came back toward me. "We're just going to get one of our buddies to keep you company while we tow your car."

I nodded.

My brain wanted to be annoyed that they weren't leaving me alone. I wanted to snoop, find the missing body parts and get out of there as soon as possible, but Christian warned me about being anxious. He said all I had to do was bide my time. They were going to be cautious of a stranger, but the more time I spent there (as long as I didn't blow it by jumping the gun), the more likely I was to succeed. I just needed to be cool.

I was cool. Cool enough to leave my winter coat on until the guy they called Chuck came in. As soon as I set eyes on him, I averted them and looked at safer-than-safe Skull Boy instead. I had to look like the appearance of Charles Lewis didn't faze me at all.

CHAPTER FOURTEEN

The Head of the Headless Horseman

Crap was a tame description for the young man who came through the break room door. Charles hardly resembled the nineteen-year-old boy I had met in Scotland. I had not liked him, but that was mostly because of the forced comparison to Christian and the request to enter into a romantic relationship. Even so, he had been healthy. That was over. Standing in the break room, his skin looked gray and his eyes had no shine. His hair practically stood up on end, the way a boy's hair does when it has a lot of product in it and it hasn't been washed lately.

The guys called him Chuck, so I followed their lead. I introduced myself and he raided the refrigerator while the other two went out into the snow.

At first, the only thing I could think about was what had happened after he saw Christian and I kiss in the conservatory. He had been talking to Brandon on the lawn, one thing led to another, and then he joined a group of crazy scientists who cut off Brandon's head? I felt sick. What happened between those two events? Rogan told me if these guys recognized me they would say anything to get me to join them. I bet that was what happened to Charles, and he had given them Brandon, who was easier to capture than Christian.

He disgusted me.

"So, you're from Edmonton?" he suddenly asked, turning toward me.

"Yep."

"Are you going to university there?"

"No," I lied. "Why? Are you planning on going there for school this fall?"

He scratched his eyebrow and frowned. "That's what I should do." After that less than revealing statement, he fell into silence.

I had to keep him talking. "Your accent is adorable. What part of Britain are you from?"

"The north. It doesn't matter. I'm boring."

"There's not even a TV in here. Come on. It's more boring not to say anything. Why do you want to go to UofA? Do you want to become a vet?"

He did a double-take. "Why would you assume I want to become a vet?"

I shrugged my shoulders. "I don't know. Everyone I talk to is trying to get into the veterinarian program. Why? What do you want to take?"

"It doesn't matter."

"Then why do you want to go?" I persisted.

"There's a girl I want to meet."

My throat felt choked up like I had strep, but I still had to act cool. "Oooh! A love interest! Tell me all about her."

"Why?"

"Because I'm bored and I'm a stranger. Your secret will be safe with me," I said as I crossed my heart with my finger.

"She's a girl I met a couple of summers ago in Scotland."

I feared that was coming. "I'll bet she had an adorable accent too," I remarked.

He frowned. "She isn't Scottish if that's what you mean. She is Canadian and she's going to UofA."

"I guess she doesn't know you like her," I said sadly.

"She did know. She just didn't fancy me. I'm sure she'd be shocked to find out that I still like her. What about you? Do you have a boyfriend?"

"Nope."

"Why not?"

I flicked my hair, but it didn't have the same effect on Charles as the other two. "I'm too busy."

"Doing what?"

"Being crazy. Come on. Tell me more about your girl. Maybe I know her. What's her name?"

"Bethany Coldwell."

I nearly fell off my chair. No one called me Bethany. Most people assumed that my name was Elizabeth. Christian never called me Bethany, not even when he was trying to act like a proper guardian. The last person who called me Bethany was my father before he died.

"Do you know her?"

I shook my head negatively. "Afraid not."

"It was a long shot."

"So why did you like her so much?"

He scratched his head. "It's hard to talk about why you like someone, isn't it?"

I snickered. "No, it isn't. Not to talk down to you, but I've been in love before. It isn't complicated at all."

"No?"

"Nope. The man I loved made me into a nutcase."

"Is that why you're crazy?"

"Happy crazy. Do you know why I loved him? I loved him because I always felt like he had a surprise waiting for me. Even if he didn't have something special to do, just having him around was enough to make live wires out of my nervous system. Every time our eyes met, I felt like I was rising off the ground. Did she make you feel like that?"

"No. She made me feel young and dumb."

"Harsh. Why do you like her again?"

"I don't know. I don't think I can explain it." It was quiet for a few seconds before he wound up for round two. "Let me ask you a question. If you had to choose between an older man who was practically your dad or a guy around your own age who liked you, which would you choose?"

"Both," I said unhelpfully.

"What?"

"Calm down. If the one guy is practically my dad why should I have to give up my relationship with him to be with the other guy? Those two things don't sound conflicting."

"What if they were?"

"I'd need more information. It depends on so many things. How old is the dad guy? Is he over forty? Is he under thirty-five? What does he look like? How much money does he make? Is he free with his money? Then I have a ton of questions about the young guy. What kind of a guy is he? Is he muscular?"

For a second Charles didn't realize I expected him to answer me. He perked up. "About average."

"Is he intelligent? Does he go to Oxford or Yale?"

"No."

"Does he have a good job?"

"No."

"Is he a rebel without a cause full of angst and energy?"

"Not so much."

"Is he so ridiculously handsome that he can scarcely step out in public without being walloped by adoring females?"

"Hardly."

"You've got no case for the young guy. He sounds like he thinks she should like him merely because he likes her, not because he's offering her anything."

Charles looked more miserable than before. "What about you? What kind of man did you fall in love with?"

"The man I liked was far from normal. He was all the things I just listed and none of them. He may have been a genuine freak. He was charming in an old-time gentleman kind of way one minute—opening doors for me and helping me with my coat—and the next he was asking me to hold a syringe full of apple juice."

"He sounds creepy. You're not still with him, are you?"

"No," I affirmed. "But I *was* in love with him."

"It's just a thing of the past now?"

I smiled. "It would be okay if I never saw his face again."

***

If I had a stopwatch measuring how long I had been on the compound, by that point, it would have said two hours and forty-three minutes. I didn't need a stopwatch. I was so tense I was counting it myself.

Skull Boy and Conroy had come back looking regretful.

"Couldn't you open it?" I asked.

"Not without scratching the paint." Skull Boy frowned.

"You scratched the paint?" I gasped.

"No," he groaned. "I think we should just let it sit in the heated garage for an hour. The whole hood must be frozen." That was what his mouth said, but he was stifling a smile. He was counting his lucky stars that I couldn't leave yet.

"I'll make some food for us," Skull Boy invited.

"Sure." I couldn't go anywhere anyway.

"It's a good day to take a break since the old men aren't here."

Charles looked glazed-over while the other guys washed up and got busy. One of them got a pizza and wings from a freezer. He popped them into the oven on different cookie sheets while the other one convinced Charles to do a beer run for them. It took me about a fifth of a second to see that whatever usefulness Charles had in the beginning, it hadn't made him an indispensable part of their group and now he was the local whipping boy.

He left and I took off my coat. I had been saving that for the right moment. My outfit underneath was gorgeous. I wore the super tight black pants Rogan bought me and a black shirt that was all horizontal in its lines. It exposed one shoulder completely, even though the neckline was intact. When my blonde hair fell on the black fabric, even I had to admit the effect was completely mesmerizing.

Without Skull Boy saying anything, I could tell he was regretting asking for cheap beer. He should have shelled out for something better. Conroy's expression was less transparent. My guess was that he was nervous about me being there when I shouldn't be.

He talked the whole time Charles was gone. I listened, smiled and laughed exactly the way I was supposed to, tilting my head and making eyes at whoever did the talking. It didn't take much of my concentration. I was actually going over the plan Rogan had outlined for me.

At a break in the conversation, I started doing what I was supposed to do. "Is there anybody else around? If we're having food, we ought to share."

"You are so classy," Skull Boy complimented. "It's only us today and tomorrow. After we eat, we'll go back out to the garage and see if we can open the hood."

The food finished cooking before Charles came back, so we started eating without him. He didn't care. He obviously lived in hell and that day was no break for him. I didn't worry about it. He could nail his own coffin shut for all I cared.

After pizza, I put on my coat at exactly the same moment Skull Boy was taking a clumsy sip from his beer and thanks to a little slip of my hand, he spilled it in a long streak down my snow-white coat.

"I'm sorry, Jill," he said in alarm. "I've only had two of these. I'm not usually a cheap drunk."

I scratched behind my ear like I was madly scraping for patience. "That's okay. Can you show me where the bathroom is, so I can get cleaned up? I think I got some on my pants." I had to make it seem natural. Like me slipping away from the group while they went to the garage was not suspicious.

Conroy told me how to get to the bathroom. "Okay," he said, taking the lead. "Let's go see if her car is unfrozen. Chuck, you come too. Maybe we need an extra set of hands."

I slipped into the bathroom, turned on the light, and closed the door. Except I wasn't inside. I was in the hallway. I ran past the bathroom to the end of the hall and down a flight of stairs. I knew where to go. Rogan had already shown me a map of the place and made me memorize it.

At the bottom of the stairs, there were three doors. I grabbed the handle of the first door and walked in. Inside, Rogan told me to look for a tiny fridge. I found it. There was a keypad attached to the door. He had given me three codes he hoped would open it.

"I know Dr. Hilliar," Rogan had said. "His passwords have a theme. Unless I'm reading him completely wrong, it should be one of the first two number sets. I've got one more that's a maybe, but if it doesn't open on the first two—ditch it. I don't want it locking you out on the third try. Try it again no sooner than twenty minutes later, at which time you can try the third number set."

If that didn't work, things were going to get messy. I'd have to find a way to take the whole fridge with me.

I typed in the first one: 66-12-19. My heart was up in my throat. Cat burgling was a terrible way to die. I was terrified one of the guys would come down and catch me any second.

The fridge opened. Rogan was a god! Inside was exactly as he said. There were two things in the fridge. One was a Tupperware container—Rogan's hand. The other was big and covered in bubble wrap—Brandon's head.

I opened my huge designer bag, pulled out the balloon that had made it look full and put Brandon's head inside. I thought I would throw up or faint, but I didn't. I just dropped it and snatched up the other container. I closed the fridge and ditched the room.

I booted up the stairs and made it to the bathroom just in time for Conroy to find me holding onto the bathroom door.

"Did you get the beer out?" he asked, looking at my coat. Seeing all the beer stains still there and the red blush on my face, he continued, "Are you okay?"

My lower lip trembled. "I really liked this coat."

"Can I have a go at it?" he asked. "I'm pretty good at getting out stains."

I wanted to get out of that place as quickly as possible, but I also knew I needed to keep to the plan. Ignoring my instincts, I nodded. "Okay, but I don't think there's much point." I took it off and handed it to him.

He looked at the stain. "Did you even get it wet?"

"You're supposed to get it wet?" I asked, playing super dumb, and biting my lower lip.

"Yeah." He smiled.

"But it's goose down."

"Geese get wet, too." He opened the bathroom door and put my coat under the tap. He put liquid hand soap and water on it and the stain sort of washed out.

I acted relieved and took it from him. "I bet it will come clean if I have it dry cleaned. I'm not mad or anything."

"Are you sure? You looked like you were going to cry a second ago."

"I'm okay. You already made me feel so much better. Anyway, it's just a coat. Which way to the garage?"

143

Without a bump in the road, Conroy took me to the massive garage. What was their building used for normally? I couldn't see a purpose and I couldn't ask.

I definitely couldn't think of the trouble these boys would be in once my theft was discovered, even though I kept thinking about the balloon I left under the conference table.

Skull Boy had become considerably less cheerful when we met him and Charles in the garage. "I don't know what's wrong. I've tried everything I can think of. I think we really will have to call a tow truck."

"Okay, but before we do that, I'd like to try starting it one more time. Can I have my keys back?"

He handed them over, but said, "I don't think it will be of much use. We already tried it twice back on the road, and three times since we brought it in here."

I got in and put my bag on the passenger side seat. Then I did exactly what Rogan told me to do. There was a button under the steering column that I should press if I could leave the scene of the crime easily. I pressed it and a half a minute later, the engine was purring. I giggled and rolled down the window.

"I guess I must have flooded it or something out on the highway. I was really upset. Maybe I was too hard on it."

Surprisingly, Skull Boy looked even more miserable. "Yeah, I guess," he muttered. Had he been hoping I would have to stay the night?

"Thanks so much for dinner and for towing the car back here. I feel like I ought to offer you some money for helping me, but would that be insulting?"

Skull Boy was about to answer when Conroy stuck his head in the way. "It wouldn't be insulting at all. We could use the cash. Up north— you know how expensive everything is."

"R-Right," I stuttered. Only at that moment did I realize my wallet was in the same bag as the human head. Almost trembling, my blind hand reached for the purse.

Skull Boy saved me. He pushed Conroy aside. "He's joking. You don't owe us a thing. It was nice to have you around. Can I visit you the next time I'm in Edmonton?"

"Yeah," I said with a smile. "That would be nice." Then I gave him the cell phone number for the cell phone I was carrying. If I really did get away without a hitch, that phone would be in the garbage in under three hours.

Charles came over to say good-bye too while Conroy happily opened the garage doors.

"It was a pleasure meeting you," the gray-faced redhead said stormily.

"Ditto," I said before I waved to them and heartily put the car into gear.

Abruptly, Skull Boy bounded up to my door and asked breathlessly, "Do you even know where you're going?"

I let out a breath. I thought he'd caught me.

***

I couldn't believe it when I was back on the highway. I told them I was going back to Edmonton. I said I'd had enough adventure and I was ready for home, so they pointed me back toward the city and off I went.

Except, I didn't go back to Edmonton. I drove directly to Hinton where I was going to meet Rogan. I sent him a text saying he was supposed to meet me. I'd done combination plan A with plan E. Plan A was to drive away in the Camaro. Plan E was to get them to spill something on me. There were a lot of plans. If only those boys had known it, Rogan had loaded me up with enough tranquilizers to make sure they were all comatose until next week.

In Hinton, I met Rogan at a gas station. I parked the Camaro next to the curb and met him by the pumps. I got into his car just as he finished filling the gas tank.

He got in, looked in my bag and said, "Thank you."

Quickly, he pulled out onto the road.

"Just out of curiosity, where did you get the Camaro."

He grinned. "I stole it."

"Today?" I gasped.

"Yes. Today. The police will pick it up from there, and they'll return it to the owner. No problem."

145

"Except my fingerprints are in it."

"Relax, they won't dust it. The compound I used to keep the hood shut will melt in a day or two and the modifications I made to the starter will go unnoticed… probably. If the owner accidentally turns on the mechanism meant to stall the starter, the worst thing that will happen is that he'll have to put in a new starter. It won't be the end of the world."

"And the CCTV on the gas station wall?" I pouted.

"Saw Rogan and Jill, and we are not either of those people. It'll be fine."

I breathed out a sigh. "You are a terrible human being."

He chuckled. "Well, yes."

CHAPTER FIFTEEN

The Selfish Girl

I stared in the mirror in Rogan's bathroom. It was lucky for me that contact lenses were easier to take out than they were to put in; otherwise, I never would have managed it. After that was done, I hacked into the makeup remover and started to look a little more like myself.

I flicked back the shower curtain and turned on the water. I smelled like beer, and I was curious as to what I looked like with blonde curly hair. I undressed and washed the straightness out of my hair. After my shower, I got out, wrapped myself in one of Rogan's blanket-sized towels and went to go find my clothes.

Back in yesterday's clothes with my hair dry, I had another look in the mirror. My hair had bounced up to my shoulders, making it look shorter than it had been when it was straight. It looked amazing!

I came out of the bathroom and went to find a snack in the kitchen. Rogan followed me.

"So, do you think you'll be able to reattach everything?" I asked.

"Yes, except there's a problem. You didn't check the body parts before you picked them up and split, did you?"

"No," I said. His expression made my mouth feel dry. "I didn't get the wrong head, did I?"

He answered wearily. "It's not that. It's my hand and his head. It's just that they weren't…" he searched for the word. "Complete."

"What do you mean?"

"My pinkie finger is missing and Brandon's tongue has been cut out. If they cut it out to stop him from talking, that doesn't explain why they cut off my pinkie."

"There was nothing else in the fridge," I argued.

"I don't think it's your fault. I think those old men may have cut out smaller parts to take with them on their trip. I bet they're trying to get sponsors to pay for their research. Showing someone a disembodied tongue and a finger that jiggle around on their own might be enough to get an investor to open their wallet. They're probably also easier to

147

smuggle onto an airplane and less shocking during a demonstration. I don't know."

"Did you know you were sending me at a time when those old men would be gone?"

"No. I thought they'd be there, but their absence is why you were able to get in and out so easily. If everyone was there, everything would have been much harder for you. Personally, I'm thankful it turned out this way. Now I have nine fingers instead of five and Henry has his head back. Even without the tongue, this is a magnificent improvement."

"And you'll give me the year you promised?"

"Sure. I don't know when. Try to understand that I probably won't be able to see you for several months. I have to help Brandon and I will be healing myself. Beth, you should head back to Edmonton tomorrow morning. I've got a lot of stitching to do and you need to get to a hair salon, so they can make you look more like you."

"But I like it," I protested. "Can't I leave it?"

He turned around and faced me. "Yes, you look cute with blonde hair. I always knew you would, but if you try to leave it, you could be in danger. You either have to go back to looking the way you did or you have to change yourself into something else."

"But my hair grows quickly. I'll have hideous roots in a month. Can't I dye it back then?"

He started moving toward me one step at a time. I backed up with each of his strides and soon I was backed up against the wall with Rogan's eyes staring into mine. "Are you really going to be like this? Do you think that once they discover they've been robbed, they won't try to find the culprit? Since we're in the Edmonton vicinity, the first person they're going to check is you. Even if you completely fooled Charles while you were there that doesn't mean he won't put the pieces together if he sees you with hair this color." Rogan flicked a ringlet with his fingers. "This is a matter of life and death and I do not want you getting in any deeper with these people. Can't you just do as I ask?"

I felt like I was losing my nerve, but I knew from experience that chickening out didn't get me anywhere, so I proceeded to be more unreasonable than I had ever been. "This is so unfair! I thought you were going to take care of me until the end, but now you're sending me to some hairdresser in the city? They won't do a good job. I'll look like crap and I'll get found out anyway. If I'm going to get caught, I might as well look fabulous."

He stuttered for a moment. "W-what just came out of your mouth?"

"I know you only have one hand and it's asking too much when you should be stitching up Brandon, but…" He waited while I got my thoughts together. "You give me all the wrong things."

He didn't answer but looked around the room like he'd rather look at anything than me.

"And to hear you tell it, I'll never be able to have blonde hair again as long as I live."

"Enough," he snapped, his breath on my forehead. "Get in the chair. I've got the stuff. I might as well do it myself since it's that important."

So he dyed my hair back to a shade resembling my ordinary color and when he was finished he said icily. "Now there's no reason for you not to go back to Edmonton tonight. Get going."

"But," I whined, conjuring a new reason to stay. "Don't you need an extra set of hands when you stitch Brandon back together?"

"No. For that, you'd only get in the way. You need to get back to your real life. You've already missed work, wedding plans, and whatever else. Also, the sooner you are back in Edmonton looking like yourself, the more innocent you look. I'll see you in a few months, and I don't know what I'll have to look like."

I nodded. "I'll know it's you. Not everyone is missing a finger."

"Hopefully, I'll have it back by then," he said grimly.

Not even a half an hour later, I stood on his snowy porch. My hair wasn't even dry, but I got into my rental car and drove back to Edmonton. It was a delightful trip. My hair kept making my cheeks wet.

***

In total, I had been gone a day and a half. I got home really late Saturday night (or really early Sunday morning) and even though I hadn't had enough sleep, I was back at work on Monday. No one mentioned that my hair looked a little different. I noticed, but it was normal that Rogan couldn't make it look exactly the same. He got the color pretty much perfect, but not even a master of disguise like him could fake sun damage.

Trinity asked me if I'd had fun when she saw me on Monday afternoon, but her mind wasn't really on it. I let it slide. Her lack of interest made things easier for me.

However, I was surprised when I was eating lunch in the food court the next day and Felicity-Ann sat down at my table. She took off her sunglasses and set them on the table beside my sushi with a flick of her hand.

"How are you, Beth?" she said nicely. She didn't have the sense to be the least bit embarrassed about what happened at New Year's, even though Trinity had told her as much of the story as she knew.

"Seen Rogan lately?" was my answer.

"I haven't. He moved or something. I thought you knew. You're not still mad at me about that, are you?"

I glared at the roots of her hair. I doubted she had to dye it to achieve that perfect sunny look. "I'm okay. There are always more men to choose from. I was merely curious to know if he had stayed in touch with you, or if he was really as fly-by-night as all that."

"No, he hasn't been in touch. Besides, I think he had another girl that he liked."

"What makes you say that?"

"I don't know. He said I wasn't his type."

I froze. "He said something like that... to you?"

"Incredible, I know." She tapped her toe and stared at the ceiling. "So, could you not be mad at me anymore?"

I looked at her. It was pretty much impossible for me to not be mad at her. I disliked her before she got in my way, but Gibson called it pretty accurately when he said it was because I was jealous of her. It still annoyed me. I let her sit there, waiting, while I thought it over.

Finally, I said, "I don't know why you care what I think."

"Because," she said, clearing her throat and showing me her profile. "You won't have a roommate in a few weeks and I've been looking for a place to live."

"But why me?" I interrupted. "You have dozens of friends. Couldn't you find someone more like you to room with? You have tons of money. If you don't want to live with mommy and daddy anymore, then why not just go into dorms and leave me out of it?"

"Well," she said quietly. "It's true that I don't want to live with any of my friends."

"Why?"

"You can't tell anyone I said this, okay?"

I nodded.

"They are a bunch of freeloaders. I couldn't believe how much money they were taking from me on a regular basis until my father showed me my financial records from last year. I have been spending five times as much on my friends as on myself. It's got to stop."

"So you don't have friends or money?" I gawked in disbelief.

She scratched her head. "Well, I have Trinity if cousins can count as friends. I also have a man I've been seeing..."

I cut her off mid-thought. "Okay, I get it. You want to tell your parents that you're living with me when you are actually going to be living with your boyfriend. I gotta tell you right now that even if you pay your rent, that situation will not do. I am not going to be your answering service explaining to your parents that you just stepped out for groceries and that's why you can't come to the door."

Felicity-Ann put both her hands in the air to stop me. "You've got it wrong. I don't plan to live with him."

"Why not? Is he a creep?" I lowered my eyebrows. "Is he mafia?"

"I can't believe this is what you think of me," she fumed, pulling her eyebrows together into a little tent on her forehead. "I would not lie to my parents about where I am living. I am a lady. I am a rich, fabulous, lady." She slowed down to explain. "But I do want to date him secretly. It's just that neither my parents, nor my friends, would like the man I'm seeing. It isn't because he's *not* educated and refined. It's because he's not wealthy, and they would not like to see me with a man who couldn't afford to circulate in our social circles."

I nodded, satisfied that her parents were rather choosy, and let her go on.

"I really liked what I saw happen to Trinity. I've heard stories about her all my life and my relatives always warned me that even though I must associate with her because of our blood relation, I must never, ever, turn out like her. But now, when I see what she and Brighton are like, I think she's going down the right path. It may not be the path my parents envision for me, but I've never had a man care for me the descent, smart way that Brighton cares for Trinity. She's becoming a better person every day."

I agreed. Trinity was really starting to shine.

"I just wanted to try dating this man without my parents watching my every step. The relationship might be nothing, over in a week, but even if it is, I still want to try to do what Trinity did. I hoped that your place would be a good place to start. Now, I know you can't stand me, and I don't understand why exactly. It is not my fault Rogan preferred me on that one night, but he left me as well as you. I've moved on, so I don't see why it should still get in the way of our friendship."

I groaned. "Rogan was very special to me."

She narrowed her eyes and informed me like it was news, "He was special to every woman. He was like a gemstone in a pile of gravel, but I don't think that kind of impression is meant to last. Just because he seemed like a gem for that instance, it doesn't mean he wasn't also gravel."

"Are you calling him a pig in your ladylike way?" I suggested.

She clenched her teeth and then neatly spat, "Yes."

I rubbed my cheek and chuckled. It was all so ridiculous. "Okay, I forgive you—completely. But you have to accept that I have a slow warm-up time. I probably won't be able to treat you as nicely as I want to for a while. If you are going to move in after Trinity leaves, we will have to make a few rules."

"Let me hear them."

"First off, I want you to be constantly a month overpaid in rent. That way, if you skip off, I won't be on the hook without a financial safety net. I do have a bit of money, but it doesn't cover all my expenses as completely as if I were rich, so money is important to me. I want you to understand that I need to be able to graduate on time with a degree that I can turn into money. Thus, even though I allowed it with Trinity, our apartment shall not be used as a place for you to giggle with your boyfriend until three in the morning when I have to be at school the next day. Thirdly, you must report to me if you're going to be late, or if you're not going to be back that night."

She looked at me like I was stupid. "I have to tell you where I am?"

I groaned. "Part of the reason for having a roommate is having someone to look out for you. I'll tell you my plans too because unlike you (who has her parents down the street), I have no one. My parents are dead and I have no family connections nearby. I was disowned by my adoptive father and Trinity has been the only one to look out for me for the last three years."

Felicity-Ann hesitated. "Is that true?"

"Course, it is. Hasn't Trinity told you all this?"

"No."

I smiled. "I like her even better now, and I didn't think that was possible." I rubbed my hands together. "And there is one more thing."

"What's that?"

"If Rogan reappears, you have to understand that if even one romantic overture happens between you two, I will throw you out on your lady-like bottom and keep your money."

"Okay." She looked so innocent. "Beth, he's really not that cool. I'll give it to you that he's handsome, charming even, but he's not dependable. He dropped me, you, and who knows who else, without an explanation. Even if I stay clear of him, you won't get him in the end. He's unattainable."

I met her warning gaze with a frightfully cold stare. "I don't care about any of his downsides. I'm warning you, I won't forgive you a second time."

For a lady, the sound that came out of her nose sounded very much like a snort. "Right, but it would be better for you if you forgot he existed."

I yawned. "Yeah, I've had that advice before. Thanks for your concern."

***

A week and a half before Trinity's wedding, brimstone began falling from the sky. Trinity's parents found out about the wedding and came to Edmonton. I wasn't there for the first rain of meteors. I was working at the print shop. Trinity wouldn't tell me who had been the one to blab, but I naturally blamed Felicity-Ann for the crime. However, I had the sense to keep the accusation to myself. After all, I didn't know anything about family. Maybe *not* telling was the bigger crime. Either way, I was still going to let the wench move in with me.

It was Gibson who constantly assuaged my doubts. He thought I was doing the right thing for the beauty queen. Actually, the stream of ridiculous crap that came out of his mouth was downright weird. He said things like Trinity never would have changed if it hadn't been for my influence. I didn't know what he was talking about. I could never influence Trinity one way or the other. She belonged to herself and the only one who could convince her of anything was Brighton, but I let Gibson go on about how great I was.

That afternoon I was standing in line for a smoothie when I caught an incredible pair of blue eyes staring at me from across the room. It was Rogan. My breath caught in my throat, and I had a hard time not breaking from the lineup. I knew he wanted me to act normal, so I didn't move. To my surprise, he got up and approached me.

"I feel like being your whore today," he said smoothly. "Buy me a drink."

It was a temptation to treat him like I would normally treat Christian, talk to him about the things I would normally talk to Christian about, ask him about his hand, and ask him if anything more had been missing from Brandon's head, but instead, I decided to take the visit at face value. He ordered something chocolaty and I ordered something with blueberries. We sat down at a table and he suddenly took a bag of pretzels out of his backpack and shared it with me as if he were still Christian. He couldn't go anywhere without bringing a gift.

He wore a tailored black coat and a tan knit turtleneck. Never once did he take his left hand out of his coat pocket, and I didn't make him.

"So, where have you been?" I asked in a friendly manner. No matter what, I had to act like I hadn't seen him recently. It had to be like it never happened.

"Here and there. What about you? Last time we talked, didn't you say something about your roommate getting married? Is that coming up soon?"

"Yeah, next week."

"Do you have a date for that?"

"No," I admitted.

"Want to take me as your date?"

"Yes," I said without hesitating. "But I'm worried about something if I take you."

He cleared his mouth before speaking. "What's that?"

"That you'll escort me just so you can see someone else."

"You're thinking I'd rather be with Felix?"

I nodded.

"You don't need to worry about that. I didn't ask her and I haven't seen her since New Year's."

I choked a little, but managed to huff, "That's good. She's going to be my roommate and if you hang out with me, you'll probably see her a lot…"

"Doesn't matter," he said blandly.

"Why not?"

"Because I'm not asking to be your date because I changed my mind about you. You are still not my type." Then he turned the impact of those blue eyes on me. "I want to be your friend. Is that okay?"

I knew I shouldn't have felt sad, but I did. Rogan promised a year with me, but he did not promise to be in love with me. Like always, he wanted distance between us.

I smiled cheerfully, even though that wasn't how I felt. "Being friends will be cool, but I should warn you."

"Warn me about what?"

"It's a wedding, so I will have to dress up. After you see me in my dress, you might feel like ravishing me. Remember to control yourself. After all, you're the one who only wants to be friends."

The look on his face was amazing. For a split second, he looked like he actually thought that was a reasonable outcome and it scared him. Expertly, he shook it off and reconstructed his confidence with a smile.

155

I smiled back. "Can you give me your number so I can call you in case there are any changes in plans? Trinity's parents just arrived on the scene and they might want a change in venue."

"Give me your phone and I'll program it in. Try not to be too disappointed in me. I often can't answer, and I have a gift for losing cell phones." I watched as he typed in my phone using only one hand.

CHAPTER SIXTEEN

Better than a Wedding Dress

Trinity stormed into the apartment. She found me fiddling in front of the mirror and blazed triumphantly, "I should have told my parents I was getting married when I was nine! This has been the greatest stunt I have ever pulled! Now I'm important! Now I'm their little girl who needs to have everything she wants. Now they feel threatened about their ownership of me because someone else wants me." She deflated onto the sofa and moaned theatrically, "I hate everybody!"

I put my mascara brush back in its tube. "Tell me all about it."

"They hate my dress. They hate my flowers. They hate the church. They hate the hall afterward. They hate that there are no bridesmaids. They hate that there are no groomsmen. They hate his parents. They hate that I'm getting married so young. They hate that Brighton hasn't been practicing corporate law in Calgary for the past five years. They hate that I didn't tell them until a week before the ceremony—"

"*You* told them!" I exclaimed.

"Yes, and no one made me. I did it all by myself. It was one of those things. You know, like high school graduation. It looks lame and you don't want to go, but even after all your rebelling, you still go. It sucks, but you still do it, because you worry that if you stay home you'll wonder all your life what would have happened if you did... the thing."

"So you did the thing?"

"Yup. Now, look at me. I'm ready to tear my hair out. My mom hates my hair. She never used to give me a hard time about the pink hair or the time half my hair was orange and the other half was green... and that was such an ugly look, parted right down the middle. Now she's super happy to play the mother of the bride and dad is just as bad. He hunkered down and talked to Uncle Max like me turning into a respectable person was all part of the plan and that was why they sent me to boarding school. Because those educators really know how to raise kids. Beth, I could die. I hate them both so much! Why weren't

157

they there when I needed them instead of only showing up for the closing act and then making such a stink about everything?"

I got up to hug her, but she was already on the couch putting her feet where her head should be and her head where her feet should be. She liked hanging upside down like that. It was her happy place. I sat cross-legged next to her and patted her arm.

"Are there going to be a lot of changes?"

"No! I'm not letting them change anything. I told them when I called them that they could come as guests. This is my wedding and I'm having it my way, but they still want to know all the details and go on and on and on about how much better it could have been if only I'd told them sooner."

"You're going to be all right. The honeymoon is right after the wedding and you'll get some peace when you go away with your new husband."

Trinity snickered. "You're just hyper because Rogan is taking you instead of Felix."

"You told her?"

"She doesn't care. She's pretty caught up with her new man. She invited him to the wedding."

"She's taking a date?"

"That's not what I said. I said she invited him to the wedding. She's not going to have a date. She's still too shy to show her parents who she likes, so she only invited him. She may not even hang out with him until her parents leave."

I rolled my eyes. "People with parents are weird."

She nodded, the blood coursing so hard in her head you could see it in her eyes. "Yes, they are."

***

The wedding was to be at five o'clock in the afternoon with the reception following that evening. Trinity didn't do her wedding day prep at our apartment. She spent the night before at Brighton's sister's house. She had already done every spa treatment her mother could think of. Aside from the final trip to the hair salon with her mother, Trinity

158

was doing everything else with Brighton's family. I felt kind of left out. She had asked me if I wanted to come and be part of all the hoopla, but I had been to Brighton's sister's house before. It gave me a headache. It was too busy. Just add all the extra relatives that would be around for the festivities, plus her parents, any staff they hired, and boom! I thought my head would split. I wasn't even in the wedding party and I was already all weddinged out.

Besides, Trinity and I had already said our goodbyes. Meaning, she had already packed all her stuff in boxes and moved them out of the apartment. I helped her. The boxes were sitting in their new place in St. Paul waiting for Trinity and Brighton to get back from their honeymoon. However, she left her bed and a few other goodies for Felicity-Ann.

I had my own preparations to do. I had to look perfect for the wedding.

The idea when I chose my dress (which was long before Rogan asked me) was to wear one that bore no resemblance to a bridesmaid's dress. Therefore, my dress was a print. It was cream with a pink and brown floral print. The neckline dove lower than anything I'd ever worn before because I had always been self-conscious about my heart surgery scars, but in the last little while, they had faded completely. I looked at myself in the mirror, thought the dress took things entirely too far and safety pinned the folds to cover a bit more. I didn't need to have a wardrobe malfunction. I wore no necklace and let my collarbone be the main attraction, which was incredibly unusual for me. I wore brown suede boots, a thick matching belt, and slid a brown leather bracelet on my left wrist.

I was ready and I wasn't. This was finally my big chance to win over the man I wanted. I tried to steady my nerves, but honestly, I felt like I was going to puke.

Rogan showed up at exactly the right time, down to the second, but he did not come upstairs. Instead, he called me from his car and asked me to come down. It wasn't very gentleman-like, but parking in that part of the city was a nightmare, so I overlooked it. He did open the car door for me.

"You look lovely," he remarked pleasantly.

He wore a coat and tie, but nothing too flashy. His coat was black, but his pants were tan. I noticed he wore gloves to drive the car and I wondered absently if he would take them off. I wouldn't say a word if he left them on all day.

Inside the church, three-quarters of the seats had been given to the groom's side. The bride's side didn't even fill up the first three rows. Rogan and I sat in the row behind Trinity's mother and Felicity-Ann's family. I looked everywhere for the man Felicity-Ann had invited, but there was no one in Trinity's part of the church that I didn't know by name.

The organ piped up and Trinity came down the aisle with no flower girl or ring bearer leading the way for her. There were no bridesmaids, but her father escorted her on the path to her soon-to-be husband. Actually, I got kind of choked up.

"Okay?" Rogan whispered tactfully.

"I'm fine," I lied.

He knew I was lying. He slipped his arm around my shoulder and gave me a little squeeze.

***

At the reception, no place cards indicated where to sit. There was no band playing. I thought I saw a stereo off to one side playing soft music. The food was simple, rather like eating at a sub sandwich restaurant. The punch tasted like someone mixed a bottle of pop with a can of concentrated juice and stirred. Instead of having a big wedding cake and a little ceremony where the couple cuts the cake, there was a table of pre-cut pieces on little saucers and the guests could take one whenever they wanted.

Rogan and I sat at a table alone. I noticed he took off his gloves to eat, but I never did see if his left pinkie was still missing.

Felicity-Ann spoke to us after the toast to the bride. She was wearing a black dress with racer-back straps. She looked overdressed and strange in the gymnasium where the reception was being held. Her platform heels made her over six feet tall. She greeted Rogan and me so sweetly, I regretted agreeing to let her move in with me.

"It's so great to see you," she beamed at Rogan. "You look fabulous." She had completely forgotten she thought he was a pig in the face of his magnetism.

"As do you," he said, taking her hand and giving her a little twirl. "Won't you join us?"

She immediately took a seat and rammed her chair so close to his it would have given anyone the impression that I was the third-wheel and not her. Then she launched into a conversation with him about his travels and why he hadn't been around.

I tolerated it for about six minutes before I got up. I knew that would happen. She hadn't done anything yet to make me cancel our arrangement to live together, but I couldn't even be mature enough to watch them talk. I moved to leave.

"Where are you going?" Rogan asked, grabbing my hand with his right one.

"Only the bathroom," I lied sweetly.

He nodded and let me go.

I wove between tables until I got to the atrium, where I got out my phone and considered calling a cab. I was about to open a search engine when Gibson came in the front doors.

Immediately, I said hi to him.

"Hi," he said, looking flustered. "I can't stop and talk right now. I have to tell Brighton what a bum I am for missing his wedding."

I let him go. Then I plunked myself down on a sofa and tapped my phone against my temple.

Two seconds later Rogan found me. "You're going the wrong way if you're going to the bathroom."

"Oh?" I said absently.

"What's your problem?" He asked the most offensive question in the world without sounding the least bit rude.

I looked at him, but couldn't answer.

"Does she irritate you that much?"

I still couldn't answer.

"If she irritates you that much, why are you letting her move in with you?"

161

I cleared my throat. "I guess I'm afraid to be alone, and I guess I'm out here because I don't like watching her flirt with you."

"So flirt with me yourself," he dared, coming right up to me so that my knees touched his shins.

"And waste my time? You already said you only want to be friends." He sat down beside me. "Okay. I understand. Today, you need support and you don't want to be exposed to another woman's attempt to get my attention. I get it."

I glared at him. "It might not be that," I said even though there was a lot of truth to what he suggested.

"We can talk about what's bothering you. Are you unhappy because your father will never walk you down the aisle?"

"No. It would make sense if that was what was bothering me, but it's not. You know, Trinity has been very preoccupied with her new life and her new family. She's been my family for the past seven years and now, she doesn't need me—not even a little bit. She's moving away and I'm left with no one but Felicity-Ann, who can't refrain from hitting on my date."

"She wasn't hitting on me. She was just being friendly. After you left she said her boyfriend hadn't gotten there yet and she was feeling anxious he wouldn't show up. She didn't mean to tick you off."

"Sure."

"Believe me. I know her type a lot better than you do."

"U-huh," I said cynically. "It doesn't matter. That doesn't stop me from feeling stung that Trinity is leaving."

"But you'll have Felicity for company, and if I'm not there, she won't always irritate you."

"And that is going to be so great," I said, getting crazier. "Even if you're not around, do you know what she's going to be like to live with? She's so pretty, I'll be consistently marginalized by her presence. There's this guy who works with me. Don't get the wrong idea. He's nothing special, but he thinks she hung the moon. If I live with her, I'll always be compared to her. I'm not even allowed to make myself as pretty as I can be," I whaled quietly.

"Why aren't you allowed to make yourself as pretty as you can be?" He looked genuinely confused.

I touched a spot on my hair. "I love that man too much to do even one thing he doesn't like."

"Whoever he is, he sounds like a jerk to me," Rogan said heartlessly, and why he said that when he was the creep I was referencing, I couldn't be sure.

"Take me home. I hate it here."

***

Back on the road in front of the main doors to my apartment building, Rogan put his car in park. "Do you want me to come up?"

"No," I said, gathering up my bag. "I should go in and get used to it."

"Used to what?"

"Being alone."

He grabbed my elbow. "I'm here. You don't have to be alone."

Gently, I removed his gloved hand. "No. Tonight, I don't want comfort from anybody who isn't willing to promise to stay in my life. Since there's no one like that, I want to be alone. I'll be in a better mood the next time we meet... probably. Though I don't know why you want to hang out with me. I'm chronically miserable these days."

"I can come in," he insisted. "You don't have to be alone tonight."

"Yes, I do! I only have a couple more days before Felicity-Ann moves in and reminds me of everything I'm not. I'm sure it will be paradise until she gets tired of sharing a room and moves back in with her mommy and daddy."

"Let me park the car and come in with you."

"Would it be at all possible for you not to see this side of me? Couldn't you wait and see me when I'm feeling a bit stronger?" I got out of the car and managed to say stiffly, "Thanks for taking me today." Then in a fit of spitefulness, I continued to say, "And you don't need to pay me back with the year. You only torture me." I shut the car door and walked away.

Rogan ditched the car and ran after me. "What are you saying?"

"Go away! You wouldn't even be here if I hadn't barged into your world and made you make that crazy promise. I have changed my mind about demanding your attention," I said fitfully.

163

"I'm not leaving."

"If you don't move your car, it's going to get towed and you'll get a huge parking ticket."

"I don't care," he persisted.

"Don't go out of your way for a girl you only made friends with a week ago. Go home," I said, reverting to the girl who didn't know he was also Christian.

He stepped between me and the door. "Please let me come up. I just want to hang out."

I stood there and thought about how immature I felt like being. It was pretty immature. "Kay," I said, getting ready to be extremely mean. I turned around and marched down the street, away from my apartment building.

He followed me. "Where are you going?"

I stopped. "You're acting out of character. Any normal guy would ditch me to save his car."

"I can't leave you alone."

"Why? Cause you feel so sorry for me? I don't want you to feel sorry for me. If you were going to come to my rescue, then you're too late." I tried to walk away, but I couldn't stop thinking about Trinity. She was the one who was there for me every single time Christian abandoned me. The forthcoming pity party was going to be ugly. I had to get rid of him before I made myself any more desperate. I walked faster.

"You need a friend right now. Why are you so against it being me?" he said, grabbing me by the arm.

"I'm upset!" I cried. "I probably would have felt differently about Trinity's wedding if I was in a similar situation as her, but I don't have a boyfriend. I've never been on a date. Could you do me a favor and stop being the guy who only wants to be my friend? I know you can't love me the way I want. Go away."

"Isn't this a date?" he said suddenly.

"Maybe it is, but it doesn't feel like much of a date when all the anticipation that it could turn into a romance was killed by your preemptive I-only-want-to-be-friends."

"You're putting me in a bad spot," he grumbled.

"I'll be fine tomorrow."

His jaw was set. He didn't believe me. "I have an idea. Let's walk to a bookstore. I'll buy you anything you want and we'll have some Italian sodas. Sound good?"

I had done that exact thing with Christian at least a dozen times. "Thanks for the offer, but nothing like that can satisfy me today."

"What about a movie? Wanna go see a movie?"

"Will you make out with me in the dark?"

His mouth twisted into a conceited smirk. "You wouldn't like it."

"I think I would, like that time I kissed you at the New Year's Eve party. I think you liked it too."

His face was unreadable, and I couldn't tell if I was giving him new information or not. Had he really not known it was me? That seemed impossible.

"Beth, I…"

"I know," I said, glaring at him. "You only want to be my friend, but I don't know if I can stand to be your friend."

Finally, he gave me an inch. "Can't we make a deal?"

"What sort of deal?" I inclined my head closer to him and he led me over to lean against the brick wall of a laundromat out of the general flow of foot traffic.

He glanced up and down the street, before relaxing against the wall. He hid his left hand behind me and let his gloved hand carass the side of my cheek until he brought my ear to his mouth. "I'm not here because of the year I promised you. I'm worried about you. Brandon thinks Charles gave him to the Argonauts in exchange for you."

"Me?" I hissed.

"Yes," he said, looking in my eyes and still whispering. "Of course, they were lying. They had no intention of turning you over to him, but he's getting impatient. He might ditch and come after you. If he turns up, he isn't going to want a date. He thinks a lot more is owed to him."

I gasped and thought about what that could mean.

Rogan leaned in and breathed hot air into my ear as he murmured, "I know you don't want me for a friend and actually, I don't want you for a friend either. We're stuck. As I explained before, I can't love, but now I can't leave you alone. I need to protect you." He slid his hand down my arm in a way that almost drew me to him. "Can we pretend to be friends?"

Heat was simmering between us now. Was he suffering like I was? I wished he would talk to me about what was wrong with him that stopped him from loving me the way I was certain both of us wanted. He wouldn't say, and the idea of Charles getting ahold of me made my skin prickle.

Rogan saw my hesitation and whispered, "I know this isn't fair and I'm sorry it has come to this."

I looked up at him and saw his perfection, everything about him I loved and couldn't get enough of. I didn't know if I could be his friend. Dressing up in something pretty with the expectation of romance always ended badly for me. What was it that Brandon had said back in Scotland? Something about how I would never be beautiful to Christian until I had blood on my face?

"Okay. Let's go back to my apartment," I said, trying to sound light. "I've got to get out of this dress."

CHAPTER SEVENTEEN

Rogan's Bad Side

Rogan wouldn't leave me alone. At the same time Felicity-Ann moved in, Rogan also moved in—not into my apartment—but one down the hall. Once his place was set up, he invited himself over whenever he wanted. He brought food too, but not the way Christian used to. Christian used to bring gourmet everything. Rogan brought over donairs in greasy paper and Vietnamese noodles in Styrofoam containers.

He also established a relationship with Felicity-Ann I could live with. She told me about it later, which surprised me.

"I just had an interesting conversation with Rogan," she said cutely. I hated it when she acted cute. "Wow, Bethie. Do you know what he said to me?"

"I can't guess."

"He told me, ever so gently, that I can't kiss his cheek anymore when I say hello. You don't like it, and since your feelings are so precious to him, he would prefer it if I stopped all together."

I didn't know she had been doing that and I felt my stomach turn At least, he'd put a stop to it before I saw it. "Was that verbatim?" I asked sourly.

"Pretty much."

I really didn't think I was going to enjoy living with Felicity-Ann. However, she did a few things right. She tidied the bathroom after every shower, never let food in the fridge rot, kept her shoes in the closet neatly in a shoe rack, and did her own dishes after each meal.

I complimented her on it, though I admit to being stingy in my praise.

Soon I realized there was something else about her that was worth complimenting and I wasn't stingy.

She answered the door. Because of the width of Trinity's circle of friends, not everyone knew she had married and moved away. Occasionally, random people would show up at the door looking for Trinity. As often as she could, Felicity-Ann took care of these people.

She had cards made up with Trinity's social media information and handed them out as she turned them away. I loved this because these people often took it for granted that I was a replacement for Trinity, even though I had not done a single thing to make them feel that way. If I answered the door, often they still thought it was okay to come in, but if Felicity-Ann answered it, they knew the party was over. She made it sound like the whole apartment was under new management and that everything was different.

It looked different. Trinity had painstakingly decorated the place with fairy lights, pillows, faux sheepskins, and plush carpets so people felt good about sitting on the floor. Trinity took most of her things with her, leaving only dishes and cookware behind. Felicity-Ann's style was different. The fairy lights were not replaced with more fairy lights. Instead, she had plants. We had a huge wall of glass on one side of the studio and she set up tropical plants at different heights. I liked it. The air smelled fresh and I felt less like a student and more like an independent woman.

In short, she was much cleaner than Trinity, and the ongoing ruckus Trinity had hosted was over. I liked a clean, quiet apartment and that was what I got with Felicity-Ann. Though I missed Trinity, it wasn't all bad.

Also, I never met Felicity-Ann's boyfriend. Not that I did much detective work to figure out who he was. It was just that sometimes I came in just as she was going out. I knew she was going to meet him, but the front atrium was desolate. Sometimes, as I leaned on the balcony railing with Rogan, we would see her. She always went out and returned home a hundred percent solo.

Even though I protested that I didn't want to be friends with Rogan, he was still excellent company. Whether he was Christian or Rogan, I was still in love with him. He was very determined to make himself pleasant and not a burden at all. His angular form on my couch was a welcome sight, and his opinion on anything was a welcome sound. I loved how he thought, how he spoke, how occasionally he would touch me, and though it was hard, I schooled myself to wait for more.

It was a nice summer. Nice in that, it was less lonely than I expected it to be after Trinity's departure.

As my fake friendship with Rogan deepened, it felt that the line between friendship and love was fading. His hands were massaging my shoulders after work. If he had something to say when we were watching TV, he whispered it in my ear filling my head with the warmth of his breath no matter what he said. If he was eating anything, he was popping half of it in my mouth. It was all very romantic, even if he said he couldn't fall in love.

Felicity-Ann had had enough. In a surprising moment when he was vacant, she asked me, "Are you dating Rogan?"

"Nope."

"Are you sure?" she persisted.

"Yes. He never kisses me and he always says we're only friends."

"Should you put up with that?"

I chuckled darkly. "Darling, it's either this or the guillotine."

She didn't know what to make of that answer, but at least it stopped her from asking any more questions.

***

It was late August. The fall term would begin in a week, and I sat in the food court. I had just finished eating my lunch and was reading a news bit on my phone when someone came over and tapped me on the shoulder. I turned around to see who it was, but he had already moved and was now standing in front of me.

"How do, stranger?" he said in his cultured British accent. His red hair was surprisingly long. He hadn't cut it since the last time I had seen him. He looked raggety. That meant, his clothes looked like they had been stored on the floor and stepped on several times rather than being hung up. Luckily, I couldn't smell him. After what Rogan said, I should have been afraid to see Charles at all, but his expression was so demure that I judged he was visiting me to test the waters.

"Why, hello!" I said as naturally as I could, considering everything. I stood up and gave him an awkward pat. "Where did you drop down from?"

"Huh?" he asked, dazed and sat down across from me.

"What brings you here? I always thought that you must be in England."

"Oh. I've been working here for the last few years, but I've wanted to go to school. I was here visiting the admission office."

"Are you starting classes this fall?"

"Probably not. I missed the deadline for applying, but I might be able to make it in by January."

I leaned in and said, like it was a secret, "I have to tell you. You've caught me on my lunch break. I can only talk for about ten minutes and then I have to get back to work. I just don't want my shortness to make it seem like I'm not delighted to see you."

"You're delighted to see me?" he asked, his bloodshot eyes staring at me in disbelief. "I thought you didn't like me very much."

Of course, I didn't like him very much. Words like 'delighted' and 'darling' were warning words in Christian's world. He didn't pick up on it. I yawned. "I embarrassed myself in front of you so many times. Please don't blame teenage-me for being shy while on vacation."

"Ah," he said like he understood.

I could have slapped him, but I kept feigning pleasantness. I only had to put up with it for another nine and a half minutes. "What were you planning on taking?"

"What are you taking?" he asked.

"Business."

"I should take that too," he said immediately.

I was going to end up slapping him. He was exactly the same as he had been when I met him at the compound. He had no idea how to improve himself, only how to screw someone else over.

At that exact moment, Rogan dropped himself into the seat next to me. "Who's your friend?" he asked, giving Charles eye-daggers.

"This is Charles. He's an old friend. I met him in Scotland when I vacationed there a few years ago."

Rogan kept his hands under the table.

"Charles," I continued. "This is my neighbor, Rogan. He's a business student too."

Charles nodded, but he looked discomfited by Rogan's appearance, not that he had been particularly comfortable before. It reminded him to

170

get to the point of his visit. "Beth, I was hoping we would run into each other. I want to show you something."

I glanced between him and Rogan. "Like what? Like, take me somewhere for a date?"

Charles opened his mouth to say something when Rogan cut him off. "She can't go."

"Why not?" Charles asked.

"Because you are a weasel."

"Excuse me?" he asked, his face becoming a completely different shade of red than his hair.

"How much did you drink last night? You hardly look sober. Showing her *something* doesn't sound like much of a date. Where do you want to take her?"

Charles cocked his head and lost what little posture he had. "What are you? Her dad? She called you her neighbor, so it's none of your business."

Rogan kept his hands under the table. "Beth, do you want to go on a date with this guy? Am I standing in the way? Or am I doing you a favor asking him to get lost?"

I stood up. "You both suck. I'm going back to work." I picked up my bag and headed for the stairs.

I heard them behind me. Charles was calling after me, and Rogan was hissing at Charles to sit back down. I knew what he was doing without looking. He was going to chase Charles away using only his mouth because he had to hide his hands and he couldn't stand up and show his height. Just like I knew what he was doing, I knew he liked what I had done. He was here in order to take care of it and I hoped he didn't take care of it too quickly.

***

Later that evening, Felicity-Ann told me that someone named Charles had buzzed the apartment looking for me.

"I told him you weren't home and he should come back later."

My spine crawled as I pictured Charles ringing the bell. Finally, I instructed her, "I'm screening my visitors. If he ever comes back, no

171

matter where I am, tell him I'm not home. I never want to see him again."

"Does he know that?"

"Look, shutting him down openly isn't a good option. I need to make it seem like he's so unimportant to me that I keep forgetting his existence. I should have pretended I didn't remember him when I met him in the food court, but I honestly didn't expect him to turn up."

"This isn't like you. You tell it like it is. Why all the deception?"

I sighed. At least, she didn't realize I lied all the time. "Listen. I don't like it either, but for once, this is the right choice."

She glanced at me disapprovingly and went to get her laundry.

Rogan came by later, but he didn't mention Charles. He was wearing navy racing gloves, but the tips of the last three fingers on his left hand were artfully covered in black fabric. He sat on the couch and read an economics textbook.

The bell rang and he leaped up like an antelope to answer it, "Hello."

"Is Beth there?" the voice asked.

"Who's asking?"

"Charles."

"Yeah, she's unavailable. Want me to have her call you?"

"Yeah."

"Does she have your number?"

"No. It's..."

Rogan let the intercom buzz off so no one could hear the number, then he buzzed back on and said, "Thanks. I'll give her that message."

The intercom buzzed a few more times, but neither Felicity-Ann nor I wanted to get on Rogan's bad side, so neither of us answered it, no matter how many times it rang. Rogan was absolutely toxic.

"Do you know this guy?" Felicity-Ann asked, finally getting brave.

"You should have seen him, Felix. He would have set all your warning systems off. He looked like the kind of sleaze that has no limits. He would probably do anything to anyone. Don't go near him and don't let him come up here."

"And how did Bethie pick up someone like that?"

I rolled my eyes. "I did not pick him up. He found me in Calgary when I ran away from boarding school when I was in grade eleven."

"Wait a second. You ran away from boarding school?" Felicity-Ann interjected. "I thought that was more Trinity's scene. Why were you running away from school?"

"I was trying to get Christian's attention."

"Who's Christian?" Felicity-Ann asked excitedly, leaning on the kitchen island. "Sounds exciting!"

Rogan snorted softly on the couch.

I ignored him. "He was my guardian after my parents died. I wanted his attention, but all I did was piss him off. I only met Charles because he was in the right place at the right time. I didn't usually cause trouble. I only wanted to be with Christian."

"Why?" Rogan asked waspishly.

I turned to him and suddenly had a thought that had never crossed my mind before. Was it possible that the way Christian acted was not always in complete harmony with how the real man wanted to behave? He was so cool as Christian. Just as Felicity-Ann thought I was truthful, I thought he was authentic when he played Christian. It was stupid. I knew he lied all the time too.

I took a breath and said what I felt deep down in my heart. It was a good time to say it, masking it in my love for a non-present character. I looked straight at Rogan and said, "Have you ever been in love with a liar?"

He returned my gaze, his jaw set.

"No. Really?" I continued leaning forward on the counter and letting my words cover the space between us. "Have you ever been in love with a liar? Have you ever been in love with someone who is completely pretentious? They're lying to you. You know they're lying, yet they could ask you for absolutely anything and you'd give it to them. Why? Because you trust that liar. You trust something in their expression, in the brush of their fingertips, and the promise of devotion in their eyes no matter what the last thing they said was. Ever since that man had to leave me, there hasn't been a day I haven't missed him."

Rogan's expression had split in half. That was what happened when a practiced liar had to play a part but still had to feel within himself. The half that was Rogan looked annoyed, while the half that had been my

Christian was visibly moved. "You shouldn't love that kind of man, Beth."

I ruffled my hair. "No kidding. How I feel about you is just as bad. I know you're wrong for me. I know you don't want to love me and you're just sitting on that couch now because you're worried I won't be safe if you don't. I love that you feel that way. Stay. I'll make you dinner."

Felicity-Ann looked horrified by my mouth. How could I have said that so calmly? She looked between the two of us like she didn't understand the interchange. I needed to make it make sense.

"He's right about Charles," I said, turning to her. "No matter what he says, don't let him up here, and don't talk to him."

"What does he look like?"

"You shouldn't have a hard time spotting him," Rogan spat. "He's a redhead who looks like he was recently run over."

***

The next day, I saw Charles in the food court during my lunch hour. I avoided him and went the other way. Back at the print center, I texted Rogan a message saying that if he wanted me to avoid Charles he needed to bring me lunch. I was astounded when he messaged me back saying that he'd have one for me in fifteen minutes. What was he doing that he could ditch with such short notice?

He showed up and deposited a Greek salad and a container full of fettuccine alfredo with grilled chicken on top.

"Wow!" I exclaimed, opening the lid and letting the aroma waft around me. "Where did you get this?"

"Yeah. Where *did* you get this?" Gibson asked, butting in.

"This was my lunch. It was what I was making for myself in my apartment when you texted me."

"The Greek salad, too?"

"Yes," he said with extreme patience.

"Wait a minute. What are you going to eat?" I asked.

"Doesn't matter," he said, straightening his glasses with both hands and moving toward the door. "Beth, return my dishes tonight, would you? And please wash them."

He left and Gibson leaned over the food. "Are you going to eat all of that?"

"Get lost," I said, picking it all up and going into the back office.

Gibson followed me. "Who was that?"

"Rogan."

"Hmm. So that's him? I thought he wasn't interested in you. Why is he going to all this trouble if he's not interested?"

I told Gibson about Charles and not a moment too soon because a minute later Charles was standing in front of our counter. I hid in the office while Gibson gave him the runaround, saying I was out to lunch. Charles said he would wait for me and took a seat. I sat there and ate, but Rogan's cooking didn't taste as good as it could have if Charles hadn't been waiting to talk to me.

A couple of minutes before my lunch hour ended, Gibson came into the office and said, "You know what? I think you should stay back here until he leaves. He is every kind of--"

"Icky?" I supplied.

"Sure. I'll make up some excuse, so stay back here. I'll see if I can figure out something for you to do. Oh, and by the way, you can pee in that empty water bottle if he doesn't leave until closing time."

"Great." I wrinkled my nose and waited.

I organized the desk, played on my phone, picked staples out of the carpet, washed the whiteboard, ate the rest of the food, fixed a ceiling tile that was out of place, and half a dozen other meaningless tasks before Gibson came in.

I stared at him. "Charles has seriously been waiting out there for two whole hours?"

"Yeah. Man, that guy is not normal. I told him you were late coming back from lunch. Then he asked me if you were in trouble for being late and I had to say yes."

"It's okay. Go out there and tell him you got a message from me saying I called in sick after lunch."

175

"All right. You're lucky it's summer and slow today." He disappeared around the corner.

I heard him relaying my lame excuse to Charles, but I didn't dare take a peek to see how he took the news. I didn't want to risk him seeing me.

Gibson came back. "The coast is clear. He bought it. Why is he stalking you like this?"

"I don't even know."

"Well, come out and do your job. After work, I'm going to walk you home. I wouldn't normally do that sort of thing, but I think I have to."

***

About an hour before quitting time, I noticed Gibson was starting to get a bit giddy. I watched him fumble around trying to finish his work for a solid ten minutes before I figured out what his damage was. He was hoping he would get to see Felicity-Ann. To my surprise, his excitement amused me.

At quitting time, we walked the stretch to my building. Before we left, he pulled my hood over my head. I tucked in my hair and we left. Like a good boy, he kept his eyes and ears open, looking behind us often to see if someone was following us. When we got to my apartment building, I showed my appreciation by inviting him up.

"Yeah, I'll come up. That guy could be waiting in the hallway," he justified. "Some people will just let anyone in who's hanging around the bell."

"I know," I agreed as we passed through the empty atrium to the elevator.

Upstairs, Felicity-Ann and Rogan were sitting around eating what seemed to be leftovers from lunch.

Felicity-Ann got up immediately and with ladylike earnestness beyond her known capacity, asked Gibson if he wanted to stay for dinner. Seconds later, he was retelling his encounter with Charles and how we eventually got him to leave.

"Unbelievable!" Rogan fumed.

176

He went on, but I took a break from the retelling by getting a can of pop out of the fridge. I was not in a good mood. I took the can out onto the balcony and stared out at the city skyline drenched in the pink-orange of an Edmonton summer evening.

I hated everything about their conversation. Charles was not someone to disdain or ridicule. He was someone to run from. The thing that made me the most uncomfortable was that he hadn't always been like that. It was hard to believe he was capable of joining those thugs in torturing anyone. Had he done everything they wanted believing I was the pot of gold at the end of the rainbow?

I was halfway through my cream soda when Rogan joined me on the balcony. "Had enough pasta?" he asked dryly.

I slid my hand into the crook of his arm and rested my head on his shoulder. "Don't tell anyone, but I am so thankful you're here," I whispered.

He kissed my temple and tapped the tip of my nose with his finger. "It's going to be all right, Beth. Nothing bad is going to happen."

"As long as you promise."

Just then, the phone in my back pocket started to ring. I picked it up. I knew what my aunt was calling to tell me as soon as I saw her name on the caller ID. I shook Rogan off and talked to her. When I was finished, I hung up and turned to him.

"What's happened?"

"My grandfather died."

CHAPTER EIGHTEEN

Empty Tombstone

My father had four sisters. The only one who mattered was Veronica, as she was the only one who ever spoke to me like I was a person. That didn't mean she was nice. It only meant she recognized I was a human being who ought to be greeted when we met. The word to describe the rest of them was negligent, even before I'd decided to cut ties.

Veronica was the aunt who called me. She told me when the funeral would be and told me that my airfare to attend in Ottawa would be paid for out of my grandfather's estate. She said I could stay at her house if I wanted to, but if I would feel more comfortable in a hotel, that bill would also be paid for.

Knowing that I would have to go there and see those people really brought back my parents' deaths. Almost seven years ago, my grandfather had been in a nursing home and no one suggested I become his responsibility. I heard he was so depressed about outliving his son that tears flowed down his cheeks. Those were the kind of tears that only fell when someone died. Grown men didn't cry.

When I told Rogan what happened, he pulled a wry expression and said conspiratorially, "Maybe it's better if you aren't here for a while. Besides, these aren't your family that have ties to Dr. Hilliar. They are just relatives. You should go."

In Ottawa, I wore black, even though quite a few of my cousins opted not to. I felt like wearing black was the only thing I could do to show respect for someone who had given part of their life to nurture my father, who in turn, nurtured me. I planned not to cry.

The funeral service was held at a church where there was a sermon given about how he would live again through the power of the resurrection and then a eulogy. My Aunt Veronica gave it. She stood tall and talked about his childhood days, his proud military service in the Second World War, his courtship and marriage to my grandmother, his career and how much he loved being a father. She spoke about the deep pain he suffered when my father died.

"He often said that when he died, he hoped he would meet his son again in heaven," Veronica said crisply. "I hope he has." She looked so confident.

At the gravesite, my cousins' children annoyed me. After the grave dedication, they cheerfully pranced around like ponies. It bothered me that they didn't have any respect for the dead. I even had to shoo a kid off my parents' gravestone.

"Get off," I said monstrously to the eight-year-old scooting her butt off the marble. I shot eye-daggers at her to stop myself from crying. I hated crying in public, so I immediately did what I always did when I was upset—I restored order. Meaning, I cleaned.

My parents only had one gravestone with both their names engraved on it. Birds had pooped on it and the caretakers of the cemetery hadn't taken care of it. I popped open my purse and produced a water bottle and a tissue. I was wiping it clean when I noticed something unusual—downright weird. My father had no death date. Immediately, I got up off the grass and went to find Aunt Veronica.

I showed her the stone.

"What's wrong?"

"Look. It says when my mother was born and when she died. Then it says when my father was born, but in the space where it is supposed to say when he died—there's nothing."

She looked at it, perplexed. "I don't know. The only thing I can say is that Christian Henderson was in charge of all that. I've never seen a single paper about your parents' death. I'm sorry. You'll have to talk to him."

"None of you organized the funeral or anything? Christian did it all?"

She put her hands up in the air innocently. "That was what your father stipulated in his will. He didn't want us to have anything to do with you beyond occasional visits. He wanted everything he had to go to Christian. We all thought it was intolerable, but that was what the lawyer said."

"And you just went with what the lawyer said?"

"No," she said, grasping for patience. "I did not blindly leave everything in the hands of the lawyer. I knew your father was planning on doing that. He told me what was in his will before he died. I thought he was joking, but when your parents passed and everything went to Christian, I wasn't surprised. Other than custody of you, he didn't get anything anyway. Why? Are you mad we let Christian take you?"

"I'm not mad. I just wonder why this has been left blank. It doesn't add up. Christian wouldn't have let something like this go…"

Just then, over my aunt's shoulder, I saw someone standing at a grave across the way, someone with red hair. He was looking at me.

Another aunt claimed Veronica's attention. "You'll have to talk to Christian about this," she said as she turned away.

Seconds later, Charles ditched the grave he was pretending to mourn at and approached me. I knew I shouldn't run. I shouldn't make a fuss. There were tons of people around for the grave dedication. He wouldn't do anything crazy. I had to act cool, just like Christian taught me.

He came to a stop beside me. "Is this your dad's tombstone?"

"Yeah."

"I heard about your grandfather."

"It's okay. He was old. Everybody has to go sometime. Did you know him?"

"No. I never met him," Charles answered with a shake of his head.

"Then why are you here?" I wanted to know.

"I came to see you," he said slowly, his voice low like he was telling me a secret. It was almost the way Christian used to speak to me when he explained something as an aside. Charles had seen him do it and was mimicking it.

I glared at him. "You flew all the way to Ottawa to see me?"

"I was having a hard time getting in touch with you in Edmonton," he explained, his hands in his pockets.

"Yes. Because I don't want to see you." I flicked my hair over my shoulder and stormed away at the fastest walk I dared. I heard his footsteps behind me.

"I have something to tell you," he called.

I kept walking and didn't turn my head.

I got two and a half steps further away from him when he barked at me, "Your father is still alive."

I turned around and angry as a wasp, I slapped him across the cheek. His face was ten times redder than normal, and his eyes were so shocked that I refrained from kneeing him in the stomach, which was going to be my next move. "Never show your face in front of me again!" I didn't wait for him to reply. Instead, I turned around and walked swiftly back to my Aunt Veronica, who ushered me into the back of a car.

Back at my aunt's, I thought about what happened and how I had acted. I wondered if what Charles said was true; if my father was still alive. It took me about ten minutes to decide that it didn't matter. The way to find answers was not through Charles. He was trying to trap me, using something I might want as bait, and the tombstone just gave him a handy idea of what to say that would, hopefully, stop me from storming off. I decided that whoever my family member was who was affiliated with the Argonauts, it couldn't be my father.

CHAPTER NINETEEN

The Last Time I saw Rogan

Back in Edmonton, I told Rogan about meeting Charles at the funeral. We stood on my balcony facing west, enjoying the late summer heat that would soon be nothing more than a memory. We leaned on the railing and I felt the secrets simmering as our eyes met. The lines around his contact lenses were very clear and I wondered for the thousandth time what color his eyes were under them. Who was he? Not Christian, not Rogan, but someone else. I tried to remember that whoever he seemed to be now, that was not who he really was.

"Gutsy little creep," Rogan rasped when he thought I had finished detailing my experience from the funeral.

"Do you know what the last thing he said to me was?"

"How could *I* know that?"

"He said my father was still alive," I whispered.

Rogan paused and cleared something out of his throat. "How long ago did your father die?" he asked, always striving to make our conversations sound normal for two people who didn't know each other well.

For my own part, it meant we had more conversation, so I answered him like he didn't already know. "Seven years. It was just weird for Charles to say that. A couple of minutes before he showed up, I was cleaning my parents' tombstone and I noticed that my mother had a death date on her side of the stone, but my father didn't have one. That's peculiar, isn't it?"

Rogan nodded.

"I was told Christian was supposed to be taking care of the engraving and all that, but I find it hard to believe he would have allowed such an important detail to slip through the cracks. Something seems fishy."

"Do you think that dirtball was telling the truth and your old man is hanging out somewhere?"

I brushed my hair out of my face. "No. It was a head-on collision. My mom wrapped their car around the support beam of a bridge in the face of on-coming traffic. It was his side of the car that was hit. If either one of my parents survived it would have been my mother because she was in the driver's seat. If anything, I think that punk would have said anything to get me to stay and talk to him. He saw the tombstone and it was an easy thing to say to get my attention. He was grasping at straws—really disrespectful straws."

"Hmm…" Rogan paused and studied me carefully. Then suddenly, his fingers started tracing the bones in the back of my hand. "Let's play pretend," he said. Those were magic words coming out of his mouth. I had to steady myself. What he said next would never be as thrilling as his tantalizing suggestion. Finally, he said, "What if your father was alive? How would you feel about that?"

My lips curved into a snarl. "I would be furious. If he were alive, then why did he leave me with a stranger? If he were alive, I wouldn't want to see him. If he ditched me to grow up alone in that crappity-crap-crap-crap boarding school, then he already betrayed me beyond understanding. The only thing I'd believe is that he treated me worse than Trinity's parents treated her, and that is very low."

"You'd feel abandoned all over again?" Rogan prompted as he removed his fingers from my hand.

"I feel abandoned all the time anyway." I glanced at Rogan's glove still present on his left hand. It looked really stupid. It was August, smoking hot outside, and he was wearing a single racing glove?

He noticed my eyes and put his left arm around my shoulder and completely abandoned the idea of composing a conversation in case someone was listening. "I'm sorry, Beth. It's been hard for you. For what it's worth, I think I was wrong."

I did a double-take. "What?"

"When I sent you away."

I gasped. I never expected him to say those words. Him saying he was sorry was not the same as him saying he was wrong. I took a breath and asked, "Why are you telling me this now?"

He rubbed his chin with his bare hand. "I have to tell you sometime."

"Are you asking me to forgive you?"

"I can't ask for that because of how much you've suffered, everything that I am, and everything that I'm not."

I looked him over. "I am pretty sure you are everything."

"But I can't give you everything. I've said it enough times."

I flicked my hair out of my face, so I could see him better. "Yes, you are very tiresome; always saying how love is out of the question when everything you do says you love me and everything you say means you don't."

"I just can't let anyone get too close to me," he admitted.

I looked at him sideways. "Are you afraid of getting hurt?"

He shook his head, a snarl on his lips. "No, darling. I'm afraid of you getting hurt."

Looking in his eyes, I had never wanted to be hurt so badly.

Then, suddenly, he held me at arm's length. "I need to go."

"Naturally," I drawled, not at all surprised.

"Yes," he said, rubbing his nose bridge with two fingers. "I have something I said I'd do. I'll see you later," he promised as he went back into the apartment. Then he popped back onto the balcony and said, "Remember, I'll come back."

I groaned. "I'm sure you will."

With that, he scooted straight out of the apartment. It was weird. Usually, Rogan didn't leave. Usually, he hung around for hours. He watched TV in the living room while I showered. He answered the phone like it was his place. He read while I did my nails and if I asked him to, he would carry my laundry back and forth. Since I didn't have a dishwasher, he dried dishes for me and always put them back in their right spots. He folded towels, killed spiders, paid the pizza guy, and sometimes did slushie runs to the convenience store a block away when Felicity-Ann and I didn't want to go ourselves. Having him leave was a bit of a downer.

I sat down on the couch and bit my thumb. His friendship did stop me from being alone, even if he didn't want me for a girlfriend. I had never gone to his apartment because I had to pretend like I didn't need him, but that afternoon, after my grandfather's funeral, when Felicity-Ann was shopping with her mother and getting the 'mommy discount', I didn't want to be alone.

I opened the door to the corridor and to my utter astonishment, I came face to face with Christian. He looked surprised to see me. On closer inspection, it looked like he had been walking the carpet outside my door debating whether or not he should knock.

"Christian!" I exclaimed. "What are you doing here? I thought you were never coming back."

He curled his lips into a smile and shrugged his shoulders. In his hands, he was carrying a single purple rose. He slipped it between my fingers at the same time he slipped his arm around mine. Then he placed a perfect kiss on my temple. I had taken just one breath of his familiar scent when he stepped behind me into the apartment.

"What's going on?" I asked as I followed him. Had our little conversation made him feel like doing something impulsive as the old him?

He put a finger to his lips to indicate quiet and went about his business. Then, without a word, he found my suitcase and packed my bag.

I opened my mouth again to question him, but he rested a gloved finger against my open lips as he passed me, heading for the bathroom. I stood in the doorway while he loaded my toiletries into my cosmetics bag. It was weird that he knew which shampoo bottle was mine and which was Felicity-Ann's. It wasn't like they were labeled.

I was very confused. Had my conversation with Rogan triggered something? After we talked, did he immediately change into his Christian costume? He was fast. He hadn't been that fast when he transformed into Charles in the hotel room. I guessed he was better at it because he played Christian more often.

I went into the front hallway, put on my shoes and grabbed my purse. Whatever was going on, I was going with him.

When he was finished packing me up, he put his hand to his face in a gesture to ask for a phone. I assumed he meant my smartphone, so I forked it over to him. Watching over his shoulder, I saw him send Felicity-Ann a message about how I was going out of town for a few days.

Five minutes later, I was in a taxi cab that was waiting outside the front door of my apartment complex. Once inside, I tried to talk to Christian again, but once again, he wasn't talking. He covered his eyes with a pair of very black sunglasses. I couldn't even see a glimmer of light in his eyes, or which way he was looking, or even the tiniest hint of his expression.

The cab driver already knew where we were going and took us to Southgate Mall. For the briefest of seconds, I was overjoyed at the idea that he was going to take *me* shopping. I hadn't been shopping in ages and that was one of the things Christian did best. My mouth was practically salivating, when surprise, he led me directly to the parking lot and into the front seat of a black sedan. He gently placed my bag in the backseat, got behind the wheel, and without a word, sped out of the parking lot.

I half expected him to take off toward the airport, thinking he was going to take me on another grand vacation, but instead, he put us on roads heading west. Once we were out of the city, it didn't take me very long to realize where we were going. I'd been there before. The old house in the woods.

***

Once inside the cottage, I thought it was safe to talk, so I started. "What are we doing back here?"

Christian didn't answer. Instead, he took my hand gently and started leading me down the hall.

Every girl thinks she's brave until she goes down that hallway. We were getting closer and closer to the room he kept locked while I was there. At the threshold, I whispered, "Is Brandon okay? Does he want to see me? Is that why I'm here?"

Christian nodded, opened the door and without even the faintest sound from his lips, he pushed me inside.

The next couple of minutes were a shock to me. I had never been attacked by a man before, and even though I had played wrestling games with Christian, this was nothing like what I'd experienced before. Either he had always been playing with me, or the man reefing on my wrists was not Christian. The problem had been his gloves. I couldn't see his hands because of the gloves and he had a perfect excuse for wearing them. The man I loved was missing a finger, so I didn't suspect anything. It was only when his wrists were fully exposed did the intense black hair on his arms show he was someone else.

"Who are you?" I hissed breathlessly as he pinned me against the wall and maneuvered both my wrists into one of his hands.

He didn't answer.

I tried to kick him, but he stopped that by crushing my thighs with his against the wall. I couldn't resist him, even when I tried with every muscle I had. I even tried to bite him, but he pushed my forehead against the wall with his free hand.

"What do you want?"

He nodded toward the hospital bed Brandon had been tied to. All the ropes were still there.

"You don't mean?" I gasped, losing all the air inside me.

I tried to fight. I tried to do everything and anything a girl could do to protect herself, but it didn't help. The man who handled me seemed like he was used to wrestling bears and winning. I cried and screamed, but it didn't matter.

After the struggle, I was very neatly tied to the bed. Once I was completely powerless, I yelled. I swore, screamed and carried on something fierce. The screaming helped me refrain from wetting myself, I was so scared.

The stranger stood on the other side of the room and slowly removed his gloves. I stopped screaming because I was interested. Was he going to show me who he was? He took off his sunglasses, which had not fallen off in the tussle. Looking at him now, I didn't see how I could have thought he was Christian. He was shorter and his chest was broad in a way my Christian's wasn't. This man was built for cage fighting. Then he took off his wig and black wavy hair fell loose. His eyes were still hazel, but he took a couple of steps closer and let me look at his face. Within three blinks of my eyes, his face changed. His eyes went from a teardrop shape to almond. His nose lost that beautiful curve in the middle and became round. His jaw went from square to round, and his lips became pale and flat. He undid the top two buttons of his shirt, and I could see part of the scar around his neck. Even with the hazel contact lenses in, I recognized who I was looking at.

Watching the transformation meant so much. It meant that Christian had not been wearing fake rubber on his nose to make himself look different. It meant that along with not dying, he could change his face the way Brandon had just done. Though it looked like he couldn't change much else. Christian had said as much when he recruited me to steal their body parts back from the compound. He said they would know him because of his height.

"Brandon, is it really you?"

He opened his mouth, showing me his severed tongue, and all ten of his fingers.

"I'm so sorry about that. I... I... uh... you don't need to tie me up like this. What do you need? Maybe we can talk about it."

Brandon arched his eyebrow doubtfully and showed me a notepad. He held it up so I could read it since my arms and legs were strapped down. The blue ink read:

Dear Beth,

Please bear with the restraints. I'm sorry to do this, but you see, my under-gardener Charles has been working with your father to hunt down Christian and me. The only thing that is valuable to your father is you, so I have arranged to exchange you for my tongue. I know it doesn't seem fair, but you were willing to make a similar exchange earlier for us, so I hoped you would be a willing participant.

Thank you very much for coming with me,
Brandon

I reread the page, gaping. I wanted to argue with him, but I knew immediately it wouldn't work. I knew Henry Brandon. We had spent that summer together in the garden, but what did I know about him? Hadn't I just talked about myself? I suddenly realized he was a stranger. Dealing with a complete unknown scared me.

"When is the exchange going to be?" I asked.

He picked up the pad and wrote hastily, "In two days."

"Does Christian know you've done this?"

He shook his head.

"And you think he won't notice or come looking for me for two days?" I growled.

Brandon breathed in an amused way through his nose. Then he scratched on the pad the words, "He's very busy. I sent him on an errand."

"And I'm just supposed to sit here quietly for two days?"

He flipped the notepad to a fresh page and scribbled, "You can handle it. I've endured much worse."

I nodded. Since he undid his shirt collar, I could see the unbelievable scar that went all the way around his neck. "And you'll really turn me over to Charles and my father in two days?"

"As long as I get what I want," he responded on paper. He pulled up a chair and wrote, "They have decided to recruit you and they didn't want to kidnap you from your place in Edmonton. Charles says you have people watching out for you everywhere, so I have kidnapped you for them. They ASKED for you. I didn't OFFER you."

I read his page angrily. "Tell me more."

"Do you know that all my trouble might have been avoided if you had befriended Charles? He was recruited to spy on us in Scotland. If you had distracted him, he would have left knowing nothing, with nothing to report. When he saw you kissing Christian he went crazy and decided to help them, because we were BAD people. A grown man was kissing a child."

I read the paper twice before I responded. "The only way I would have distracted Charles is if I had been told to do that," I panted. At that moment, I couldn't remember if I had been or not. I tapped my forehead with my bound hands clenched together. I might have been. I just hadn't understood what those indirect words had meant. "I would have done it, if I had understood that I needed to," I muttered.

"Doesn't matter anymore," he wrote. "I speak thirteen languages. Having my tongue cut out is worse than losing a finger. If you want anything to eat, shout. My ears still work."

***

"On top of spaghetti! All covered in cheese! I lost my poor meatball when somebody sneezed! It rolled off the table and onto the floor! And then my poor meatball rolled straight out the door!" I had started singing because Brandon wouldn't untie me. He wrote that he had his reasons for wanting me tied up, and excused himself by adding that he had tried to make it as comfortable as possible. Except, I wasn't comfortable, so I was determined he shouldn't be comfortable either, and I made as much noise as I could.

I was singing at maximum volume, but he didn't plug his ears. He didn't tape my mouth. He didn't write me nasty letters telling me to shut up. I sang the entire score for *The Little Mermaid* and all of the Queen songs I could think of (there were three). Even with the ear-piercing racket, he didn't leave me alone very often. He sat in an armchair in the corner and read. Sometimes he slept when I was quiet, but I didn't like being quiet. I liked being noisy as it stopped me from crying pitifully.

After the spaghetti song, he set up a tablet on the table and turned on a movie. Oddly enough, even though there were a lot of movies to choose from, he didn't let me pick. Instead, he put on *Blade Runner* and refilled my water bottle.

I watched it, completely helpless to turn it off or leave and wondered why he wanted me to watch a movie about living in fear. Okay, I didn't wonder that long. Brandon and Christian didn't live knowing that their lives were set to expire once they reached a particular age. They lived knowing that death would never come for them, no matter how much they suffered.

When it was over, Brandon took me to the bathroom. On the first bathroom break, he gave me a note before we got started. "I'm going to untie you and escort you to the bathroom. As you probably know, there is no escape route in that room. You can have a shower or whatever you want whenever I take you. I will wait outside. If you try to run or attack me, you'll find out how nice I have been treating you. But if your pride insists that you make the attempt, do as you must."

I looked at him. With the hazel contacts out, his blue eyes were totally clear. His conscience didn't bother him.

I nodded and the ordeal was exactly as he described. I didn't fight.

When Brandon brought me food, he untied one of my hands, but he guarded me like a bulldog. *Logan's Run* was the next movie he played, and I stopped wondering what his taste in movies was.

When it was over, I whispered to him, "If I do what you say, will you make sure I'm safe?"

He languidly approached me with his pad in hand. Slowly, wrote something I was sure he regretted and then flipped it over for me to see. "You are not mine to protect."

"Why not?" I bellowed. "Why does everyone want to be rid of the responsibility of me?"

On the paper, he wrote, "Not everyone does."

"Really?" I gawked sarcastically, fighting back the tears.

Brandon did not hand me a tissue. Instead, he looked like he was going to strangle me. He took a couple of calming breaths, smirked and then wrote, "I've decided to give you a gift. I'll let you look at Christian. He's almost always dressed up as someone else, but I'll let you see him in the two minutes when he won't be."

"Why would you do that for me?" I sputtered.

He closed the notebook and turned on another film. This time it was a space movie about ice being the most valuable thing in the galaxy. I didn't understand. Weren't there comets and plenty of planets that were mostly made of ice? Old science fiction was weird. But then, what people knew about the universe was a lot different thirty years ago compared to what they understood now. I glanced at Brandon. What did he know about the way nature worked that the rest of humanity hadn't figured out yet?

CHAPTER TWENTY

Without the Mask

The morning of the second day, Brandon did not write me a note explaining what would happen. He probably didn't know himself. He brought me breakfast, watched me eat it, and then disappeared into the front of the house. Undoubtedly, he was watching the road. He was expecting Christian and the Argonauts. Exchanging a whole person for only a tongue made less sense to me than it had on the first day.

Brandon opened the door quietly when he went outside and even more quietly when he came inside. I probably wouldn't have heard him moving at all, except that the air was so still, there was nothing to hear except his movements.

I heard the engine of a vehicle approach. Brandon was on the roof. Unless I was mistaken, he had been assembling guns and arranging ammunition for the last hour.

The engine cut and the vehicle door slammed shut. I didn't hear the footsteps up the walk, but I heard the front door click open and bang closed.

"Brandon!" a male voice called out. "Are you in here? I got the package you wanted. I'm opening it. If it's material used for making explosives, I'm going to kick your ass until it burns. Where are you?"

I heard paper ripping. The voice was familiar and yet not an exact match. The edge of my awareness was prickling. Was it him?

I didn't know if I should call out. I wasn't certain it was Christian. I waited.

"The package is empty!" the guy yelled. "I thought it was too light," he muttered to himself just as he opened the door to the room I was tied up in.

I saw him and at that second, I knew exactly who he was. This was Christian when he didn't look like Christian. This was who he really was. Now I understood that when he played Rogan, or Christian, or any other man, there was a pinched quality to his face like he was flexing a muscle that was not normally flexed, a muscle that a normal person could not flex. He had much more control over his expression and form than anyone average. It must have been the reason the scientists wanted to cut off Brandon's head, to examine not only why these men didn't die, but also why they could change the shape of their features so completely that they could essentially become someone new.

The man in front of me looked very different from the Christian I had always known. Christian wore a smirk, a playful, adorable smirk, that made you think of games and danger and trouble. He didn't look like Rogan either. Rogan looked disinterested, bored, and blank because you made him blank. He blamed you for his boredom. As I examined his actual face, I realized it wasn't just his expressions either, he could change his features, so he looked different, even if he didn't smirk or sigh.

However, it didn't look like he had the power to change his coloring. He had to dye his hair and wear contact lenses if he wanted to change color. I had already seen what he could do when he made me into Jill.

The man in front of me had Rogan's dark hair and haircut, though it was obviously in need of a touch-up, the pitch-black had dulled. His jaw joint under his ear was higher than his mouth; his chin distinguishing and pointed. If I thought his nose was sharp when he played Christian Henderson, I was to be surprised, as his nose was even sharper. His beard had grown in, filling in Rogan's goatee, and the dark blue contact lenses were gone. Now his eyes were a grayish green and wide like seeing me tied up on a bed meant something to him.

Other than that, he wore no expression at all, like a person whose eyes reflect the ocean. His hand went to his throat as if to stop himself from speaking. I knew the back of that hand, square knuckles, long fingers, nine fingers, and a line around his wrist.

My mouth wasn't taped, but I couldn't say anything. I was too stunned. It was him; the man I had waited all my life to meet.

He glanced down the hallway, as though he were still looking for Brandon. Directing his focus back to me, he approached the bed and touched the nylon binding my ankles together. "This," he said, "all this," he motioned to the whole room, "means something disastrous has happened, doesn't it?"

"Brandon is trading me for his tongue. Was it supposed to be in the package you brought?"

"It probably was. He had me driving for two days to pick it up. He said the only way to get the delivery safely was if I did it. In exchange, he would make sure you were safe," he said, examining the knots around my ankles. He found one of the ends tied underneath the bed and pulled on it. The entire thing came loose in one motion. "Why didn't I think of tying you up? It would have solved everything," he said, like joking around was the best he could offer me.

"Would it have?" I said sarcastically as I slipped my legs under me and raised myself into a kneeling position. He freed my wrists and I looked around, commenting on what I saw, "This room is kind of familiar to me. The green paint on the walls feels very nostalgic. I like it in a sick sort of way. Do you ever like something you shouldn't?"

"All the time," he breathed.

"Do you think you can get me away from here before Charles and my father come get me?"

"I doubt there's much time for any other action than to meet them when they arrive. It's easier to defend the house than to meet them on the road. They have probably blocked the roads and we wouldn't get far on foot. Since the package was empty, this has obviously been a trap. Well, it worked since all three of us are in the same place at the same time. They're trying to capture us all. I doubt Brandon intended to turn you over to them, but he had to have you here to show them he was in earnest. Nobody wants to give up their leverage. Not your father either if he didn't send the tongue."

"And you knew my father was alive? He was the family member interested in my safety all this time?" I questioned.

"I didn't know he faked his death. At first, I was as fooled as you. I wasn't there when they buried him. It was slow getting the information necessary to be the executor of his will and I was very busy with you for the first six months after his death, but I grew suspicious when they couldn't produce a death certificate for him. I didn't see him immediately either. That was how the Argonauts got me the first time. He contacted me and said he wanted to meet. Obviously, for your sake, I agreed. They caught me, but they were sloppy and I escaped quickly."

I took a painful breath. "I don't want to see him."

"I don't want you to see him either, which is why I never took you to pay your respects at his grave. Even if I didn't tell you, there was always a chance he'd reenter your life, but he also might not."

I didn't know how to answer him, or how to move forward.

Suddenly, he smiled. "You'll have to tell me how you feel about all this. Seeing my face, learning what I've kept from you? My secrets unbuckling themselves without my permission? How are you taking it?"

"I'm not even remotely shocked. If you had approached me in the middle of a crowded street, I would have recognized you," I said cautiously. "I've spent a long time studying you."

He breathed deeply and looked back at me. His eyes full of mischief, like the Christian I had known was not completely erased from him. "I've shown you my last face. It's always the last face I show anyone. My sixteenth face." His eyes met mine and his expression was curious, as it was at least half challenging.

I tried to meet his challenge and remarked grouchily, "I thought you said you were old. You look about the same age you did before."

"That's because there's more wrong here than I'm willing to admit." He cupped the back of my head with his palm. "Are you scared?"

I shook my head, portraying false confidence.

"Brandon will have a plan, but he's a bit bad at explaining his plans at the moment. We probably don't have much time." he groaned, putting a hand to his forehead. "If things go badly and they manage to get you, remember; I'm bad news. I wasn't there when I should have been. I threw money at you rather than giving you the life you deserved. Remember, you are better off without me. That's what you have to tell them."

"Don't worry," I soothed. "Things won't go badly, but if they do, I'll tell them all the right things. I'll be your girl and do everything you would want me to do. Everything you taught me to do."

He paused. "You'll be mine?"

I looked at him and realized suddenly what an incredibly intimate thing that had been to say.

"Even if that should happen, don't worry too much. You're very precious to them. I believe that was the reason your father entrusted you

195

to me in the first place, but a lot has happened since then. His feelings have probably changed more than either of us realizes."

"Do we have much time? Can you tell me one more thing before you go?"

"What?"

"Your name."

He rolled his eyes. "It's Damen."

"Damen Cross?" I squeaked in surprise. "That's your real name?"

He tugged at his collar like he was choking. "No. It's Damen Christianus, but I always have a few aliases with my real names in them, so I don't forget, and so I hear something familiar once and awhile."

I felt a great settling in my chest. Something that had bothered me forever was finally settled. I smiled. Damen had been my favorite alias. Finally, I had opened one of the secrets, like a present he had kept from me. "Can I call you that?"

"No."

"Why not?"

He scoffed. "Because you have to call me Christian, or Rogan, or Louis, or whatever I tell you to call me. But you can know it, and remember it for me."

"And when we're alone like this?"

"You may as well keep calling me Christian. I like the way it sounds when you say it."

I loved being the keeper of his secret. "Are there more secrets you're keeping from me?"

"Not many," he said softly. "Maybe a hundred. Maybe a thousand. I really can't keep track of all the things I'm supposed to know and keep quiet."

We heard the vehicles rumble up the driveway.

"There isn't time for this," he muttered. "Stay here, stay quiet, and try to hide if you can."

Though I wasn't tied down, I was again locked in the room. I was worried at first, about what could be going on outside. He was up on the roof.

There was talking in the yard and then a shot was fired. Then multiple shots were fired. The noise was coming from every direction. What could I do?

An enormous crash sounded outside. Something had exploded. I pinned myself against the wall. I didn't even hear the window break because there were too many other sounds coming from everywhere. It was impossible to isolate that particular sound or to know it was vital to my safety, so I hadn't moved from under the window when a hand reached in to grab me. It curled around my chin and hefted me up through the broken window frame. As he pulled, my back was dragged across a thick piece of broken glass. It cut from my shoulder blade down to my hip. I screamed. He raised me to my feet and put a pistol to my head. With the barrel of the gun pressed against my skull, he walked me around the side of the house, disregarding my pain and blood.

I saw two men propped up against the far side of the roof, I could only assume it was Christian and Brandon looking like people I'd never seen before (but with hair I recognized). Each had a rifle positioned in front of him. As the front yard came into view, I saw army vehicles. They weren't really the army, as the men did not have Canadian insignia on their shoulders. They were a private army. Once I was in view, they began their retreat.

Christian changed the direction of his rifle and shot the man holding me at gunpoint through the neck. The blood splattered against my back. Before I could run, my elbow was yanked backward by someone firing their gun blindly at the roof. I saw Christian and Brandon duck behind separate chimneys, as a vehicle swung around to collect me.

I didn't see Christian or Brandon as I was hauled off into the back of a van. Once inside, there was nothing to see. I was handcuffed, with cold painful rings around my wrists. They hurt all the more because of the nylon ones Brandon had used, keeping me tied up for days. My back was bleeding and a pool of blood was forming behind me, enough for me to feel the wetness soaking through my pants.

The anger that besieged me was unmanageable. This couldn't be just because my father wanted to see me. He had had millions of opportunities to get in touch with me if he had wanted to talk. What did he want now that he hadn't wanted before?

I breathed slowly and didn't even feel the pain in my back as I kicked the man who had abducted me.

CHAPTER TWENTY ONE

The Argonauts

The guys I was with didn't play games and they drove us directly to the compound. This time, I was not taken through the break room or the garage. I was brought to the front facade, which had had some construction since the last time I had seen. It was built to impress with large cement steps and overly large windows letting in the western sunset.

After I barked some choice words at the guys in the van about my injury, they brought me a stretcher and carried me in with several other men who were wounded or dead. It was hard to tell if they were dead since they weren't screaming and swearing the way I was.

My first stop was their sick room, which was completely unprepared for the slaughter they brought home with them. Christian and Brandon were good shots. It didn't take the doctor a minute to flip me on my stomach, cut my shirt and bra up the back and cover me with gauze. He instructed them to take me to a private room prepared for me. He would be up as soon as he could to stitch the wound shut.

On the third floor, I lay on a bed on my stomach and pulled at my chain. I was handcuffed to the rail. The room I was in was stupid. White feather duvet? Please. I was toying with the idea of taking off my bandage and rolling around on the cover to stain it red, when someone came into the room.

"Who's there?" I asked like it was the last thing in the world that mattered.

"It's me," Charles said, doing me the courtesy of entering my field of vision.

I greeted him icily. "Does my slap still hurt?"

"Yes," he said. I felt his hand on my back as he pulled back the gauze to see my injury. I felt his eyes linger on my bare skin and the parts of me that should have been covered by my shirt.

"Get away from me," I hissed.

"This could have been avoided if you'd just let me talk to you and explain things," he said, mumbling and confusing his sounds.

"Shut up. Kindly replace my bandage."

I felt it drop.

He sat down on the floor next to the bed with his back to the wall. "I thought you might like some company while you waited for the doctor."

I rolled my eyes. I didn't need to say I would prefer anyone to him because my expression said it for me.

"If it helps, I could pretend to be someone else. You really seem turned on by that—duplicity," he said the words as if he'd finally managed to say something smart.

"I can wait alone."

"Would you like to hear why Christian was pretending to be me?"

My breath caught and betrayed me. I did want to hear.

"Your father tried to contact me after the first summer I worked at Christian's home in Belfron. Christian intercepted it and went to visit Lance in Toronto in order to tell them off in my place. He had a fake passport made with fake numbers and everything. That was the exact moment you had your hissy fit and ran away from school. They got footage of him kissing you (in my place) in front of your school. They tried to contact me again, but went through a different channel and got me—the real me. I didn't know who you were, but they showed me the video of a man who looked just like me kissing you. Did you know it was Christian you were kissing?"

I groaned. "Of course, I knew."

"Pervert!" Charles scorned, denouncing Christian so violently it made my fillings rattle.

"I think you're the pervert. You saw that video and thought it should have been you I saw kissing?" I ridiculed. "You watched all that video footage of me and you think Christian is the one who is wrong?"

His lip quivered as he tried to think up a retort.

"You spied on us through windows and decided he was the monster?"

Charles didn't answer. That was how he felt.

"Because of that, he sent me away. What he and I had was none of your business and for what you did, I hate your guts."

He got up and for a moment, I thought he was going to leave as I asked, but instead, I felt him lean on my back. The pressure felt good. "Will you remember I did this for you?"

I refrained from snorting, and retorted, "Still trying to score points with me?"

He hesitated. "Maybe."

"Hello, Bethany," the doctor said cheerfully when he came in. He strode over to my side of the bed and seemingly unaware of my metal restraints, introduced himself. "I'm Dr. Hilliar." He had painfully straight teeth, cheeks so round he almost looked boyish and hair two shades off pure white. His wrinkles fanned out from his eyes and mouth. "I'm your father's doctor," he explained.

"Oh, you were in charge of bringing him back from the dead. Very impressive," I said, my voice laced in toxicity.

"Not at all," he said with a grin like he knew how to take a joke. His eyes twinkled like the glint of his teeth. He was an extremely dangerous man, and now he was going to touch me. I felt my whole body involuntarily quake.

"Let's have a look at your back, shall we?" he said as he donned a fresh pair of latex gloves and removed my gauze. "That's a nasty-looking cut." Charles was soon setting out items from the doctor's bag. My wound was soon wetter and felt fresh. "That was an antiseptic," he explained. "Here's the anesthetic."

I felt the prick of a needle. Soon afterward, I was under a magnifying glass while Dr. Hilliar pulled fragments of glass from the wound.

"Do you think you'll be able to get it all?" I asked, through sweat and set teeth.

"Yes. We'll get it all. We just need to be thorough," he said patiently.

"Don't you have other patients to see in worse shape than me?" I wondered aloud. "There were quite a few wounded men that came in with me."

"It's good of you to be worried about them. I'm not the only doctor on site. There are others to care for them." Then he started stitching. "We'll have to do more than one layer. Those will dissolve and then the ones on the outside will need to be removed later. How are you feeling? How's the anesthetic working for you?"

201

I was not in a great deal of pain. The wound looked worse than it felt. The tricky part was staying still when I wanted to run. "It's fine," I said.

He began stitching. With such a long cut, the stitching would be time-consuming. The only moment of interest was when I heard him smack his lips and say, "You have such beautiful tissue in your back."

I thought of a few scathing replies but kept my mouth shut. However repulsed I was by him, I needed him to finish.

As he stitched, I thought back to when I heard that my father and mother had died. Their funeral had been in Toronto, and I had been too sick to travel. I didn't see them die or see their bodies in their coffins at the funeral. It was shameful how little I had thought about him or my mother since Christian had taken charge of me. But what should I have thought? I didn't miss them, because I didn't know them. Once they were dead, they just sort of fell out of importance in my mind. Except now I was going to meet my dead father.

Afterward, Charles appeared in the doorway with a fresh nightgown and slippers for me, and I glared at him wondering how I was going to change with my hand handcuffed to the bed.

Doctor Hilliar got a call on his phone, something about one of the other patients, and he swept through the exit, leaving me alone with the last person I ever wanted to be alone with.

I sat up and put my free hand out. "I think I can manage it myself."

He frowned. "I realize you don't like it, but you are completely unable to put your arm through the sleeve if I don't unlock you."

I didn't say anything and instead concentrated on keeping what was left of the front of my shirt pinned to my chest. He sat down next to me on the bed and took my wrist between his fingers.

I knocked his hand aside. "You may unlock my handcuff. I will not run and you will leave the room while I change. If anything else other than this happens, I will kill you."

His expression was amused. Who knew how many times he had seen me undressed? If he got one good clip, all he had to do was hit *play* again. He had even made recordings of me himself in Scotland. He laughed because it was too late for me to keep anything sacred.

I tried again. "Whatever you people want from me, this is the worst way in the world to get it. Let me put on my own clothes."

Apparently, that convinced him. He undid the locks and reluctantly left the room. Before he left he casually glanced at two places on the walls: a vent and a framed picture. Undoubtedly, that's where the cameras were planted. Between the two places, there were no blind spots in the room. Hefting myself stiffly off the bed, I ambled over to the picture frame. I found the camera behind the glass. With a great amount of effort for a girl with a back injury, I pulled it off the wall and leaned the picture facing the wall. Then I tugged a pillowcase free and hung it over the vent.

Only then, did I change. The nightgown was white and hardly constituted more than a shirt, barely covering my butt. I left my jeans on, even though they were blood-stained. There was a housecoat too, that was so meager in fabric it was practically a hoodie, but it was stupid too and barely covered my elbows.

I carefully lowered myself onto the bed and enjoyed the pressure of my own body on my back, but I didn't have the energy for much more.

I was still like that when Dr. Hilliar returned. He glanced around the room, noticing the changes I had made, but refrained from commenting. "It's great to finally meet you, Beth. Your father has been in my care for almost seven years. He never fully recovered after the accident. Did you know he is confined to a wheelchair?"

"No," I said blankly.

"He's waiting just outside. Do you have any questions for me before I ask him to join us?"

I considered what he said. "When do you think I'll be able to get my stitches out?"

"We'll play it by ear, shall we?"

"Then, by all means, let him in."

The door was automatic and my father wheeled forward. He looked the same as I remembered him. Perhaps there were a few more wrinkles, but it had to be him. Hanging out with Christian and Brandon had taught me to look for other identifiers and even though I couldn't capture his height with him sitting in a chair, his hands were the same as I remembered. His hair was immaculately groomed, the same as it had always been with not a single hair fell out of place.

"Hello, Bethany," he said.

"Hello, Dad," I said, my own voice sounding strange to me. "I want you to know that I take exception to this invitation. Kidnapping your own daughter? What do you want?"

"After all these years, this is how you say hello?"

"You want me to get up and swoon over you after the good doctor here just finished putting over four hundred stitches in my back?"

"Was it over four hundred?" my dad mouthed.

"I didn't count," he muttered.

"Well, I *was* counting and it was over four hundred. So, no, I don't imagine this is the reunion you imagined. I thought this day would never come because I thought you were dead. Silly me!"

He rolled his eyes. "I guess Christian didn't teach you to be respectful."

"Christian was hardly around. He didn't teach me anything except how to use a debit card. Did you go to boarding school? Do you know how attentive they are toward each and every child? So much more efficient than parents! You bastard! You were alive all this time and you choose to contact me now, when I'm an adult?"

"I had my reasons," he said grimly.

"Which I would undoubtedly find fascinating... if I were still fourteen. You brought me here because you want something from me. Let's avoid the mushy crap sandwich where you explain how difficult your circumstances were only to top it off with some pretty promises you never plan on fulfilling."

He frowned. "I guess you haven't had an easy time either."

"Don't act like you care what I've been through," I snapped. "I have been let down and ignored and neglected until absolutely nothing you say could have the least effect. Just tell me what you want."

He smiled. "I want you to stay with me for a few weeks."

"Like hell, I'll do that. In case you haven't seen a calendar lately, it's September in two days. I have classes. I have work, and I am really not willing to take a break from either of those things for you."

"I'll compensate you," he said, reaching into the inner pocket of his suit coat for his checkbook.

"Put that away. I don't take checks."

"Cash?" he asked, looking hopeful.

"You don't get it. I don't want money. There are only two things in this world I want. First, I want you to drive me home and end this madness."

"What's the second thing?"

I clenched my teeth. "To never see Christian Henderson again as long as I live."

He leaned back in his wheelchair and stroked his chin. "What a surprise! Charles thinks you're still quite enamored with him."

"Charles thinks I must be in love with Christian because I hate him differently than I hate all of you."

"Ah, Bethany. You can't trick me into believing you aren't interested in the whole story of Christian Henderson."

I grit my teeth and flicked my eyes away, irritation radiating from me. "There's no trick. His reasons for abandoning me matter about as much as yours. Whatever the reasons were, I'm not interested. I got over you and I got over him. Just like that."

He put his hand back on the armrest of his wheelchair and drew his eyebrows together. "What has happened to you? I would never have believed that a daughter of mine could be so jaded. Where's the Coldwell optimism?"

"Losing both your parents at a young age can make you forget whatever they wanted you to remember most." I met his eyes crossly.

"And you don't believe I just want to spend time with you?"

"I don't care what you want. *I* don't want to spend time with you. If you don't take me home immediately, I'm going to report you to the police for kidnapping me at gunpoint."

Dr. Hilliar and my father exchanged looks.

"Aren't you a little worried about what might happen if you get kidnapped by Henry Brandon again?" my father suggested.

I snorted in the ladylike way Felicity-Ann had taught me. "Yeah, he's terrifying."

"What about this, daughter?" my dad said as he showed me a print out of the letter Brandon sent him.

I wasn't surprised. Looking at it, it was exactly what Brandon told me he was doing, except that the part about exchanging his tongue had been replaced with some nonsense about money.

I shrugged my shoulders and dropped the letter on the floor like I couldn't wait to stop touching it.

"Oh, Bethany," he sighed, retrieving the letter and putting it back in the pocket on the side of his wheelchair. "You are more innocent than I supposed. There's no doubt about it. You were being held as a hostage. We rescued you. I just want you to stay here until things with Henry Brandon are settled, so he can't use you as a hostage. I can't let you leave. So, even if you call the police after we free you—that's fine. I just want my little girl to be safe."

I knew it was going to come down to that. I couldn't leave no matter what. "Give him back his tongue and he'll leave everyone alone."

"I don't know what that means," he said, pretending to be too out of the loop to understand the latest slang.

I glared at my dad. "Do you have anybody else locked up, or will I be the only one?"

"You're not going to be locked up," he said cheerfully. "You are our guest. Lobster tails and something bubbly?"

That was the kind of food I used to like, long ago, when I was a kid and money was in everything, even in the food.

"I've hired a chef," he continued. "You'll be well taken care of." He moved to roll out.

I glanced at Dr. Hilliar. He was unsatisfied. My father looked unhappy too, but not ready to give up. Charles looked like he was finally about to get what he had been working for all along.

"Dad, I'll be pleasant... ish, if you can give me one thing," I volunteered.

He blinked, surprised. "What is it?"

"You'll keep *that*," I said, pointing at Charles, "away from me."

The air hung heavy for a full minute, while my father decided whether or not to give in to my demand. Finally, having made up his mind, he instructed, "Charles, stand guard outside my daughter's room and please do not enter without permission, but first, pull that pillowcase off the wall and fix that picture."

After a strangely pitiable look, Charles did as he was told.

Before my father could turn his back on me I piped up. "Why must you spy on me?"

Clearly, I'd hit the plot square on the head. My father's expression was aghast. He didn't have the poker face Dr. Hilliar had. "The cameras are for your safety," he argued.

I continued. "I'm awfully tired of having a video feed of me given as a reward to low-level goons. You won't get my cooperation that way."

My father was feeling a little panicked by this point. He said nothing about what I accused him of, but instead gave instructions. "Charles, remove the picture. Call Steven in maintenance and get him to unscrew the vent."

I smiled at that. I was getting Skull Boy Steve. He was my favorite of the boys I had met at the compound. I felt a little like I was winning, but I couldn't let up for a second. "I want the audio equipment removed as well. It's a violation of my privacy like I can't go to the bathroom without a bunch of thugs listening to me flush."

He shook his head like he had to explain something to a child. "You don't understand why we need them, but if you desire it, I'll have them removed."

"Thank you," I said, sounding somewhat tamed.

"He has another girlfriend, you know," he said because he wanted to show me something I wouldn't like.

"Who does?"

"Christian." He got out a folder. I knew what it was before he showed it to me. It was a picture of me playing blonde Jill taken from a surveillance camera. Daddy didn't know it was me!

I smirked. "Why should I care about that? He should have some blonde bombshell. I bet they make a great couple."

He scowled in reply.

I crossed my arms over my chest and frowned. The nightmare was never going to be over.

CHAPTER TWENTY TWO

Picture Show

The room they prepared for me was done up in raspberry, white and navy. It was perfect, like a pin on Pinterest. I looked around pricing out the furniture, the blankets, and the artwork. Did they feel they had to do this because of the room Christian had made for me in Scotland? There was a telephone I quickly discovered was only connected to the reception desk. There was a TV and I could watch thousands of channels. No books. There was a desk for writing, but no supplies. Did they seriously think a TV would be enough to entertain me, when I was looking for ways to be a bad hostage?

Not long after, I was escorted to a conference room for dinner with my father and Dr. Hilliar. At the table, Charles took a seat beside me, even though I had asked for distance.

Dr. Hilliar took charge. "Bethany," he said after he sat down. "I've been thinking that perhaps you don't know much about the man who calls himself Christian Henderson. I think you need a lesson about him."

"Are you sure you want to go through the trouble of telling me all this stuff? I have nothing to do with him anymore and I'm not interested in whatever he kept from me. He kept a lot more than secrets from me. I'm over this and I want to go home," I said, making my promised effort to be polite.

Dr. Hilliar gazed about the room like he didn't know where to begin if I shut him down after his opening remarks. He had been counting on my interest. He smiled wryly as he continued, "Please humor me. You won't be bored at all. Christian Henderson is, without a doubt, the most interesting man alive. I have a slide show."

"Over dinner?" I asked skeptically.

"Why not over dinner?"

I glanced at the table. It was the sort of food a person in university never got because they didn't serve roast beef with horseradish and mashed potatoes anywhere I normally frequented. In the interest of being a bad hostage, I decided not to eat anything. I busied my hands by placing my napkin in my lap, as they dimmed the lights.

A picture of Christian popped up: hazel eyes, strong jaw, and wavy, tawny hair. I used to think he was gorgeous, but the appearance of the real him had killed the effect for me. That face was only a pinched mask he wore to hide his true face.

Then they showed me a picture of Damen Cross. "Do you know who this is?"

"Damen Cross. He's a banker."

"It's extraordinary, isn't it? Would you believe it's the same man as this?" He flipped back to Christian.

"I'll believe anything you say to get this over quicker, or I won't believe a thing if it'll get you to stop... whichever."

"Aren't you interested in the man you've been living with?" my father inquired.

"'Living with' are strong words," I said with palpable disgust. "They are also incorrect words. I hardly call vacationing a few times a year 'living with' him. Besides, he and I aren't on speaking terms."

Father piped up again. "But more importantly, do you think these two pictures look like the same man?"

I shrugged. "If you say they do."

Dr. Hilliar and my father exchanged glances. From their expressions, my father thought it was time to put the projector away, but Dr. Hilliar wanted to press on. He flipped to the next picture.

It was of a man with extremely blond hair and dark eyes. He looked like a surfer with messy bleached hair below his collarbone. The picture had been taken at a beach resort. He looked a little like a raccoon because he had a slight tan line where his sunglasses had been sitting. I examined his bone structure carefully. I thought he did something to make his eyebrow ridge bigger. The slight lamb chop sideburns were also meant to throw a person off, but none of it threw me off anymore, not since I had seen his real face.

"This is Riley Fulks."

"And he is Christian Henderson in disguise too?" I huffed.

My father looked deterred, but no amount of lip threw the doctor. He was probably better at judging my subtler nonverbal communication. I had heard all these names before, and I might not be able to hide my lack of surprise from someone who was trained to look for such things.

"He might be," the doctor said noncommittally. "This is William Farris."

I glanced at the new picture on the screen. He had wrapped something around his torso to make himself look beefier. He also wore shoulder pads, but to me, his neck looked disproportionately thin. His hair was the most boring color of brown and his eyes the most boring color of blue. I could see how that getup could be useful to a man who wanted to disappear, as he looked like an extra in a movie.

"This is one of his less convincing disguises, don't you think?"

I turned away. "You tell me."

"Those are only a few of the aliases he uses now. What do you think of this?" The doctor flipped to the next picture. This one was yellow. He had curly grayish-brown hair and a mustache, but he looked more like the original man under the grubbiness. He still had that fantastic twinkle in his eye, like he knew all the fun things. He was at a BBQ in someone's backyard. He was wearing flip flops and holding a red plastic cup. He looked really happy. I wasn't sure I'd ever seen his posture so relaxed.

"This picture was taken in 1968."

I squinted my eyes. "If you want to feed me horse manure, you could at least tell me it's chocolate. It's his dad or his uncle. So what?"

"It's not his dad or his uncle. It's him," my father said quietly. "This was what he looked like before he started messing with his face so that he could disappear into the crowd. The way the world worked back then was less exact. Someone could fudge their identity much easier. What do you think, Bethany? Do you still think he's handsome?"

I shrugged my shoulders.

"He was going by the name Clint Johnson."

"Riveting," I said drolly.

"What about this?" the doctor asked as he moved onto the next slide in the photo tour.

This one was a black and white shot of him looking over his shoulder. He was wearing a military uniform and he had a cigarette sticking out of his mouth. There was no disguise unless a uniform was a disguise. They flipped to an enlarged version of his face. It was grainy and monochrome, but it was him.

"This was taken in 1915. He was Harold Martens back then."

I didn't answer the question they didn't ask. Why did he look the same in the two pictures when over forty years had passed? And why did he look the same in 1915 as now? Christian had told me he was alive when he shouldn't be. He did not tell me he was over a hundred years old.

But he was.

I believed them instantly. It explained everything. It explained his classic tastes, his chivalrous attitude, and perhaps how he felt when he told me that he had expected to watch me die. How many people had died in his arms?

I had to mask my interest, hide my curiosity, even though he was the only person I'd ever been curious about.

I pitched my voice to a bored drone. "And all this has something to do with me because?" I waited for them to fill in the blank.

"Bethany, after all this time with him, we wonder if you know the answer to a few of his darker secrets."

I glared at them. Suddenly, I understood something Rogan had told me. He said that they wouldn't come after him if I was with him. They were trying to get him to confide in me, because I would be an easier nut to crack than him. It wasn't that I was precious to them. It was that I was unwittingly their mole. They had come to get me because I was out of contact with Christian, so they thought I couldn't learn more about him. It was time to harvest what they'd planted. I scoffed at my father. "I don't know any of his secrets if he has them. I've tried to explain it to you. He neglected me. All the years I was with him, he neglected me."

"But you still have some lingering affection for him?" the doctor questioned.

"Right. I like him more than I like any of you. That isn't saying much."

My father rolled his wheelchair sideways so he could face the doctor. "I'm sick of this cloak and dagger. Christian already knows what we want. She might as well know too if she's going to cooperate."

Dr. Hilliar inclined his head. "If that's what you want to do, but we might not be able to go back."

"We already can't go back," my old father said bitterly. He turned to me and raised his voice, "Bethany, show us your heart surgery scars."

That was a strange turn for our discussion to take, but since I knew no reason to hide the truth, I left it open. "I can't. They're gone. Over the years, they faded."

Doctor Hilliar leaned in toward my father and tried to whisper unsuccessfully. "All our questions should be answered in the next few days. We don't need to convince her of anything more right now."

It was then that dad noticed my dinner plate. Everyone else at the table had cleaned their plates, while I had eaten nothing. "Why haven't you eaten?"

I looked at the food. "I have vowed to eat nothing until I am released."

Dad looked at Dr. Hilliar for his opinion. The doctor shook his head. "Bethany, we can't send you home in that state. We have to keep you here for treatment. Any hospital would do the same."

"No. They wouldn't. They would send me home to my own bed since I require no further treatment until the stitches come out," I answered bravely. "And though I am grateful to Dr. Hilliar for stitching me up, surely I don't need a doctor of his expertise to remove my stitches."

"Bethany, we don't want to risk infection," the doctor said, again using my full name in that infuriating way. "You must eat so your body can heal."

I glared at them. "I don't need to heal. I need to leave."

"She *knows*," my father rasped. He started speaking into his smartwatch and within a second I was completely surrounded by their army drones in military uniforms.

They were ordered to escort me back to my room. I walked, albeit slowly, because of my injury. Charles followed behind them, carrying my dinner plate.

Outside the room, I flipped it over so the mashed potatoes and meat splattered across the carpet. I was so feeble they hadn't expected me to do something like that. "I'm not eating that!" I spat angrily.

Before I could register his reaction, I was thrown headfirst into the room. The door was slammed shut with finality behind me. A few of my stitches ripped open and I bled through my gauze and into the white nightgown.

CHAPTER TWENTY THREE

Tongue and Toothpicks

I lowered myself onto the bed and thought of what else I could do to be a bad hostage. Thinking of Trinity and her trouble-making, I realized I had to meet specific criteria. I needed to tick them off without making my room unlivable. I didn't know how long they wanted to keep me there. I bet they had changed their mind about getting Skull Boy Steve to take the camera out from behind the vent. My outburst didn't make them want to do any favors for me.

The lights in the room went off by themselves at exactly 10:20. I was scared to sleep. I remembered how Rogan had coached me not to fall asleep when I was Jill. I worried that falling asleep might be the worst thing I could do. I was very tired, very bored, and when I tried to turn on the lights, they wouldn't go.

I thought about making noise as I had with Brandon. It had not worked with him, and looking around at the walls, I thought it had less of a chance of working here. Besides, my throat was chapped from all the yowling I'd done when I saw with him, just to be annoying.

Hours passed and the night grew quieter as staff outside the room retired. Footsteps down the hall ceased, and the quiet came. Then suddenly, something was familiar. I was basically in a hospital room, moonlight shone through the one window, light shone from under the door, and there was a slight humming in the air. The door creaked open and a man quietly entered.

Without making a sound, he approached the bed, took my hand in his and placed my right hand on his left. Allowing me to feel the place where he was missing a finger, he whispered, "Beth?"

"Did you come here to rock me to sleep?" I asked, as more of a password than anything else. After Brandan had convinced me he was Christian, I needed to make sure I trusted the right man.

"It would be wrong if I didn't," he said. The way he said 'wrong' was exactly the way he had said, 'This is wrong,' when he dropped me on the bed all those years ago.

"Christian!" I exclaimed, reaching for him, but my other hand found nothing but air. Resting my hand on the bed, my expression fell in dismay. Wasn't he supposed to hold me? Wasn't he supposed to draw me to him like he had that night long ago?

Instead, I heard his silky voice across the darkness. "We have to hurry."

"How can we get out of here?" I asked, clasping his mutilated hand like he was my salvation.

He sat on the edge of the bed. "I gassed the security guards and shut off the locks. You know the layout of this building because I taught it to you. Go out through the break room," he whispered under his brimmed camouflage hat. "Go straight through the woods to the road. Hide if you see headlights. Head north until you get to a farmhouse that has a barn door painted like a Scandinavian cross. Brandon will meet you there. Wait for me." He turned to leave.

"What does that look like?" I mouthed with hardly any sound.

"A sideways cross," he said patiently. "Leave quickly, Beth, and do not turn back." He slid his smooth fingers from mine and fifteen seconds later, I saw the light in the doorway expand enough for him to slip through the crack. He moved so quietly, I didn't hear which way he went after that. He had to be searching for the missing body parts.

Two seconds after that, I was on my feet, searching for something to wear, so I wouldn't freeze outside.

***

Picking through the forest was hard. The place was wild, nothing had been cleared away. There were no obvious paths. I always thought they were joking when Snow White ran through the woods and tore her clothes. She was lucky the branches didn't gouge her heart out.

I hoped I was going in the right direction, but I had been walking forever and I hadn't made it to the road yet. My progress was slow and the trees were like shredded toothpicks. I worried someone would see me because actually, there was no place to hide except to crouch on the ground.

Taking a break on a fallen tree trunk, I let my head loll back and I looked directly up. The stars were fading in the growing light. I breathed and tried to let the air that filled me be enough. The wind was perfumed with the scent of things living and dying simultaneously. I hoped Christian would catch up to me soon.

Finally, the sun's light came over the treetops and I could see the road. At the edge of the treeline, I came to a barbed-wire fence. I planted my foot on it the way I had seen Christian-of-old step on blackberry vines and I stepped through it like a pro. I climbed the incline to the paved road.

Turning around, I could still see the compound! I must have walked in circles! A black SUV pulled onto the road. I tried to duck into the ditch, but I knew it didn't work when they stopped and came after me on foot.

Charles was in the front. "Bethany, come on. Running away? Did you think that would pay off?" he said in a friendly tone. "Doesn't your back hurt?"

It did.

Grabbing my elbow, he spun me around to face him.

"What were you thinking?" he demanded as he frog-marched me to the car, his grip on my arm tight and painful. In the early morning light, he lectured me. "Do I really have to chase you down before sunrise? We're not animals. Did we hurt you once?"

I refrained from mentioning the cut on my back, the three other cuts I had that hadn't warranted stitches, the stitches that had been torn out and the way Charles twisted my arm. I could feel him getting revenge for every single time I had talked down to him. His satisfaction was unmistakable.

The early morning birds' voices rang shrilly through the trees and a moment later a gunshot was heard cracking through that same air. The birds' wings panicked them into the air. One of the windows had been shot out of the SUV.

My eyes scanned the area frantically to see where it had come from. Had Christian come after me? A second later my question was answered and not by him. Another person appeared from a dense patch of foliage. The black cap on his head hid his identity for a second, but the black shotgun in his hands revealed his nature before I could see his face. It was a face I recognized.

"It's Brandon!"

"Huh?" Charles grunted. He was still scanning the treeline. He hadn't seen him yet.

"Let's go!" the driver called to Charles.

Another shot went off. This one hit one of the men in the shoulder. I pounded my heel onto Charles' foot, and he let go of me.

He yowled as he reached for me again, bouncing on one foot.

"He wants his tongue back," I said, twisting out of his reach.

The SUV was moving now. They were leaving without Charles and me! The guy in the passenger seat had pulled out a revolver and he shot at Brandon, but missed. Brandon fired again and hit the driver. The SUV spun out of control and stopped with a skid.

Charles dove for cover while I limped toward Brandon. I had only gone a few steps when I saw him deliver death shots to both the driver of the SUV and the passenger.

My stomach flipped. I had just seen two people murdered. My hand involuntarily cradled my heart and the other one covered my mouth. I turned and fumbled my way toward the forest. I had seen both Christian and Brandon shoot people before. I shouldn't have been so shocked, but I was as I stumbled away.

When the hand fell on my shoulder, I jumped. Brandon's blue eyes stared into mine. He couldn't call me. He couldn't tell me what he wanted. He just looked apologetic as he put a small silver gun to my head.

I winced. "We're going to do this kidnapping thing again?" I moaned. "Can't you think of another way?"

He ground the barrel into my temple like he was grinding out a cigarette. He didn't care, he was going to use whatever leverage he had to get what he wanted. If I understood right, he didn't care about what happened to me because whether I died that day or with the natural course of time, I was still a dead woman. He, on the other hand, had to live forever and he did not want to live forever without his tongue. So he put my life, that would expire with or without his intervention, on the line.

Brandon put his arm around my neck and kept the barrel of his gun pointed at my head. He led me down the compound and to the front doors of the building. They had no warning. Charles hadn't made it back and the other two guys were dead. The boy sitting at the reception desk had his feet up and he was watching something on his monitor. Brandon walked me right up to the desk. The receptionist almost fell off his chair when he saw us.

"Hi," I said, with my head in a headlock. "Remember me? Can you please call Dr. Hilliar and tell him Henry Brandon is here and he would like his tongue back?"

The receptionist recovered quickly. One hand went to his phone and the other went for a gun in a holster under his coat.

Brandon pulled the gun on him before he could reach it.

I spoke for Brandon. "You'd better give me your gun. He really will kill you."

The boy hesitated.

"Hand it over!" I screeched. I did not want to see another one of these hooligans shot to death in front of me.

Reluctantly, he did. I took it, and twisting a little to look at Brandon, he indicated with his eyes what I should do. I slipped it into the pocket of his jacket.

"If you have any more guns," I continued. "Better give them to me."

The boy shook his head and picked up the phone. His voice into the receiver was clear like nothing out of the ordinary had just taken place. "Mr. Henry Brandon is here. He's here to pick up a parcel. Something about a tongue…"

Brandon lightly smacked me on the side of his head with his gun.

"He wants Christian Henderson's finger, too," I inferred.

The person on the other end of the line commented though I couldn't hear it. "Yes, it's Bethany," the receptionist said. "He's got a gun to her head. She's okay. You're coming? I'll tell them." He hung up the phone and turned to us. "Dr. Hilliar says security has been tightened since we were robbed in the spring and it will take some time to get those things out of cold storage. Would you mind waiting ten minutes or so?"

Brandon didn't get a chance to show whether he was willing to wait ten minutes or not before I piped up. "You were robbed last spring? What was stolen, if you don't mind me asking?"

The guy looked uncomfortable, probably because Brandon pointed the gun at him again. I guessed he was interested in his answer as well. He shrugged. "I don't know. I didn't work here then."

I frowned deeply. "Are there lots of body parts on ice downstairs?"

The receptionist gawked at me. "You're not much of a hostage, are you? It seems like you're *his* friend and not ours. Aren't you Lance Coldwell's daughter?"

I glanced at Brandon. "Yeah, I like this guy better than I like all of you, but I do think he'll shoot me if it comes to that."

"Why?"

"He wants his tongue back more than he wants me to live, moron."

The guy didn't understand. "What's the big deal? They borrowed one of his specimens."

"Specimens? That sounds like the truth bent a hundred and eighty degrees. Is that what Dr. Hilliar told you?"

"Yeah, just now on the phone."

I sighed. It was probably better if the receptionist didn't know the truth.

Exactly ten minutes later, Dr. Hilliar came through the back door, carrying a Tupperware container. The sides of it were foggy like it had just come out of the freezer.

Brandon shook his gun at Dr. Hilliar, but the old codger didn't seem to know what he wanted until I shouted, "Open it!"

With the lid off, Brandon looked inside. He turned and whispered in my ear. "Put it in my mouth." His voice was terribly garbled and the only reason I could understand was because of the movement of his lips, which touched my ear.

I looked away, unwilling to help.

He noticed my hesitation and encouraged, "Only way to check if it's mine."

Quick as a bunny, I stuck my fingers into the container and wrapped them around the cold tongue. I shuddered and rocketed it into Brandon's open mouth.

I gagged and I couldn't look at him. The thing was frozen. How could he possibly tell if it was his or not?

The doctor put the lid back on the container that had Christian's finger in it and handed it to me. I put it in Brandon's coat.

"Satisfied?" the doctor asked blandly.

Brandon shifted his severed tongue into his left cheek and then into his right.

"Aw! Come on! I'm gonna throw up. Is that your tongue or not? If it's not…" I put a hand over my mouth to stop the gagging.

The doctor chimed in. "It's the correct tongue. If you are satisfied, could you please turn Bethany over to me? Her father is unable to come downstairs and is most anxious."

Brandon pinched his lips together and nodded.

He walked backward, still holding me with a gun to my head until he made it to the door. Checking the area, he mumbled something.

"I think he wants you to walk him to his car," the doctor interpreted. "It's unnecessary. No one is going to come after you, Brandon, but if you must, I'll allow it."

Slamming his back against the glass doors, he opened them and we were back outside. I looked around the compound. Did Brandon even have a car? I had seen him come out of the bushes. Were we going back to the bushes?

He muscled me off the property line and across the road. From there, he checked in all directions to make sure no one was following us on foot, or had us in their sniper scope, or were otherwise waiting for us. When he was satisfied, he let me go.

For a second, I thought about following him rather than going back to my wretched father and his cronies. I only took one step before Brandon turned around and pointed his gun between my eyes. I stopped dead in my tracks. The feeling was completely different than when he had held me at gunpoint just seconds before. His eyes were steely and cold. He lowered his black eyebrows and shook his head. He pointed toward the compound with his free hand and I felt exactly like a dog being told to reenter a burning building when I'd just pulled someone clear.

With my head low, I walked back to the road. From there, I got picked up by the receptionist and Charles. That sweet little receptionist boy was packing a machine gun and Charles was holding a revolver.

I jumped when I saw them. "He's gone. Put those away."

Charles looked spurned. "The guns aren't for him. They're for you. You've got to come back with us."

I threw my hands into the air. "I can't believe this place. Do you know how many guns I've had pointed at me since I got here? It's getting out of hand. I'm going to end up getting shot, even if I cooperate."

"No you won't," Charles soothed, not sounding reassuring at all. "Just come along and everything will be fine."

"Whatever," I fumed as I was hauled back into their hideout.

Not more than five minutes later, I was back in my lovely suite, with the door triple bolted behind me. The room was the same, except that there was one addition. Christian was sprawled out on my couch. Approaching him, I saw he was hurt. His face was badly bruised and one of his eyes was swollen shut. His hands were bare and the stub where his finger was missing was showing. The knuckles on his hands were cut and dark with bruises.

I knelt next to him, totally confused. Hadn't he gotten away?

CHAPTER TWENTY FOUR

That Kind of Love

Since there was an attached bathroom, I moistened a face cloth with cold water. I wrung it out as best I could and draped it across Christian's face.

"Thanks," he said as he pressed the cloth deeper into his eyes. "That's a relief. Don't let me sleep."

"How am I supposed to keep you awake?"

"Talk to me. Is there a game we can play?" he asked, shifting onto his side.

"No. There is not even a pen or paper here."

"You're hilarious. You think I need a pen or paper to play a game with you?"

I chuckled, but my voice was dry and flat. "Obviously not."

He adjusted the wet cloth on his face and made sure his eyes were completely covered. "This is new to you, but it is not new to me. I have already been through several rounds with these people. The first stop is measuring how long it takes to heal. They cut me, and watch my blood clot a hundred times faster than an average person. Second stop, they drowned me. It's very similar to being waterboarded. No fancy pool. They just put my head in a barrel of water to see how good I am at static apnea." He smiled sickly. "I'm very good at it. Third stop, they tried to cut out my kidney. It didn't work. The fourth stop might be beheading. I never got as far as step four before I escaped."

I looked around warily. "I am deeply concerned about why we have been locked in this room together. They must not want to cut off your head."

He took the cloth off his face and looked at me. "I can make a very educated guess as to why they have done this."

"They're hoping we'll get bored and start fooling around?" I muttered unpleasantly, thinking of the camera that was still set up in the vent.

Christian replaced the cloth on his face. "They don't need you for experiments like that."

"What?"

"I don't think these guys are very interested in that at the moment."

"What do you mean?" I gawked.

"I mean that I have met a lot of other people who didn't cut me, drown me or try to steal my organs. Those are all new things. Trying to get me to father a child is usually the first thing anyone tries. After all, for thousands of years, that was the best way to harness another person's power."

"Does it work?"

Removing the cloth, he met my eyes and the smile that played upon his lips was unreadable. "Does *what* work?"

"You being a father?"

"I really couldn't say. I don't remember."

"But you remember the seduction attempts?" I sneered.

"I remember the one that struck me the deepest," he said slowly. "I remember the one that got me. It undid me, ruined me, and made me fall apart. I remember that one."

"What happened?" I asked quietly, very afraid of what he would say.

"I think it worked so well because it wasn't intended to be a seduction. A long time ago, a girl was a woman at fourteen. People died young. A woman of thirty could be a grandmother in those days, but this story didn't happen in those days. All those old customs had died and out of nowhere a man came to me and asked me to watch over his dying daughter," Christian's voice was slow and measured. "I refused, but he convinced me to visit her in the hospital once. Only once."

My heart thumped in a pattern like wild bunny feet racing everywhere. He was talking about me.

"When I saw you, limp in your hospital bed, I was reminded of something very old, something I had forgotten. History was unfolding before me afresh. To me, you were not a child. I remembered something—a tiny flash of something important and it was happening again. I had to promise to take care of you, but I couldn't figure out what I was supposed to remember fast enough. You were dying." He paused and rearranged the wet cloth between his fingers. "That last night in the hospital… I worked it out."

"What?" I breathed in heavy anticipation.

"Love, and it was a love I had not felt for a very long time."

I stared in wonder. "You love me?"

His eyes were like diamonds, full of points of light and shadow. "More than I have ever loved anything, and I would not call the love I have experienced little."

I moved to dive into his arms, but he held me at bay with a single hand on my collarbone. "I have never been brave enough to believe you could love me when I was always lying," he continued. "The situation you and I lived with was maddening. If romantic love has to be like you and me, it explains perfectly why I always chose to love something else."

"What?" I asked, my voice dry.

"I like the kind of love where you believe in something so strongly, you're willing to let every day pass while you work for it. This past hundred years—I know Dr. Hilliar showed you my picture from a hundred years ago. Those years—they were supposed to be my holiday. The reward I gave myself for exceptional vigilance."

"What did you do to earn a holiday that lasted a hundred years?"

He grinned and shook his head. "I can't remember. It was important. I was important. Not just for one person, but for all people. I can't remember. The only thing I know is that I couldn't work anymore."

I wondered what happened to him that he couldn't remember, but I refused to interrupt.

"And then that night, the one where I held you, I didn't want any more holiday. As a matter of fact, I didn't want anything but you. I wanted you so fiercely, I was willing to take you under any circumstances, even if it meant agreeing to the disagreeable post as your guardian. How could you have asked me to kiss you? It felt like I almost died kissing you."

"You can't die!" I exclaimed.

"Perhaps not, but I have never felt closer to real death than in those moments. My heart stopped almost like it was doing a demonstration of what it would be like to die, of exactly what it would be like for you to die."

He was close. He had never been closer to telling me the secret. What had he done to save my life? I waited, afraid to move, afraid to breathe.

He lazily leaned his head toward me. "It's one of those days when I feel like admitting how I have lived through loving you so much…" His voice petered off. Then he seemed to wake up again. "I think they gave me something."

"Like what?"

"Drugs."

"Like a truth serum?"

He rested his head on the arm of the couch. "Maybe. I felt a pinch when they brought me here. There were so many hands on me, pain coming from so many different directions, I didn't think one of them could have been a needle. Something isn't right. I've been talking. I never feel like talking."

I covered his mouth with my hand. I had been letting him talk because he was telling me all the things I wanted to hear, but now he had to stop. "Shhh… Christian. There are cameras and bugs in here. You have to keep your secrets"

I thought he understood, so I took my hand away from his mouth, but whatever they had given him, it was deep in his blood by then. He was mumbling, "I've never felt like this, Beth. Not even I remember the way back to my secrets. I leave. I cross the bridge and burn it. That's the only way I can keep going, is if I can't remember and I never will."

I got up. I had to find something to gag him with. I snatched up the housecoat they'd given me and pulled the belt free.

Christian was still talking. His sentences were breaking down. "I didn't like your father the first time I saw him. The dent in his cheek and the shape of his eyes belonged to his grandfather, but… he was nothing like him. Like something awful had taken possession of my friend's features. I didn't want to help Lance, but he knew my reputation for helping… and begged me."

I didn't listen to him. "You have to stop talking." I straddled him to get the belt across his face.

He was still talking. "Did I tell you these guys didn't cut my hand off?"

225

"What?" I asked, pausing in my work. I had assumed they had. He said his hand had been cut off by a spiteful man.

"No. I cut it off myself. It wasn't the first time. It's just that I can usually get it back immediately afterward. I've cut it off, put it in my back pocket and headed out only to sew it back on after I was free. Only that one time, when I rescued Brandon, I couldn't get it back. I lost it."

"Stop talking," I pleaded. I grabbed his head, covered his mouth, and tied the belt tightly. I got off him and sat next to him on the couch. He grabbed my hands and held them tight in his. The fabric across his lips turned dark with saliva. Slowly, his breathing settled.

His eyes went glassy and then closed. I didn't know what to do to keep him awake. I thought of slapping him, but his face was already purple in patches from his capture. His grip on my fingers slackened. He was fading. He was going to be unconscious in a moment if I didn't do something, but I didn't know what to do.

Suddenly, I decided to check his pulse. I reached for his wrist. He didn't feel me touch him. Impatiently, I ran my fingers up to the place I could find it. I didn't feel anything. How deep was it? I pressed harder, but felt nothing. Panicked, I gouged my fingertips under his chin to feel it. Again I felt nothing. Finally, I put my head against his chest and tried to feel it the way I had all those years ago in my hospital room.

I heard nothing.

I pulled back and stared at him in confusion. He was immortal. What did it mean if he had no heartbeat? His eyelashes fluttered and his chest still heaved slightly with his breath.

I placed my head on his chest a second time and heard nothing.

Then, it all came together. He said his heart stopped when we kissed that night. He must have got the idea that he could survive without his heart. I shuddered, but once I made the connection, I remembered more. I thought of those moments before I saw Brandon, headless and strapped to the bed. I had expected to see a complete person, and to be told he was missing organs. I expected the injury to be something that couldn't be proven in a way that would satisfy me. I would never have guessed that Christian was the one who was missing an organ. My mind flashed to another moment when Christian talked to me about Charles' little love and that some men loved so deeply they would allow their hearts to be cut out. I remembered myself in *his* arms being rocked back and forth as he promised me he wouldn't let me die.

My hand went to my chest and I felt the heart inside beat a rhythm it had beat so many times. I had thought it was ordinary.

That was the secret.

I looked at him, crumpled on the couch, and thought of that daredevil gleam he sometimes had in his eyes. Eyes that looked inside me, challenged me, and dared me to become something amazing. What was amazing? What was I?

He really was alive when he shouldn't have been.

Suddenly, his hand reached out with electrifying speed and he caught my wrist.

CHAPTER TWENTY FIVE

The Heartless Man

With strength, Christian pulled me to him and gazed penetratingly into my eyes, as if to discern if I had uncovered his secret. His gag was still in place, but one of his eyebrows was slightly lower than the other as he tried to gauge the damage.

I couldn't think of what to say to him.

He never held me. All those years, all through the closeness we had always shared, I was never once close enough to him to feel that his heartbeat was gone. I thought of what he said, that he couldn't love, that if I ever got really close to him, I wouldn't like it. He had to keep me at arm's length if he was going to keep the truth hidden from me. Because of what he had done, he couldn't even hold me, let alone love me.

"Do they know?" I whispered finally. "Do they know your secret?" I asked, looking meaningfully at the middle button of his shirt, because I could not return his gaze.

He nodded, barely moving his head. He groaned and he pulled his gag free from his mouth and let it fall in a soggy circle around his neck. "They pieced it together the last time they examined m-me," he stuttered. "I can't. I can't undo it," he said and the look in his eyes terrified me. This was Christian's worst nightmare. He had suddenly become helpless and didn't know how to meet me.

I knit my eyebrows together, getting courageous. "I don't understand. You saved me. I owe you everything. Why are you so afraid of what I'll think and how I'll act?"

"Beth, I feel sick. How could a little needle have left me unguarded enough that I spilled my secret to you so easily? I never wanted you to know what I had done. You were meant to lead an ordinary life."

"You mean, I was meant to die at age fourteen," I said.

"No. You were meant to live a life where your lover/boyfriend/husband/partner was not me."

"Without you, I'd be dead," I corrected sternly.

228

"Perhaps, but when you woke up healed, didn't you feel that you suddenly adored me?" he suggested, like the answer would be as distasteful as a plate of worms.

"No," I said impatiently. "It wasn't sudden. I adored you before the surgery. A heart is not actually the home of all our emotions. Why would you think my feelings changed after the surgery?"

His left hand went to his chest. "Because of what I felt."

I exclaimed my surprise in a gasp. He didn't have an empty place in his chest where a heart should have been. He had exchanged hearts with me! He had my shriveled broken heart in his chest and it wasn't beating.

"Did it ever beat for you?"

"It did, and when it did, I was happier than I can remember. I was in love and it was a love I never expected to feel. Just looking at you, I knew that what I had done changed everything."

I gave him a shadow of a smile. "You never said anything."

"How could I say anything? You were fourteen. Even though it has been completely acceptable to fall in love with a fourteen-year-old for most of human history, it isn't now. How could I confess to loving you?"

"I would have felt less lonely," I argued dully.

"I had to make it clear to anyone who saw us that there was no romance between us. The whole world had to know that your guardian, Christian Henderson, was without fault. It didn't work well. The older you got, it didn't matter how appropriately I behaved, people believed the worst of me constantly. It was almost like it was true when I couldn't let it be. I had my own troubles..." he said rubbing his chest where my heart was. "This heart has not worked well."

"Of course it wouldn't," I said numbly.

"It beat on and off for several years, but it eventually stopped altogether. I remember the last time it beat. It was that last day in Scotland when I sent you away and the car you were in went out of view. It stopped and then the pain came. After all these years, it hurts more than ever."

My eyebrows flew upwards. "That was the last time it beat? When I left?"

He nodded.

I looked at him and tried to put the pieces together in my mind. I thought of Brandon and how he had lived when he was headless. I remembered the tubes in his neck that kept air flowing to his lungs and what was happening in his body when he had no brain connected to send commands. He wasn't connected to the system and he could still transmit instructions. Was that what was happening now? I had Christian's heart in my body and it beat because he told it to?

Then I wondered if the individual cells in their immortal bodies could respond to other commands, other than muscles and tendons. Could Christian order his blood cells to receive the oxygen he brought into his lungs? Ask those same blood cells to circulate throughout the body, not under the control of the heart pumping them, but under their own control? There would be no heartbeat, but there would be red and blue blood moving along the veins and arteries, moving oxygen and forcing life, because each one of those cells did as they were commanded?

It was only a theory, one I didn't feel comfortable running by him at the moment in which we found ourselves, but I felt the truth burn in my heart. He was alive when he shouldn't be because he was better at organizing his own cells.

"Beth," he breathed, allowing the slightest sound to escape from his lips. "Have you figured out why you're here?"

I stared at him, uncomprehending, for a moment. I was locked in a room, no one was interviewing me, and when they had talked to me in the conference room they gave me Christian's history and decided they didn't need to talk to me anymore. I just had to be locked up.

"I'm scared to talk because they're listening," I muttered angrily.

"Whisper, Bethie. Whisper in my ear," he said, finally drawing his body closer so we could talk.

For the first time since he took charge of me, he drew me as close to him as I could go and with our arms wrapped around each other tightly, we put our heads together and began to quietly conspire like the closest of allies.

"Are they doing the first experiment where they see how long it takes for me to heal? Except they didn't have to cut me because I was already cut?" I asked.

230

Christian nodded.

"They think I'm immortal because you gave me your heart?"

He clenched his jaw and nodded again.

"Do you think I am?" I asked.

Sliding his fingers in my hair, he tilted my head and spoke gently into my ear. "I haven't been certain. Brandon says you are. He's been saying you are since Scotland, but Beth, if you are like us, it isn't a good thing."

"Because of all the running?"

"Yes, because of all the running, all the torture and all the hangups that go along with how I have to live. I recognize I may be guilty of glamorizing a normal life, but this kind of life is undoubtedly more dangerous. Everywhere you go is a figurative minefield. Brandon says that not everyone who receives an organ transplant from an immortal donor becomes immortal themselves. I hoped you wouldn't be one of them."

I listened. When he was finished, I whispered to him. "What does it mean for us if I am or if I'm not."

"If you aren't, I can't be with you. I'll only bring harm upon you, in the form of people like Dr. Hilliar who can't let the question of why I can't die rest. Even if we kill each and every one of these people, there will be others."

"And if I am?" I asked gravely.

"Then I did my best to give you a taste of the normal life before you had no choice but to join me in this... thing I do."

The corners of my eyes crinkled with amusement at how he managed to diminish a gift most people would consider to be priceless. "What will that be like? Will you finally give me what I want?"

He chuckled. "I shudder to think of all the girlish fantasies you've concocted regarding me. I'm more normal than you make me out to be. You're bound to be disappointed when you discover I'm pretty much like any other man, except for my face and the perpetual pain in my heart."

"Can't we do anything about that?"

"You could give me my heart back. My chest would feel much better." He gave me a sideways glance to make sure I knew that what he was suggesting was a joke he found rather tasteless.

"So, if I am immortal, we'll finally be able to love each other? You won't be off-limits anymore?"

His breathing became staggered. "Darling, it has been hard enough for me to keep my hands to myself. You can have me, but I promise you, it will come at a grave price. Being with me can only end in misery and that's true whether we finish this day in this locked room or if we don't. Immortality is irrevocably joined with misfortune."

"Because my heart won't beat for you?"

He muttered his next words under his breath, "Yes, but also because I have lived too long. I don't know how long I've worked, how many wives I've had, how many children I've fathered, or how many different lives I've led. A body like mine is perfect. The only way I could forget would be if I…"

"Damaged your brain on purpose?" I suggested, thinking of how empty headed he generally was in regards to his past.

He nodded. "Living forever means seeing a million things you wish you hadn't. Their cut test is a legitimate way to test the truth. If we stay here longer than a day, their questions about you will be answered."

I shook my head. "I don't want them to find out. How can we get out of here?"

"They know me. They know what I can do, which is why I'm not bound hand and foot. It wouldn't surprise me if we started reefing on the walls, we'd find a steel cage on the other side of the drywall. I've escaped many different rooms, broken many locks, shattered windows, jumped from high places, and they would have prepared for the things I've done in the past. I'm gonna be honest, I'm not sure what's left to try."

He pulled me closer to him, but after touching my back, his face suddenly fell. He rubbed fresh blood between his fingers and thumb. "You're bleeding. Didn't Dr. Hilliar stitch you up properly?"

"The excitement of last night and this morning have torn it open," I admitted, before explaining what happened.

232

"Let me see." He got off the floor and led me to the bed like Prince Charming leading his princess onto the dance floor. He helped me down on the mattress, face down, and with my permission, he lifted my shirt to see my wound.

He gasped. "You're not healing. You've torn out quite a few of your stitches. You are going to need more bandages. You shouldn't have been moving. Clearly, I should have accompanied you out last night instead of merely pointing you in the right direction."

"It's okay. Brandon got your finger and his tongue before he escaped and I was recaptured."

"Of course." Christian procured some clean pillowcases from the closet and cleaned my wound with what oddities he could find in the bathroom. "Way to kill the mood," he joked.

"You seem like you're all better from the drugs they gave you. Even the bruises on your face look better," I countered.

"Yeah, all better," he said, stroking the side of my face with his four-fingered hand. "Do you want a clean shirt?"

"I'm not changing my shirt. I'm going to roll around on the carpet in a second, and then I'm going to let my blood pool up and I'm going to write, 'help me' in blood all over the walls. If I stop bleeding, I'll cut myself and keep going."

"What exactly do you think that will do?" he asked, perplexed.

"When you tried everything, did you try this?"

He shook his head in the negative.

"I am a hostage, not a guest. I'm not going to sit nicely and watch TV like I was fine with being here. I want whoever looks in this room to think that the people who kept me here were monsters. I already started a hunger strike and I haven't had a bite to eat or a sip of water to drink since they brought me here. Now, let's make a mess. How's my blood, is there a lot of it?" I didn't dare think of what a lot of blood might mean for our future.

He lifted the pillowcase bandage. "You're bleeding afresh."

"Great," I said wetting the tip of my finger and starting to write the letter h on the wall.

Then suddenly a voice came on a loudspeaker I hadn't known was there, but then, all microphones were also speakers. "Bethany," my father's voice said. "Stop that. We aren't torturing you."

"Yes, you are!" I exclaimed. "I have asked repeatedly to be released and you have kept me here against my will. I have been brought here with a gun to my head thrice. Let us go."

"Christian was caught trespassing and thieving!" my father retorted.

"Then turn him over to the police," I snapped. I turned back to the sound and finished my h.

"Bethany," he said, not knowing that hearing my name pronounced that way made me hate whoever was speaking. "We want to measure how fast you heal. That's all we want. If you would please stop hurting yourself deliberately, we could be done a lot quicker."

"Shut up!" I snapped.

"I think we should check the news," Christian suddenly said slowly, picking up the remote control.

"The news?" both my father and I questioned at the same time in the same tone. I flinched angrily. I hated having anything in common with him.

"Yeah. Felicity-Ann should be missing you. I told her if you went missing for more than two days, she needed to report it, and she should report Charles Lewis as the culprit. I wouldn't be surprised if the Edmonton police are looking for you.

The speaker went dead as my father and his goons went to see if such a thing had happened under their noses. I glanced at Christian, still pacing. He hadn't turned on the TV.

"Did you know this would happen?"

"I've been in a lot of these scrapes. A Google search will be faster than channel surfing, so they'll know whether it happened or not in minutes. Just to warn you though, it might be hours before your father and Dr. Hilliar come back with an answer. They'll disagree and talk amongst themselves to figure out the best thing to do."

"Then there's plenty of time to make a mess." I shook my head and continued to write in blood.

"Are you just doing that to annoy them?"

"It obviously does annoy them, otherwise my father wouldn't have spoken to us at all," I fumed.

"Your back is bleeding alarmingly, and most of it is soaking into your shirt, so you're not using it for your mural."

I growled and rolled my shirt up, so my midriff was bare.

"Doesn't it hurt?"

It didn't, but I didn't like to say anything about it not hurting. That seemed abnormal, which was exactly what these psychos were trying to learn about me. I also didn't feel hungry or thirsty and I really should have been both after everything that had happened. Instead, I felt energetic, but wasn't that wrong? I pulled my finger away from the wall and pretended to feel sapped of my strength. It was an act for them.

"Are you all right?" Christian moved to catch me if such a thing was needed.

"I need to lie down," I muttered. Whatever the truth was, I had to hide it from them.

Five minutes later the door swung open with my father on the other side. He flicked the switch on his armrest and wheeled in the room with a sour look on his face.

CHAPTER TWENTY SIX

The Red Forest

"Bethany," my father began. "Let's get the story straight. You are not a hostage here and you never were."

"Gunpoint!" I exclaimed weakly. "I was brought here at gunpoint." I lifted three fingers to enhance my point. "Three times!"

"You were rescued from a madman who kidnapped you," he corrected with a stern voice.

"That's not the story I'll tell," I said in a sing-song whine. "I'll tell the police and anyone else that you were the one to kidnap me." Suddenly, my teeth were chattering. I grasped at a blanket and tried to cover my shivering frame.

"She's going into shock," Christian muttered. "She needs to go to a real hospital."

"Look," my father said, wheeling closer to me. "I need you to prove that my theories about immortality are correct. You have this man's heart inside you and it has made you immortal. There is a lot of money riding on this and some extremely hostile people waiting for the answer."

I wanted to reply, but the chattering of my teeth was overriding my ability to talk or listen or reason with whatever he was saying. Instead, I closed my eyes and felt the blanket around me. I had to get a grip on myself. At the very moment I decided I had to get a grip, I did. My teeth stopped chattering, and my body did what I told it to do, instead of what it did naturally.

"It's not that we want to live forever. It's because of things this man," he said pointing at Christian, "has done during warfare. With his unique ability, he has been a perfect message system since he simply cannot be persuaded to give up information, or die. He has probably done it for centuries. He's a hero, but why should he have to shoulder the burden by himself? If we could learn what's special about him, what stops him from dying, from being bothered by torture, he could pass his diplomacy baton on to the next generation of immortals, and he would be free."

"Free?" I muttered.

"Yes," he said, smiling. Even I thought it was a rather convincing smile. "Free. He would be free to travel, to be with you, to live without always having to look over his shoulder. Others would take over for him."

I looked him straight in the eye. "I want to be free, too. Send me home."

"You're not looking at the bigger picture. Can't you see how exciting all this is? How exciting it could be for you? You would be the first!"

"Look, I never had a heart transplant. I had surgery and it saved me," I lied, not caring how outrageous it sounded to my father, who already knew differently. "You see, Christian wasn't afraid to bring out the big bucks to pay for special treatment, which was something you could never do. It was shocking when you died and had so little money to leave your daughter." I glanced at Christian. "Wait a minute! He died," I said, pointing at my father. "But he's not dead! How do we know you're not immortal, dad?"

He grumbled and shook his head. "I'm an old man in a wheelchair."

"You could just be pretending," I said with a smug smile.

"I'm not immortal. Bethany," he said, pulling something from his pocket and ignoring the nonsense I had spouted. "Have you seen my tombstone?"

"Yes."

"Then you know it's been blank because there was never a death certificate for me. I had a closed casket funeral and they buried an empty box. Just this last week, someone did this." He showed me a photograph of his tombstone. It now had a death date, and unless I was completely confused, that day was today. "If you don't cooperate, they'll kill me. The men I'm working for; they're dangerous."

I never felt sorry for people who asked me to. I found pleas for pity pathetic, even when I wanted pity for myself. "Yeah," I said, examining the work. "They hired an actual engraver. Only cold-blooded killers do that."

Christian laughed, but dad kept talking like I hadn't said anything. "I owed them a lot of money before I faked my death, but now I owe them much more."

"And I'm supposed to protect you from the consequences of what you did? Perhaps you could explain why."

"They were the ones who told me about *him*," he said, indicating Christian and sticking to his original story. "They told me if I moved you to Edmonton and used my grandfather as an excuse to make friends with him, he would save your life and he did. Surely, knowing that will help you to understand that they are people with incredible resources. It's not for nothing that I've worked for them all these years."

His argument was conflicting. Either the people he worked for were good people, who would not kill a crippled man, or they were monsters who didn't deserve to know whether I was immortal or not. He might have been able to find a way to convince me if he had not mentioned 'all these years'. I thought of the bugs and cameras I had found in my room and the hungry way Charles looked at me. I remembered the fake army guys, their automatic weapons and how I had once expected my whole life to twirl by me without ever having a gun pointed at my nose.

I sighed. "You're wrong about me. I'm not immortal. If I were immortal I would not be this terrified of dying, which will surely happen to me if I stay here with you. You're worried about your own life. Your greed will kill us both. They'll kill you and keep me around to 'test' on, and when I turn out to be as fragile as you, they'll kill me too. If you want me to live, you're going to have to help me leave. Right now." This was the last appeal I could make. He had to have some desire for my safety. I was his child!

My father took the news the same way I had and his fingers started to tremble like he too was in shock. He had a blanket on his lap and legs. It was brown and black plaid and he hid his shaking hands under the blanket.

"You have no idea how committed I have been to this project," my father said in a small voice. "I've given everything I had over and over again to see this through to the end." I heard the sound of something crack under the blanket and I thought he was cracking his knuckles as a nervous habit.

Christian knew better and dove to stop what was about to happen. I didn't see it. I didn't know what was happening until it was too late. Christian knew that the sound was the sound of a hammer being pulled on a gun. My father didn't take the gun out from under his blanket because he needed those precious seconds so he could pull the trigger before Christian stopped him. Christian didn't make it in time and the gun fired. The bullet hit me in the middle of my forehead and the bullet lodged itself in my brain.

***

I had never had something in my brain before. To put it mildly, it really messed me up. I couldn't see or hear. It was like I was thrown into the place that exists only when you're bored. It's sunny outside, you close your eyes, and still try to look out as if you could see something through your eyelids. The world there is dark, but there are shapes, blood vessels like the limbs of a tree, stretching just out of your reach. It's a place you can sort of see, if you use your imagination, but it isn't a place you can go, unless you get shot in the head.

I suddenly felt that I was there, in that place. The sky was brown and the trees were leafless and red barked. I was there, walking in a black dress.

In my dreams before, I had always worn a white dress, like a little girl going to sleep. I don't mean it when I say 'sleep'. I'm referring to the drug-induced sleep of a girl who is about to be cut open on an operating room table. I wore a white hospital gown that did up in the back, but when I imagined the dress, it was something you slid over your head, something with a lot of skirt you would have to pick up if you were to run. Something you wore when you wanted to feel the sun on your shoulders.

But now, the dress was black, and it was exactly the same dress. It had been white when my body was repaired under a thousand tiny concentrated lights. Now it was the black of a woman who repairs herself in the dark of a starless night.

I was not dead.

I could still feel the heart Christian had given me and it was beating strong, undisturbed by what was happening in my head.

I tried to see the forest around me as it seemed like the only clue for curing myself as I felt cut off from most of my senses, except my heart. Red vines hung all around me and everything was dark, but aligned correctly, growing the way it was intended until I came to the problem. It was like a torpedo crashed through a forest at high speeds and the limbs of the scarlet trees had broken when they collided. The shell was enormous and some part of me knew that it was the bullet inside my mind, but I didn't know how to remove it. It was huge, like a helicopter.

I rubbed my hands against the dark fabric of my dress and reminded myself that I was not there the way it appeared. My body was showing me the problem in a way I could understand so I could fix it. What part of me was seeing this if my brain had a bullet in it? If it wasn't my brain, then I could repair even that. It was a part of me that lived, perhaps my spirit that saw the damage, and if I could instruct my cells to repair themselves, perhaps I would again be able to open my eyes.

There was no muscle in my mind to push the bullet out. Maybe I didn't need muscle, tendon or bone. Christian didn't need those things to keep his blood flowing. He commanded the cells to move and they moved.

I wondered whether or not I ought to try anything. Maybe it was better if I pretended to be dead. I didn't feel that death was close. The black of the dress didn't mean I was dead. It just signified how much I had changed.

In the end, I decided against it. Even if I wanted to lay still and pretend to be dead, my heart was still beating. Any idiot who could take a pulse would know the truth.

I had to learn to take control of my body.

I put out a hand to touch the length of the tree beside me. It felt nothing like a tree, but instead slick, warm, and pulsing. Then I saw the bugs. They were not insects, but spheres with tiny white wings. They were not blood. What was I looking at? They were everywhere, and they were suddenly coming in huge quantities, like a plague of Egypt. What were they? They weren't winged creatures any more than the trees were trees. I put my hands out and caught one. I caught a cube floating in a liquid droplet, with wings. It was a square crystal. It was salt water and it was flooding the area. The brain was a sterile place. It made sense there was something like saline there.

Then suddenly, there were other bugs. These were red with longer wings. These had to be individual blood cells I was spilling.

I needed to try something. I was now up to my knees in white and red bugs that were starting to seem more like streams of slugs.

I suddenly understood that I could still die. If I refused to take charge of the situation and fix the problem, then I could go braindead and die. I had to act.

I felt a tree quiver when I touched it. I touched one of the trees partly crushed by the bullet. It tried to bend, but its branches were pinned. I turned and placed my hands on an unbent tree and said, "Move."

It moved.

Everything around it moved.

I moved.

And suddenly, I knew for certain that my body could move absolutely any way I wanted it to. I could get the trees to push the bullet back out where it came from. I could repair what was damaged and make myself whole.

My father shot me because he was desperate and he was gambling on the idea that I was immortal. I had to take the chance that I would be better off with my nervous system repaired, but if I pushed the bullet out, it would roll down my face. Everyone would see it. They might even be recording it. That would remove all doubt. What if I could get the bullet to fall a different way? What if it fell down through my sinuses and the roof on my mouth so it landed on my tongue?

Could I do such a thing?

As a way of focusing my thoughts, I told my body, "Make it fall. Make it fall."

All at once, I knew I was disturbing my brain far more by what I was ordering it to do than the bullet had done. This was more invasive, but I heard little voices and connections in my body telling me I could let the bullet fall into the back of my throat and either cough it out or force it down my esophagus.

I chose the esophagus and felt the world around me tremor as the bullet sunk into the forest floor until it was out of sight. My whole body in the real world must have trembled with the force of it, but that was probably not important. The important part was that the people there must not know that the bullet had changed locations. I was surprised at how many of the winged insects disappeared with the bullet. Blood and saline were dripping from my nose and aiding the bullet on its journey downwards.

When the ground replaced itself, I walked around the forest touching the wounded parts and healing them with only my touch. It wasn't really my touch. It was my focus on each, individual part. I thought about Brandon putting his tongue in his mouth and insisting that he would know if it was his tongue. I understood the feeling now. Your body would follow your commands, each bit would do exactly what you asked it to do, even if it wasn't in that part's nature to do what you asked. His tongue was probably half-way knit back together before he disappeared and left me there.

With those thoughts, I finished healing my head and thought about the stitches in my back. With a bat of my virtual eyelashes, I was there in my black dress examining the four hundred stitches from a vantage point of inside my body. Each one was enormous, like a suspension bridge overhead with each of those bits of thread appearing like ironworks.

The blood here was the blood I had used as paint. I had done some of this damage by commanding myself to bleed more on purpose. Now I needed to stop the blood, seal the breaches and heal the whole area. The trees were here too, and I knew how they worked, but I didn't feel like that was what I needed. I needed the ground to rise to meet those stitches. Only when the floor and the ceiling of this space met would I not need those stitches anymore.

I considered how I ought to touch the floor to make it obey my command and decided to get down and rest my whole body flat against it with my view pointed upwards. I got down and put my head back, extended my arms slightly, palms up and called out, "Seal this up!"

To my great surprise, the floor didn't move. The walls did. The opposite walls rushed to each other and as they did, the stitches snapped one by one. It was like being in the middle of a horrific disaster, like the Red Sea coming down on the Egyptian army after Moses parted it. There were over four hundred of them, and each one of them broke with a satisfying snap.

I watched the remainder of my stitches snap. It was over quickly, like fireworks. Fireworks that stopped blood.

I got to my feet and felt a surge of triumph lift me. It didn't matter what world I met when I opened my eyes. The gift Christian gave me was the greatest gift anyone had ever given. He had cut off his own hand without fear, and I wondered how far his gift extended.

Perhaps it didn't have an end.

CHAPTER TWENTY SEVEN

Spitting up a Bullet

Back in the real world, there were only distant voices at first. Military men barking orders far away. I was in a wheelchair and being pushed with haste. A sheet covered my face and I reminded myself to make my breath shallow. Whatever was going on, I felt strongly that it was in my best interest to go along with it and to stay still. Opening my eyes, I could see the outline of the windows in the front entrance.

Suddenly, the chair stopped. I saw the outline of two men approaching. Then I heard Charles' voice. "The army guys are coming," he said. "There's nowhere to run, Christian."

"Except, I'm going out the front door, because it doesn't matter if you shoot me, but it's going to matter a lot if I shoot you. Get out of the way."

Through the cloth, I saw the receptionist step out of the way, but Charles paused, hesitating.

"Whatever," Christian said emotionlessly before he shot Charles.

The receptionist moved to shoot Christian, but Christian shot him too. I didn't twitch and I didn't make a sound. Neither of them was dead, as they wriggled on the floor. Christian moved from behind me and kicked their guns out of their reach before bending to take a set of keys from Charles. Once they were in hand, he returned to the wheelchair and wheeled me out of the building.

Outside, he pressed the unlock button on the keychain to point out which vehicle he could take. He wheeled me across the gravel and just like I was that little girl in the hospital bed, he lifted me and placed me in the backseat. He didn't check my pulse or make sure I was okay. He simply set me inside and got in the driver's seat.

I pulled the sheet off my face. There was blood on my face, seeping from my wound and my nose. "How did those guys keep you captive before?" I chirped. "They seem like pushovers."

Christian jumped. He turned back and saw me lying on the backseat. I saw at a glance how messed up he was. He was sweating and red in

244

the face. I had never once seen Christian sweat before. He was trying to hold it back, but he was crying. I realized that when he wheeled me out of the building, he didn't know if I was okay. His heart still beat inside my chest, but it probably would have continued to beat even if I were dead. Men only cried in my world when someone was dead.

"I'm okay," I whispered. "The bullet is lodged in my esophagus."

He reached out to touch the blood on my face. The blood from my forehead parted on my nose bridge into two streams and the blood from my nose clotted in a blotch on my upper lip. "You're beautiful," he said, getting emotional. "So very beautiful."

Just as Brandon foresaw, there was blood on my face, and Christian was finally mine. I reached out to touch him.

Movement out the back window caught his attention. I sat up and peeked over the seat. Army men were beginning to spill out the front doors, but none of them were firing at us. One stood in the forefront talking on a walkie talkie. His hand signal ordered the men to stand down, but why?

"Can you spit it out?" Christian asked me, starting the SUV and moving it onto the road.

To my surprise, I could spit it out and immediately did so. "Here it is," I said pushing my palm between the two front seats and showing it to him.

He wiped his forehead and held his hand to his mouth as he got a grip on himself. "Good girl," he praised as he merged onto the highway and picked up speed.

I pushed myself between the seats and sat next to him. "Why do you think they let us go?" I asked, trying to close the window in the passenger seat, only to realize that the window didn't close, because Brandon had shot out the window a few hours earlier.

Christian flipped his hand like it wasn't important. "Because they were mercenaries and I already killed the man who was paying them."

"You killed Dr. Hilliar?"

"Yes, and your father," he said, staring with dead eyes onto the road in front of us. "That's the gun," he said, pointing to the pistol propped barrel-down in the cupholder between us. "That's the gun he shot you with."

I looked at it, but did not touch it. I did not feel like crying or mourning. A man who was willing to play chicken by shooting his own daughter in the head was not a man I would claim as my father. He had been hopelessly poisoned by greed and I felt relief wash over me that the problem was buried.

"It's a wonder you didn't get gun-happy when they cut Brandon's head off," I said.

"That is to be avoided... as often as possible. Easier to do when I haven't had time to calm myself and talk myself into rationality. Undoubtedly, I've killed people before. I don't remember doing it, but my hands do and my reflexes do. And you..." he said, turning to look at me. "You're alive. It's a miracle and a catastrophe."

"Aren't you a little bit pleased?" I asked hopefully.

"I am," he said, glancing at me with a dangerous glint in his eyes. "But first things first. We need to get rid of this car. I have a Nissan Micra we can pick up."

"Is it far?"

"Other side of Edmonton. We'll ditch this and get a cab once we're in the city."

"Where can we go?" I whispered, unsure about the future. "What will we do?"

"It's going to be okay, Beth," he said, putting his hand on mine.

I glanced around, not knowing where to look. "I can't tell Felicity-Ann that I'm okay before we go on the run, can I?"

"You must. One of the problems with being us is that if we disappear without a trace, that gets noticed and people get curious. You can call her when we stop."

I groaned. "What should I tell her? Not the truth!"

"It doesn't matter what you tell her as long as she knows you aren't coming back and that you're safe."

"What would you tell her?"

He pulled a face. "Something definitive. Something you will not want to tell her. I'd tell her that you've been sleeping with Rogan and you just found out you're pregnant. Tell her you're sick with the pregnancy and even though you and Rogan are not a couple, and never have been, you're going to stay with his mother for the time being because you have no parents and she's going to help you raise the baby."

"Where is the real Rogan Cormack?' I suddenly asked.

"Half the year, he works the oil fields and the other half, he travels. To my knowledge, he's gotten two women pregnant, so we won't be smearing his name."

"He sounds awful. Why did you decide to be him?"

"Because he's handsome and whatever I did, I wasn't going to ruin his life. In a few months, you can email Felicity and tell her you had a miscarriage and decided to move back to Toronto. Rogan's mother lives in Winnipeg, so you don't need to worry about Felicity-Ann coming to find you."

"What about Trinity? Don't you think she'll come looking for me?"

"It would be sweet if she did, but she won't. She already moved on with her life. That's the way this works, and one of the reasons why it will be painful to live forever. Everything here is temporary, except us."

"But I'll be able to watch out for her children in the future and be a guardian for them, won't I?"

Christian let his breath out slowly. "That was what I thought. Your great-grandfather, Forrester, was one of my best friends. I just shot his grandson in the head, threw his dead body thoughtlessly on the floor, and stole his wheelchair."

That did sound bad, spoken on its own that way. I bit my lips together and refused to speak for a bit.

Finally, he said quietly, "Do you want to get married before we go to bed tonight?"

"Can we?"

He nodded. "It won't be fancy like Trinity's wedding."

I snorted. Trinity's wedding had not been fancy and I said as much.

"Yes, but weddings that take place quickly mean that we'll be rushed and it will be the furthest thing from romantic. I'll get you out of those blood-soaked rags, but nothing about our wedding will be the wedding of your dreams. Unless you're like me and believe in wedding vows completely, that we'll be each other's through everything, and then it will be everything we need."

"That's what I want."

He looked at me with his gray-green eyes, and I felt he would have stopped the car and kissed me, fell on his knee to propose to me properly, but we were on the run and there wasn't time. His eyes promised that there would be time. Later that night, after we had checked all the boxes, by abandoning the SUV, calling Felicity-Ann, getting a car that would be safe to drive, getting to the courthouse to get married and eventually stopping for the night.

He let go of the steering wheel with his right hand and reached for me. My hand touched his fingers and I held them the rest of the way to Edmonton.

***

Christian stopped the SUV in front of an office building with boarded windows. He let go of my hand and cut the ignition. Leaving the keys in, he got out and came around to meet me at my door.

Carefully, he used the sleeve of his shirt to wipe the blood from my face. He didn't do a good job, but I saw that I looked less alarming in the side view mirror.

"You know," he said, taking me in his arms in a way that was completely different from how he had touched me at any other time. "My selfish side is really going to enjoy this." He bent his head low and I felt the angle of his arm enclose me.

The kiss he gave me was not like our other kisses had been, shrouded in the other faces he wore. He was not Christian Henderson, not pretending to be Charles Lewis or Rogan Cormack. He was himself, and he was letting the guard he had kept up all those years slip. He kissed me softly like I was the dearest thing he had ever known. It was that feeling that made him give his heart to me.

I felt the secrets between us vanish like smoke.

Then, he seemed to have a thought. I felt his hands under my shirt as he quit kissing me and turned me around. He pulled my shirt up and bent to look at my back. His fingertips were on the place that had been cut.

"You've done well healing it this fast. There's still a scar," he murmured. "It will fade faster if you concentrate on healing it."

"Do I have to go to the Red Forest to do that?"

He shrugged. "The Red Forest? Just wish the mark would disappear. I'm sure it worked that way when your surgery scars disappeared." He tugged on my collar and looked down the front of my shirt.

Instinctively, I pushed his hand away and he let the fabric fall back into place.

"See? That's all gone," he said with a grin. "And you're going to need to get used to that."

I sighed, wished I hadn't gotten so defensive with him taking a peek at my chest, and unconsciously touched my forehead. There was a scar there too, but the wound had closed. I supposed it would go away too. "Is it noticeable?"

He nodded. "I can cut you some bangs before the wedding. It's probably faster than teaching you how to change your face."

He slid his arms around me and pointed me down the sidewalk. He told me he was taking me to a coffee shop and dipped to kiss the side of my face. All the time we walked, he stopped and kissed me at every interval he could. Briefly, he slid his fingers into my hair, under my clothes, and massaged my shoulders as we walked. He took my fingers in his and kissed each one of them like he'd wanted to do it for ages and had only now allowed himself the pleasure.

At the coffee shop, he bought us sandwiches and ducked out again to buy a cell phone from the store next door. I had no idea he knew Edmonton so well that he could find everything he needed within walking distance once he dropped off the vehicle. When he returned, he had a phone.

"I'm going to call for a taxi with this. There's a phone in the corner you can use to call Felicity-Ann, so it won't show our new number on her caller ID. I'll give you five minutes to explain, then you've got to say goodbye."

"And I can explain any way I want to?" I asked hesitantly as I moved over to the phone.

"As long as you don't tell her anything that might make her curious about where you've gone." As he said those words, one of his hands brushed his forehead, while the other snaked around his torso to rub his back.

I knew what he was saying. I was different now and I couldn't say goodbye in person. I dragged my feet the rest of the way to the phone. I picked up the receiver and paused because I didn't know her number.

Christian was by my side in a moment. His hand was over mine on the number pad as he carefully entered in the ten digits. He knew the number.

The phone rang and rang. No one answered. The beep came and I said my piece, "Hi, Felicity-Ann, it's Beth. I know you're really worried about me. I'm okay, but I can't come home. There's been a family emergency and I can't explain. Sell my stuff and keep the money. You were a great roommate."

Christian leaned in and said in Rogan's voice, "Congratulate her and Gibson for me."

"What?"

"They're a couple. Didn't she tell you?"

I turned back to the receiver and said something I never thought I'd say. "Way to keep a secret, Felix! Gibson's a great guy. Please tell him I won't be back to work. Thanks for everything," I said, before I leaned in and whispered. "I want you to pass something onto Trinity for me. Tell her that Christian needs me and I had to go. Tell her I'm well, that I love her, and that I… I hope she has a perfect life with Brighton."

It took all my strength to replace the receiver because as I did so, I gave up Trinity, Felicity-Ann, Gibson, everything that I had, everything I'd been working for and, actually I said goodbye to the version of myself that I had been.

Christian was all angles when I turned back to him. He was hovering over me with his elbow leaning against a wall and his hand gripping the back of his neck. His other hand was free and he reached for me, catching me, because I was about to fall.

"I don't think I said everything I needed to," I whispered into his chest.

He stroked my hair. "You weren't going to be able to say everything. You're just going to have to trust that Trinity knows you and loves you well enough that she can say whatever needs to be said to assuage Felicity-Ann's feelings. I, for one, think she'll do well."

And then I cried.

***

Christian had the taxi stop a block away from the house where the car was parked.

"Where are the keys?" I asked as we padded down the sidewalk. We were in a rather ritzy area. It was not gated, but each of the houses spoke of wealth and taste. It seemed a million miles from where we had been earlier that day at the compound.

"They're in the shed. I used to rent a suite in the attic here as Rogan before I got the apartment down the hall from you. We need to hurry if we're going to make it to the mall and the courthouse before they close."

"We're going to a mall?" I gasped.

"We both look like crap. I look ex-military and you look..." he hesitated.

There was rust-colored blood all over the back of my shirt. I wasn't even wearing a coat. No one had paid much attention to the bloodstains on my clothes at the coffee shop. It had been dimly lit and people up north often looked rough. Not that rough, but no one had been looking very closely. I should have been wearing a coat to cover my back.

"Like you just murdered me?" I supplied.

"Sure," he said, looking around the hedge. "I know the people here. I've been paying them to let me park the car, but I'd like it if they didn't see you. They're likely to be more curious about who I'm with than any of the people we've seen. Stay here."

"Can I watch you change into Rogan?" I blurted, looking into his face expectantly.

"I'd prefer it if you didn't. I'll change it on my way up the drive. Just wait here. I'll only be a second."

He had been touching me the whole time, kissing me in the backseat of the cab like the driver wasn't there. I'd been kissing him, letting my fingers dance on the back of his neck, and pinching myself to make sure it wasn't a dream.

As he stepped out of sight, I was breathless and overwhelmed. Even though it was still summer, I felt a chill when he stepped away from me

251

and took his body heat with him. As he rounded the corner, I felt cold. Maybe even afraid. I told myself it was normal. It had been a big day, being betrayed by my only living relative, the shock my body had received when I'd been shot. I started to wonder if there were scars inside my head where the bullet had traveled, the way there were scars on my skin.

I stood there, holding my arms tightly across my chest and waited. He was taking too long. I started counting to gauge the time. I counted to a hundred six times and realized the counting wasn't working. I could count several numbers in one second. My panic was rising. Why wasn't he back? If I hadn't been bloodstained, I would have gone up to the house to see what was keeping him.

Instead, a police cruiser quietly drove up beside me and stopped. I hadn't even noticed it before it was too late to hide.

"Beth Coldwell?" the driver said as he got out of the car.

I didn't know what to do. Should I run? Should I talk to them? What? I just stared, until both officers had got out of the cruiser and approached me. "What's the problem?" I asked.

"Has there been an incident?" he asked, looking at my clothes.

"Nothing," I said, knowing it sounded ridiculous and cursing myself for not being able to think of anything better to say.

"Are you aware that every officer in the city has been looking for you for two days?" the other one asked.

"I wonder why," I said blankly.

The first one spoke again. "We're going to need to bring you to the station with us."

"No, you don't. I'm fine. Just tell whoever's interested that I'm fine. You saw me. Everything is cool."

"What are you doing here?" the second officer said, getting out a notepad and scratching off a few notes.

"Excuse me. Are you here to get me? You weren't patrolling?" I asked.

"A lady across the street saw you and made the call. A girl splattered in blood loitering might make some people nervous."

"Well, she needn't have worried and needn't have bothered you. I'm fine. I'm just waiting."

"For what?"

The other cop glanced at his partner. "It doesn't matter. Take her."

The second officer put his notepad back in his pocket and to my ultimate surprise, I was dragged kicking and screaming into the back of their cruiser. One of them followed me into the back and a heartbeat later, I had a wad of smelly cloth shoved up my nose. The last thing I saw before I passed out was a scar that encircled the man's neck. Brandon?

Then nothing.

CHAPTER TWENTY EIGHT

My Tombstone was a Mountain

When I finally woke up, I couldn't understand it. I had been able to wake up after I had been shot in the head, but not when I was chloroformed?

What did Brandon want with me now? Didn't he have his tongue back? Hadn't Christian killed everyone Brandon wanted dead?

I couldn't open my eyes immediately, and when I did, the entire world was different. I was on a bed, a comfortable bed. My person had not been touched or changed, so I was still splattered in dry blood. My head hurt and my sinuses were raw.

As I looked around, I realized I was not in a normal room or a normal building. I was somewhere else, like a different world. It looked like the walls around me had been assembled by a mad man. They were made of rock slabs, and placed out of alignment so the pattern and the walls were not flat. The ceiling was too high, with large windows almost as tall. Heavy curtains were pulled aside and I could see rugged mountain faces. In every direction, there were windows and out those windows, I saw mountains that looked like they were pulled directly from the heart of the planet. Flat plains met almost vertical climbs. The crooked castle was built high on the side of the mountain and as I looked down, I couldn't see how a person could get in or out at that impossible angle.

I moved and noticed another problem. My ankle was tied. Sitting down on the bed, I put my ankle on my knee to examine it. It was not like the nylon Brandon had tied me with before. It was a metal circlet that would only come off if I cut my foot off. What was the point of this?

I rubbed my eyes, looked around and found a note in Brandon's hand writing on the bed in the place Christian should have been.

The scrawl read:

Dear Beth,

Congratulations, you'll never die. If I were Christian I would tell you this is the fate of everyone immortal. Someone will catch you and do experiments on you to see how far your immortality goes. That is exactly what has happened here. You have been placed by yourself in a mansion on the dark side of Tombstone Mountain.

Your mission, while you are here, is to figure out how to command the metal around your leg to release its grip on your ankle. If you can do that, you are free to join our group of immortals.

If you saw your leg off in your haste to be free of us, you'll find we won't tolerate your lack of cooperation and we will replace the brace as many times as it takes.

We did not kidnap Christian. He does not know where you are. He's not coming for you. He already knows how to do what we're asking of you, he's just forgotten.

The house is heated and there is a water reservoir. There will be food delivered from time to time, but I do hope you enjoy canned and dried food because that is what your diet will be until you accomplish your task.

This doesn't need to take forever, Beth. You took a bullet to the head and woke out of it in under an hour. You are powerful. Take care and no one, not even us, will be able to stop you. You might even save the world.

All the best,
Henry Brandon

I shuddered. This was the very opposite of what I wanted. Christian had asked me to marry him! I was supposed to be somewhere feeling his kiss, getting under his clothes and completely giving up being a lady. He didn't know where I was.

Aside from Brandon's habit of tricking me into believing he was someone else, once the gig was up, he always told me the truth, no matter how unpleasant that truth might be.

I fingered the ring around my ankle. I didn't even know what kind of metal it was, and I didn't feel like crying or screaming.

In the bedroom, there were clothes hung up on wall hooks. They weren't pretty and they were too big for me. I grabbed a dress to wear after I washed and went to the bathroom to clean myself.

Wherever Christian was, he was pulling his hair out. They may have stashed me on a mountaintop to hide me, but it wouldn't be forever and they would pay for having done this to me on my wedding day.

The End

Dearest Reader,

Thank you so much for reading *His 16th Face*! I hope you enjoyed reading it as much as I enjoyed writing it.

Now seems like the proper time to confess something to you. I'm an independent writer, which means I need your support to keep writing. If you want to support me, it would be helpful if you'd post a positive review on the site where you received your copy. It would also be helpful if you posted something on your social media about enjoying the book. The more momentum is gained, the faster I'll write the sequel. It's already in the works. For now, the working title is *If Diamonds Could Talk*. I can crack out a book in a year for the right readers!

Thank you again for reading! I hope your imagination was ignited and your spirits lifted.

All the Love in the World,
Stephanie Van Orman